DRAGON FORTUNE

THE DRAGONS OF HARBOR CRAG
BOOK TWO

T.M. BAUMGARTNER

CHAPTER I
PERFECTING TECHNIQUE

The charred ruins of Lord Hanley's estate glittered in the dawn light, dewdrops and shards of glass gleaming like precious jewels in the wreckage. At the edge of the rubble, Lisette stood and sipped from the mug of spiced tea she and Remy were sharing. It was also possible that was *magic* gleaming in the debris, a worrying thought. Sane people avoided magic and gods. "I guess we should do this." She didn't move.

"Since we're here," Remy agreed. He rubbed his palms together, looking for all the world like a child deciding which of his nameday gifts to play with first. At the motion, Simi poked her head out of the satchel at his hip, where she'd been napping since they'd left the freeholder quarter. The cat's whiskers twitched.

It had been two months since the dragon Aarat had burned Lord Hanley's mansion to the ground, more than enough time for the wreckage to cool — if it had been a normal building and a normal fire. But *something* had kept the rubble radiating heat until now. It was a stark contrast to the duke's palace; the magic that had kept Harbor Crag's residents from noticing the duke's peculiarities had dissipated quickly. Smoke damaged paintings of chickens had graced the market within days.

Though Lisette had spent time inside Lord Hanley's mansion before it had burned, it was difficult to picture the layout with three stories collapsed into the basement. "If the kitchen entrance was there," she said, pointing to the end of a flagstone path where blackened sticks showed the remains of the kitchen garden, "the main staircase should have been over *there*."

Most of the magical items would have been in Lord Hanley's workroom a few dozen paces beyond the staircase landing. That was what Remy cared about. Though Lisette agreed it was important to recover anything Harbor Crag's enemies might use against them — or an unsuspecting citizen might accidentally use against themself — Lisette was more interested to learn if any part of the dog-shaped automaton had survived. Bralinost had been built by Lisette's ancestor, and though it had likely melted in the fire, Lisette's fingers itched to find and disassemble the creature.

Using his staff to test the rubble in front of him, Remy picked his way across the stone and brick. "The strongest magic is coming from this area." He turned in a circle, drawing invisible walls around him. Then he climbed over a heap of stone, mimed opening a door, and turned left down the ghost of a hallway. "The last we saw of Bralinost, it was here. There's an echo..." He unslung his satchel, setting it down carefully. "Excuse me, Simi," he murmured as he reached under the calico for his gloves.

Simi yawned, stretched, and climbed onto a brick mound before settling again.

Lisette pulled on her own work gloves, lifted her scarf

over her nose to keep from inhaling soot, and tried to be practical. One of them ought to be. "We should probably clear the workroom first. Nobody's going to steal a bunch of metal."

"Think of this as an opportunity to perfect our technique," Remy offered.

Lisette flashed him a grateful smile from under the scarf and shifted a heap of roofing slates, slinging them toward the remains of the staircase. Within a few minutes, both she and Remy were covered with soot, and a depression was forming in the rubble where they'd cleared away debris. Simi watched them from her perch, grooming a front paw.

Grabbing what she thought was another stone, Lisette felt it crunch and bend under her gloves. "That's not..." When she rotated her wrist to get a better view, the charred leather cover of a book cracked and shifted. Lisette snatched her hand back. "One for you, I think." Any book that had survived the fire might contain enough magic to be dangerous. Besides, Remy loved books.

"What's that?" Remy paused in his excavation to look where she pointed. He picked up the book and brushed chunks of ash and clay from the cover. "Ah, *Control of Air and Water for Novice Mages*. Written by Jehan the Bland, which isn't the *worst* sobriquet, but I'll admit, I'm really hoping for something better." He smiled fondly at the book. "The spells are unnecessarily complicated and the prose would cure the toughest insomnia, but the recipe for fish stew is worth trying." Blackened pages drifted down to the rubble. "There isn't much magic attached. I think it just survived the fire — as much as it *did* — through luck. Someone probably hid it years ago in a protected place and then forgot about it. The book is often used to teach small children, so I wouldn't be surprised if the recipient 'lost' it."

As far as Lisette knew, there hadn't been any children living in the house before it burned, which meant it had probably been the young Lord Hanley who had hidden the book away decades ago. After being stalked and threatened by the man for years, Lisette had a hard time picturing him as an innocent child. Logically, though, he must have been — before he'd been warped into the adult he'd become.

To avoid thinking about that transformation, Lisette dug into what Remy had said. "*You* didn't read it as a child." It was a safe guess. Remy hadn't come from a family of mages, and his first years at the college of magic had been spent trying to catch up.

Laughter ended in a cough that dislodged ash from Remy's scarf. "No. I got into enough trouble as a child without formal training." He tossed the disintegrating book to the side and crouched. "Aha! Here." Wiping gloved fingers over a spot at his feet, he uncovered the dull gleam of metal. "I think this is it."

Lisette excavated bricks around it. "That's more than I had any right to expect."

"Oh, I don't know. Anything that lasted hundreds of years had to have some spells of protection on it." Remy slipped on the edge of the hole they were digging, keeping his feet by a cat-like twist that would have made Simi proud. "Though I don't expect they had considered dragon fire."

This was definitely Bralinost. Lisette cleared brick dust away from the side of its body and got her hands underneath. "*Can* you protect against dragon fire?" She strained to raise the automaton, but the back legs were still trapped.

"Let me... Hold on, I've got it." Remy levered a slab of

marble onto its side. "Try now." He stepped back to give Lisette room. "Can *I* protect against dragon fire? Definitely not. During my first year at school, my fire-starting spells were so unpredictable, my professor made me learn how to protect a surface from burning before moving on with my lessons. But it only worked below a certain temperature."

"How many buildings did you burn down finding that out?" The automaton came free when Lisette heaved a second time. The legs were warped and crushed, but the rest of the machine looked mostly intact.

Remy helped lift Bralinost out of the hole, then pulled Lisette up. "None, though I was banned from practicing in the dormitory." He lowered his scarf to take a sip of water from his flask. "We had to cook a meal using magic for our final project. The other students showed off with seared meat and braised vegetables. One person caramelized sugar around an apple for dessert."

"And you?" Lisette accepted the proffered flask, letting the water wash away the ash coating her mouth.

"The professor and I went out to a patch of mud near a pond, and I cooked her the worst scrambled eggs she'd ever eaten. But I passed the class." He recapped the flask and set it down next to Simi. "But to answer your original question, I did read a book with a spell that claimed to protect the mage from dragon fire."

"So maybe it's possible."

"Well..." His voice took on a doubtful tone. "The writer also claimed to have found a spring of immortality, so I'm not sure I would trust it." He shrugged. "Even if he wasn't completely unhinged — a common state for mages, as you well know — how could he be sure it was the spell that protected him from dragon fire and not the immortality?"

"An important distinction to make." Lisette checked the

angle of the sun before pulling her scarf back over her face. "We still have an hour before I need to get back to clean up and open the shop." Though she would have preferred to stay and make sure Remy didn't run into trouble, at least she could help him shift anything too heavy for one person before she left. "How much do you think we can recover from the workroom?"

"Let's find out."

They climbed over the wreckage to the area Remy had previously indicated. Shifting the debris over the workroom and stabilizing the edges of the hole were easier than Lisette had anticipated, probably because Aarat had destroyed the top floor of the building before setting it on fire. But *something* in the rubble sent up gouts of flame every time Lisette or Remy stepped too near.

After fifteen minutes of trying to approach that corner, Remy wiped his face with the back of one glove, smearing ash and sweat in a band across his eyelids. "The good news is we don't have to worry about thieves making off with dangerous artifacts." His left eyebrow was singed, giving him a quizzical look.

"Surely, it will run out of fuel soon." Lisette's boots had burn marks on both toes. "Or is that a purely magical flame?"

"Magical. I think I'll have to come at it from the other direction." He sighed and drank more water. "I'm fairly certain it's not a new small god anyhow."

Lisette took a deep breath and slowly let it out. "Please don't even suggest that sort of thing." The last thing Harbor Crag needed was a shrine adding magic to the mix. There were a few old ones scattered throughout the city, ruins where the magic had faded enough to be harmless, but most parents still taught the old rhymes to warn children away.

Remy was amused by her reaction, but he didn't argue. "I'll let you know how it goes."

"Be careful." Ignoring the grime covering his face, Lisette leaned in for a kiss. "Don't forget Tiffany is coming over at lunch to measure the spare room."

He put an arm around her waist to prolong the contact. "Never fear. I shall be there to distract the minions while the two of you work." Tiffany's daughters adored Remy, and he mostly stayed out of trouble when entrusted with small children.

The spare bedroom refit was part of their preparations to host Remy's mother, whenever she arrived. She had accepted their invitation, but one unanticipated consequence of freeing Aarat was the current shipping chaos.

The mages of Harbor Crag had been using stolen dragon magic to protect the city's merchant fleet from the creatures of the deep. As those spells faded, ships were forced to stay closer to the coast, lengthening voyages. That, in turn, wreaked havoc on carefully planned dock schedules and caused further delays. In her last letter, Remy's mother said she was planning to leave soon, but that meant she might arrive any time over the next three months.

After scratching Simi's chin, Lisette hefted the remains of Bralinost over one shoulder and crunched across the rubble to the street, where pedestrians and horse-drawn carts passed with barely a glance. Lord Hanley had been the most powerful person in Harbor Crag, but it had been months since he'd fled. Life went on.

Then a collective gasp sounded. A horse bolted and people scattered. Lisette stopped moving, looking up just in time to see the massive amber and black form of a dragon land in front of her, his wings throwing up a cloud of dirt and soot.

Lisette blinked rapidly to clear her eyes. "Hello, Aarat."

"Lisette." The dragon's musical voice was nearly too beautiful to hear without weeping, but at least he hadn't tugged on their bond. She had freely given him her name, not knowing what that meant. It had been both a blessing and a curse. Now he had power over her, but the bond also protected her from most spells.

A calico blur streaked past and scrambled onto the dragon's head, purring so loudly the fish in the harbor could probably hear. Lisette heard Remy's footsteps in the rubble behind her. "Hello, dragon. The egg is well?"

A few weeks before, Remy and Lisette had tracked down the dragon's egg and brought it to Aarat's cavern. Since then, the dragon's protective instincts had made him even grouchier than usual, so the humans had kept their distance.

"The egg is well," Aarat agreed. He tipped his head back, causing Simi to slide over his shoulder and down to the ground. "There is a mage on the ship sailing into the harbor. The *Fool's Errand*. Say the word and I will sink the vessel before it docks."

Lisette glanced at Remy. Could Lord Hanley be sneaking back to Harbor Crag? She knew in her bones that he would return one day, but she'd assumed it would be with the backing of the Island of Light and their powerful mages, not alone. This didn't feel like the beginning of an invasion.

Before she could reply, Remy clicked to call Simi to him. "Thank you for the warning," he said. "We'll meet the *Fool's Errand* when it docks and let you know if there's a problem."

"I will not have those mages return," Aarat grumbled. Then he ran two steps and took to the sky, a fresh cloud of soot billowing up around the ruins of the mansion.

Remy followed the dragon's path until he had to shade his eyes from the sun. "Well. I guess excavating the workroom will have to wait." He opened his satchel so Simi could jump in. "Let's find out who just arrived."

CHAPTER 2
FOOL'S ERRAND

The *Fool's Errand* carried cargo as well as passengers. Instead of dropping anchor in deeper water and rowing people ashore on smaller boats, it had sailed near the largest pier and was currently finishing the docking process by warping, four large men pushing the capstan bars to wind in the line attached to the pier.

Lisette stood next to Remy on the waterfront, watching as the ship slowly dragged itself closer. "This seems like one of those things that should be easier with magic."

"A good mage can make a very comfortable living bringing ships in." Remy scrubbed at his face with a rag he'd pulled from his satchel. "A classmate lives at Bleeding Rocks and they shower him with coins." He shrugged. "*I* wouldn't live anywhere that sacrifices a goat to the monsters of the deep every full moon, but I doubt they'd have me anyhow. My magic would probably create a whirlpool and drag the ships under."

Lisette ignored his self-deprecation — Remy's magic might work a little oddly and occasionally have unintended consequences, but it had always come through when she'd needed it. "Why goats? Wouldn't that just draw the creatures closer for a free meal?"

"That's what I wondered. Every few years, they lose the boat that carries the sacrifice, and they blame it on impiety and close all the taverns for a week." He turned to face her. "Better?"

Taking the rag from him, Lisette wiped a black streak from the bridge of his nose. "There. Now you can uphold the reputation of your mage college." She was still covered in ash and held a battered automaton under one arm, but any mage coming to Harbor Crag would overlook her.

"I'm fairly certain the college would be happy enough to forget I was ever there, especially after..." He made a gesture that encompassed the whole of Harbor Crag. He'd been sent as a spy to ferret out the secret to Harbor Crag's increase in magic with the ultimate goal of having Wendsmouth replicate it. Instead, Remy had helped Lisette unchain Aarat, forcing the mages enslaving the dragon to flee. Then, he promptly quit his job as a spy to stay and help free the remaining dragons.

Lisette thought the Galfigon College for Magecraft in Wendsmouth should be proud of Remy, but suspected they would have a different view of the matter. "So, if some evil mage walks off the ship, what's the plan?"

"Run away?" He put an arm around her waist. "It's probably just a recent graduate who came to meet a dragon. If so, I'll introduce them to Aarat and either the dragon approves or there will be one less mage in Harbor Crag."

As the ship drew inexorably closer, Lisette tried to identify the visible cargo. Pots with tiny trees on the main deck obstructed half the passage between the masts, but she supposed trees couldn't be kept in the hold. Baskets of nuts and a barrel of whisky in a distinctive red cask told her the ship had come from the north. "They came by way of Safeman's Harbor." Because of the winds and currents, ships rarely stopped at both the Island of Light and Safeman's Harbor on the mainland.

"The whiskey?" Remy shaded his eyes with his free hand. "I can't see the Safeman's stamp on it from here, but I think you're right." Dropping his hand down, he scratched Simi's chin. "Hopefully, that's a good sign." He cocked his head. "It could be my replacement."

"If they're here as a spy, they're doing a terrible job," Lisette pointed out. "They haven't even set foot in the city yet and we know they're here."

"I had an advantage. When I arrived, everyone was rushing around getting ready for the Festival of Secrets and the city was awash in magic. I blended in."

Lisette snorted. Remy's idea of blending in was committing a series of high-profile thefts dressed as the Black Fox, which left the whole city gossiping. Though that *had* left the guard looking for a thief, not a mage. Now that Aarat's magic wasn't being stolen and squandered on pretty illusions, it was easier to pick out a mage.

The pier shuddered when the ship made contact, and two sailors jumped down to anchor lines. As the gangway was lowered, passengers milled about on deck. A tall man in a velvet coat and trousers elbowed his way to the front, oblivious of the resentful stares he engendered. Lisette considered him. He certainly *acted* like Lord Hanley, the only mage she'd spent much time around other than Remy.

A young woman herded three children into the makeshift line, and while her charges appeared well-behaved, that itself probably wasn't evidence of coercive magic. Two older women stood near the back of the crowd, laughing and talking animatedly. Nearby, three young men wearing the embroidered shirts of journeyman chefs yawned and leaned on the mast. A middle-aged woman wearing a protective linen shirt over a satin dress inspected the trees carefully, speaking quietly to the sailor undoing the knots that held them in place. On the pier, a row of stevedores waited, more or less patiently, for the passengers to disembark so they could begin working.

Lisette sighed. The mage could be any of them, really.

"Oh, no." Remy gave a strangled laugh. "This might be a disaster."

After glancing at him, then back at the ship, Lisette still couldn't tell who he was looking at. But her gaze followed Remy's pointing finger to the back of the crowd of passengers, where the two women were still speaking and laughing. "You know the mage?"

"See the woman with the blue tunic and long gray hair? That's Giselle, one of my professors. She helped me figure out how to graduate."

Though Giselle's hair was braided close to her scalp, wisps had escaped all over, giving her a halo that reflected the sun. She didn't look particularly grand, though Lisette noticed she moved with the confidence of one who expected to get her own way. Her companion looked a few years younger, and had an oddly familiar smile.

Remy cleared his throat. "And the woman she's talking to is my mother."

CHAPTER 3
A LITTLE TOUCHY

Meeting Remy's mother while covered in soot and holding a half-melted killer automaton under one arm hadn't been Lisette's plan when she'd urged Remy to extend the invitation. "So much for first impressions." An offshore breeze added a note of brine to the odors of drying fish, roasted nuts, and water-logged wood.

Remy grinned and waved to the two women waiting to disembark. "Nonsense. We look like two people who dropped everything to rush down to greet them."

"We look like a couple of chimney sweeps mid-shift," Lisette corrected. With another sigh, she let go of her dreams of impressing Remy's mother. "Ah, well, my attempts to look like a sensible adult wouldn't have lasted long under scrutiny anyhow."

"Be brave. My mother has been forced to deal with *me* all this time. *You* are the pinnacle of respectability in comparison."

Lisette watched the women talking, their stances showing the ease of close companions. "I know why your mother is here, but why is Giselle?" Though the citizens of Harbor Crag needed allies, a mage with ties to the college was automatically suspect.

"Good question. I wrote to her for advice on how to free the chained dragons, but I was expecting her to send along a book or two, not show up in person." Remy considered for a moment. "Of all the mages I know, I would think Giselle the least likely to exploit this situation, but people do surprising things."

As soon as the gangway had been lashed in place, the wealthy passengers hurried across, headed for the shore and its waiting carts. Most ignored Remy and Lisette. One boy was transfixed by Simi, who had moved onto Remy's shoulder. The cat blinked slowly and watched the boy as the child was pulled along by his mother. After the first rush, the remaining passengers and luggage-burdened servants crossed more slowly, though they seemed intent on reaching solid ground as quickly as possible.

The two older women waited until the rest of the passengers had cleared the gangway before they descended and strode the length of the pier.

Remy performed the introductions. His mother gave Lisette a welcoming smile, waving away her apologies for the state of her clothes. "Call me Anna. I've been looking forward to meeting you." She bumped her cheek against Simi's when the cat jumped to her shoulder. "Hello, silly cat."

Giselle eyed the automaton Lisette held. "Is that what's left of Bralinost?" Then she brushed Lisette's shoulder with one hand and cocked her head. "You're not a mage, but... Is that the dragon's magic on you?"

Like most people, Lisette could sense some forms of magic, but she'd never learned more than that. Until she'd met Remy and fallen into Aarat's cavern, Lisette had maintained that the most important thing to know about magic was how to avoid it. "Probably?"

Remy nodded as the four of them moved away from the pier. "You'll get a chance to compare when you meet Aarat."

Giselle raised one grizzled eyebrow. "Aarat allows people to talk to him?"

"I'm not sure you'll have a choice." Remy gestured toward the dragon warrens visible near the top of the steep slope of Harbor Crag. The ancient ruins were a contrast to the built-up remainder of the town. "Aarat felt you on the ship. He's a little touchy about new mages arriving."

"Understandable." The wind playing with Giselle's hair made her look like she might take flight at any moment. The motion fit her, as if she were part dragon herself. Perhaps she would be able to talk to Aarat after all.

They stepped onto the paving stones near the chaotic shoreline road, with food carts, merchants, and sailors carrying bulky loads all jostling for space. Remy was correct — Giselle needed to be introduced to Aarat before any more time had passed. And while she didn't exactly consider Aarat a *friend*, Lisette irritated the grumpy dragon less than Remy did.

Tugging Remy's arm, Lisette stepped to the side. "Why don't I take Giselle to meet Aarat while you get your mother settled in?"

Remy looked over Lisette's shoulder and murmured, "My mother hasn't scared you off already, has she? Because we can always take Rye and Barlow up on their offer." The uncles had a spare bedroom available as long as Lisette helped clear out the stock packed into it.

"No. It's just that you seem fond of your professor, so I'd hate for her to fall victim to an irritated dragon before she has a chance to unpack." Lisette also wanted to get a better sense of why the professor was here — Remy's fond memories might keep him from asking the right questions.

"Fair enough." He leaned forward to kiss her cheek and theatrically whispered, "Don't believe anything she says about me." Then he stood, took Bralinost from Lisette, and spoke more loudly. "Professor, Lisette is going to give you the 'meet the dragon' tour since she's less likely to inspire a conflagration. You're invited to come see the freeholder quarter afterward if you don't have other plans."

HURRYING up the hill after Giselle, Lisette tried to think of a question that would keep the other woman talking. In retrospect, she should have found a less direct way of asking if the steep hike would be a problem. She'd meant it as a courtesy, not knowing if Giselle had any physical limitations that would make travel in a carriage more comfortable, but the mage had taken it as a slight about her age. Now, Giselle seemed determined to leave Lisette behind her as they climbed the hill toward the dragon warrens.

Trotting to catch up, Lisette panted, "Remy says you helped him figure out how to graduate."

Giselle smiled and slowed just enough for Lisette to keep abreast. "He was always one of my more *interesting* students. Not necessarily the strongest magic user, but he thought about things in a different way. I just nudged him in the right direction." She resettled her bag over her shoulder. "I thought sending him here would keep him out of trouble, but..."

Lisette snorted. "I think Remy would find trouble no matter where he went."

"Ha!" Giselle's bark of laughter turned a few heads. "You're correct, of course. Though I wouldn't have thought he would take on unchaining a dragon by himself. I thought he had a bit more self-preservation than that."

Lisette hummed in the back of her throat, trying to decide how much to tell this professor of Remy's. It hadn't been Remy who had broken the spells on the dagger of Aarat. Lisette had done so accidentally and had nearly died in the process.

She'd waited too long to respond. Giselle stopped walking and fixed her with piercing black eyes. "Was it *not* Remy, then?"

But before Lisette could decide what to say, screams came from the road ahead. A flood of people ran down the hill toward them, abandoning possessions and wares as they ran. The scent of bruised oranges trailed behind them. Somewhere close to the dragon warrens, a plume of smoke rose.

"Another dragon!" a burly man yelled as he passed them.

"Run!" a woman screamed. "It's attacking people!"

Lisette and Giselle glanced at each other, then sprinted uphill, rushing toward the source of the fire.

CHAPTER 4

SELF-PRESERVATION

With no maintenance for decades, the wall surrounding the dragon warrens had a snag-gletoothed look, but the carts of vendors and travelers usually formed an orderly row outside the boundary. Nobody was foolish enough to enter the warrens uninvited, especially now that Aarat patrolled the area.

Now, carts lay smashed, chickens squawking in their overturned cages. Flames licked at the cobbler's awning. Not one person had stayed to fight the fire, though to be fair, the attached structure was built of earth and stone and unlikely to burn.

In the middle of the destruction, a dragon crouched, tail lashing from side to side. The dragon's blue-green scales shimmered in the sunlight, the color varying from teal near her belly and turquoise on her wings to a lighter sea foam on her dorsal spine. The effect was like watching a wave crash over the beach as she breathed. She limped forward two steps and crouched again. From one back leg, the end of a broken chain clattered on the cobblestones.

Lisette and Giselle peeked around the corner of the

wine shop. The professor smelled of lemon and pepper, in the same way that Remy always smelled of vanilla and pepper. Did that have something to do with being a mage? Lisette had never noticed it with Lord Hanley, but she'd always done her best to avoid being anywhere near him.

"Oh! She's beautiful," Giselle breathed.

Lisette suppressed a sigh. She'd thought it was just Remy, but maybe all mages were prone to getting distracted when they should have been worrying about their safety. Though this dragon was only a third of Aarat's length, Lisette was sure it could kill them just as quickly. "Why doesn't she just fly away?"

When Aarat had broken free, he'd flown to the free-holder quarter to accost Lord Hanley, the mage who had helped keep the dragons in chains. But Lord Hanley had fled weeks ago, along with the rest of Harbor Crag's mages. There was nothing keeping this dragon from leaving.

"I don't think she can." Giselle leaned forward. "There's a nasty spell on that chain."

The dragon turned her head toward them and inhaled. Only Lisette dragging the older woman backward saved her from being incinerated. Flames roared by, blocked by the building.

Giselle stood and straightened her clothing. "Thank you, dear." Some of her wilder strands of hair were now decidedly shorter.

Wishing Remy was there, Lisette decided the more Giselle knew about the chain, the better. "Aarat had a similar chain. Sunny, the dragon-born girl —"

Giselle's eyes widened. "You have a dragon-born here? In Harbor Crag?" Her voice rose in pitch and volume as she became more excited. "Do you know what that *means*?"

It meant there was a dragon egg nearby, the first in a

generation. Once, dragons had traveled more freely and raised their young in the warrens within cities. But something peculiar happened when human children were carried to term and then raised near a dragon egg. They were *different*, somehow, attuned to the dragons in a way most people weren't. They were able to soothe and heal the dragons. But mages had discovered the blood of a dragon-born could be used against the dragons, so dragons had begun raising their young elsewhere. The egg that had changed Sunny had been stolen by a mage and hidden away in the heart of Harbor Crag.

Remy and Lisette had tracked down the egg and brought it back to Aarat's cavern. But she didn't want Giselle to know that. Not until Lisette was sure this new mage could be trusted. "If we can find Sunny, she might be able to calm this dragon. She was able to heal Aarat's leg under the shackle."

"Where is she?"

Lisette opened her mouth, then closed it again. "I don't know. She's been sleeping in Aarat's cavern, but during the day..." She looked around. "The other street children could probably find her..." Lisette didn't bother stating the obvious — the street children had run at the first sight of the dragon. *They* had a sense of self-preservation. "I would imagine she'll come here as soon as she hears about it, but I don't know when that will be."

And where was Aarat? Surely, he could hear the disturbance.

A child's voice, quickly muffled, called out from the other side of the road. "Help!" Lisette darted another look around the corner. Two barefoot children in dirty clothes huddled next to an overturned cart, trapped by the wall behind them. Their only avenues of escape were to run in front of the dragon or scale the wall and take their chances in the warrens.

The dragon turned her head to investigate the noise.

Lisette abandoned her plan to wait for Sunny or Aarat to arrive. "Whatever you do, don't give the dragon your name," she whispered to Giselle. Then she raised her voice. "Excuse me? Dragon?"

The dragon turned her head and took a deep breath.

Lisette ducked back to let a gout of flame go by. "I guess she doesn't want to talk." The stones near her head radiated heat. She had to keep the dragon's attention away from the children. "I don't suppose you have any way to protect us from dragon fire?" Remy had said he couldn't, but he also claimed to be a terrible mage.

Giselle dropped her bag and squatted next to it, pulling out clothes and other personal items. "Yes, but it takes two days to set up, so it's not terribly helpful. Maybe I can... Ah, here it is." She stood again. "Let me see if I can buy us some good will." Ducking around the wall, she tapped the pouch she was holding, then hurled it at the dragon.

The bundle dropped to the ground, bronze smoke pouring out. Giselle called loudly, "That should make your leg better. We only want to help!"

Lisette waited, sweating from the heat of the stones next to her face. Magic rippled over the dragon's body, from her nose to the tip of her tail, and then she took a cautious step forward. Then another. The limp was gone, though the chain still dragged on the ground behind her.

After letting out a cautious breath, Lisette called, "Please, dragon. We need some time to find the dragon-born who can help you."

Something was wrong with this encounter. Aarat would

22

never have let her talk this long before cutting in with his acerbic wit. Did this dragon not speak the language?

The smaller child across the road whimpered. The dragon turned her head and spat fire, setting the cart aflame. Both children screamed and pressed against the wall.

Giselle swore under her breath. "Creatures from the deep! That should have helped!"

"She may not be sane after all the time she's spent chained." Lisette looked at the older woman. "Is there any way you can remove that shackle so she can fly away?"

"Not without getting close enough to touch it. And maybe not even then." Giselle rummaged through her things. "I have a sleeping spell ready to go, but I don't know if it will work on dragons." She looked up, thinking about it. "In fact, I doubt it will. The mechanism of —"

Having seen Remy get lost in the theory, Lisette knew this explanation could take some time. "Forget the sleeping spell for now. Can you create a distraction?"

Giselle's face lit up. "*That* I can do!" She plucked two pouches from the items strewn on the ground. "Close your eyes and cover your ears."

Lisette took two steps back, crouched, and obeyed Giselle's instructions. A tremendous boom shook the earth, and light flashed in front of her, painful even through closed eyelids. When she opened her eyes, blinking to clear the afterimage, smoke and steam filled the air and there was a crater filled with water in the road. Hundreds of tiny glowing newts scrambled away from the center of destruction.

The dragon pawed at its eyes, temporarily blinded.

"I'll meet you at the freeholder quarter," Lisette yelled as she dashed toward the dragon and the children beyond.

CHAPTER 5

SPEECH

Glowing newts scattered as Lisette sprinted past the dragon. Her eyes watered from the smoke, but she focused on the two children ahead. The older child, a girl, had wrapped her skinny frame around the younger boy to shield him from dragon fire.

Lisette considered her options as she jumped over smashed pottery. Ideally, she would get the kids across the road so they could run toward the harbor, but she didn't trust Giselle's distraction to last for long. Already the dragon was blinking her eyes and looking around. The only other choice was to get the kids over the man-high wall into the dragon warrens. It wasn't a place Lisette would generally suggest going, but this was an emergency.

She slid to a stop next to the children. "Up, over the wall."

The girl drew back. "But the dragons!"

"We'll walk next to the wall until we can get out. We'll be fine." The boy weighed next to nothing, and she nearly tossed him over the top when she boosted him. The girl was a little heavier, but she grabbed the top of the wall and scrambled over when Lisette lifted her.

Now that the children were relatively safe, Lisette jumped to grab the lip of the wall, ignoring the sharp rocks cutting into her fingers and using the loose bricks and stones as toeholds to climb. But an inhalation from the dragon told her she'd run out of time. She dropped flat to the ground behind the burning cart. An instant later, fire blasted the wall where she'd been.

Lisette kept her head down and yelled at the dragon. "You know, I'm trying to *help* you!"

Curling up on the ground wouldn't save her — the dragon knew where she was. And the wall was now too hot to climb, even if the dragon could be distracted long enough for Lisette to pull herself over. She couldn't outrun the dragon, and any attempt to do so would leave her dodging flames.

But could she get *closer* to the dragon?

It would never have worked with Aarat. He was too fast and agile. But *this* dragon seemed slower and more uncertain. The blue dragon had done nothing other than crash into things and burn them. If Lisette stayed near the dragon's shoulder, she'd be safe from the flames. Probably.

Lisette wished Remy was here to give his opinion of this plan.

Before she could consider all the things that might go wrong, Lisette rolled to her feet and dashed to the dragon's side. The dragon turned her head and sidled away, but Lisette shifted to maintain her position. If the dragon kept moving and turned around, Lisette could pick her moment and dart to safety between buildings.

Even better would be if Lisette could convince the dragon to stop. "Can we talk about this?"

Instead of turning again, the dragon sidestepped *into* Lisette, knocking her off her feet. Lisette grabbed at the dragon to keep upright. The razor-sharp edge of a scale sliced into her fingers, but she regained her footing. When she pulled her hand back, her little finger caught on something.

A flare of magic ran up her arm.

Ever since Lisette had given Aarat her name, something in their bond had protected her from magic being used against her. But this magic seemed to cling, as if it had been made just for her.

Lisette opened her mouth to complain, but nothing came out. All words had fled. She gaped, forgot about her immediate danger, and almost got trampled when the blue dragon moved.

Then the dragon moved again, yanking Lisette's hand free. Speech flooded back to her in a rush. "Oh, dragon," she breathed, dancing sideways to keep close. "What have they done to you?"

Decades ago, the mages of Harbor Crag had banded together and trapped the dragons, chaining them in the warrens and siphoning their magic so it could be frittered away on spells of illusion and light. Binding the dragons had been torture enough, but this made it worse. To be a creature of the skies, bound underground and without the ability to communicate...

The mages hadn't done this to Aarat. Later, she'd have to puzzle out why. For now, Lisette needed to free the blue dragon from this spell.

Not for the first time, Lisette wished that she could work magic if she was forced to be around it. But even though she couldn't, she *could* study whatever had snagged her finger so she could describe it to Remy. Lisette stopped plotting her escape route and lifted a scale on the dragon's shoulder, trying to see what she had touched.

It took three scales and a gavotte's worth of stepping to stay in place, but she found it. Just above the point of the shoulder, a silver spike pierced a blue scale streaked with orange, a chain looping around the rear of the scale to attach to the spike underneath. Even without touching it again, Lisette could tell the spell called to the dragon bond within her.

"If you would just hold still..." she muttered. The dragon's steps had slowed, either because she was tiring or because she realized Lisette wasn't hurting her.

Remy or Giselle might create a counter-spell, allowing them to safely work with the dragon to remove this thing. But Lisette didn't know if she could give them all the information they needed. And she'd noticed mages sometimes forgot things could be done *without* magic.

Plus, she was already here.

The chain was fastened to the spike with a simple cotter pin. She *should* be able to pull out the pin, then yank the spike from the scale. With any luck, that would free the dragon from this spell.

Magic flared when Lisette grabbed the cotter pin, and she nearly jerked her hand back. In another moment, her grasp of language had faded and disappeared like grains of salt dropped in boiling water. Her bloody fingers slipped the first time she tried to withdraw the pin. Her second attempt was more successful, and the chain swung free. Grasping the spike, she pushed up. It stuck. Lisette twisted and pushed harder.

Splinters of blue and orange dragon scale flaked away. Lisette grabbed the chain and yanked.

With a roar, the dragon crashed into Lisette, slamming

her into the ground. But Lisette had the chain wound around her hand, and the spike ripped out of the dragon's scale.

Flat on her back with the breath knocked out of her, Lisette could only watch as the dragon turned and faced her, head lowered. She waited to be incinerated. Instead, strange noises came from the dragon, loud and frantic.

Giselle appeared, moving warily around the dragon and making different noises.

Nothing made sense. Then Lisette realized she was still holding the spike and chain in her bloody hand. She dropped the spelled metal in the dirt. Suddenly the dragon's noises snapped into focus.

"The dragon-born has been taken!"

CHAPTER 6

BRAATLE

L isette sprawled on the road staring up at the blue-green dragon, the creature's words echoing in her mind.

Sunny had been taken. How?

Next to her, Giselle said, "When?" As if responding to her mood, her gray hair looked even wilder than it had before.

The dragon's head swiveled as she looked at the surrounding buildings. "The dragon-born cried out in the tunnel." Her voice held the same musical tones as Aarat, but the effect was muted. "Then I couldn't feel her anymore. By the time I broke the chain..." She swiveled again. "We must find the dragon-born."

The mage dug through her pack again, pulling out bags and jars. "Do we have anything she's recently touched? I may be able to get a tracking spell working."

Pushing herself to her feet, Lisette wrapped her bleeding hand in the hem of her shirt. If nothing else, being around dragons had taught her that her own blood could be used against her. "I'll get something. Stay right here!"

Hopefully, the dragon would take the hint. And with any luck, the dragon wouldn't take offense. Lisette didn't stop to find out, but ran down the road to the main entrance of the dragon warrens. She knew two ways to get to Aarat's burrow — the closest was unmarked, and she wanted to make sure she slid down the correct hole in the ground. Landing in a different dragon's warren would be a quick way to die.

Lisette wondered why Aarat wasn't already above ground. If he was in the dragon warrens, he *had* to have heard the noise this new dragon was making, and he wouldn't have flown away from Harbor Crag before finding out if the mage on the ship was a threat.

The opening to Aarat's warren loomed ahead. "Aarat, it's Lisette! I'm coming down!" Jumping feet-first, she slid down the incline into the cavern. Normally, when she visited Aarat here, she went through the other entrance, which led to an underground passage she could walk through. This way was definitely undignified, but at least she kept from tumbling over. When she came to a stop at the bottom of the ramp, the first thing she saw was Aarat, curled in a circle, magic pulsing along his amber and black scales.

"Aarat?"

His massive head rose and turned to her. "The new dragon emerges. An intruder came to steal the egg. They failed."

"Oh. *Oh!*" Belatedly, Lisette saw the charred lump of what had once been a human near the other entrance to the cavern. That explained why Aarat hadn't investigated the disturbance in front of the dragon warrens — the dragon's first priority was ensuring the safety of the egg and the tiny dragon within.

Or possibly no longer within. Lisette took a step closer so she could look over Aarat. The glowing purple egg now had a crack visible along the meridian. As she watched, a tiny gold claw punctured the membrane.

Entranced by the scene, Lisette wanted nothing more than to stay and watch. But there were other people depending on her. She stored the image in her heart to describe to Remy later, then stepped away.

"The blue-green dragon broke her chain. There was a... *thing* that was keeping her from speaking. When I removed it, she said the dragon-born had been taken."

The waves of magic rippling over Aarat's spine grew in strength. Lisette took another step back and kept speaking.

"Giselle — she's the mage that was on the ship, one of Remy's professors — she's going to use a tracking spell to find Sunny, but we need something she's touched recently."

Aarat's body curled more tightly in on itself, as if he could protect the new dragon with his bulk. Then one limb stretched out, snagging a gold coin from the edge of the cavern and dropping it by Lisette's toes before she could move. "The dragon-born sleeps on gold. This should allow your spell of tracking."

"Thank you." Pulling a rag from her pocket, Lisette stooped to retrieve the disk. The coin was old, the pattern stamped into it one of a ruler dead and forgotten, but there was enough gold to fund the freeholder quarter for a week. The dragon-born had the same taste in precious metals as dragons.

Aarat lowered his head again. "Make no mistake, Lisette," and this time his musical voice tugged on her soul, "this is an attack on the dragons. It will not stand. Find the dragon-born and return her to safety."

The implicit threat sped Lisette up the ramp and out

through the gates of the dragon warrens, a fortune in gold clutched in one bloody fist. Giselle and the blue-green dragon waited where she'd left them.

Giselle was looking down at the spike and chain lying in the dirt, brows furrowed. "*That's* a nasty piece of work, no doubt about it." She crouched to examine it. "We may be able to use the residual magic to power this spell."

"Here," Lisette said, holding up the gold coin. "Aarat says Sunny slept on this recently."

The older woman glanced over. "Ah, yes. That will do nicely. Put it down here. Careful. Don't get your blood... Ah, I see you've learned that lesson." She sat cross-legged on the road in front of the items. "Braatle here tells me it's been less than an hour since the girl cried out. She must still be in Harbor Crag."

Or dead, Lisette thought, but she didn't say it. Aarat might destroy the city if the dragon-born had been killed. The blue-green dragon was apparently called Braatle, though how Giselle had learned that Lisette didn't know. Dragons held power through names.

Once again, Lisette wished Remy were present. She looked around for someone to send with a message, but the street was empty — anyone with sense had put space between themself and an angry dragon. Still, news of a second dragon would spread through Harbor Crag faster than flames. Remy would show up on his own soon.

The spike and chain flashed red and then crumbled to dust.

Giselle stood, the coin hovering above her palm. "She's alive, but they have her cloaked for now. She'll only stay hidden until she awakes. The instant the cloaking spell releases, we'll know her direction." The coin remained in place above her hand as she began repacking her bag. "In the meantime, I suggest we head down to the waterfront. If *I* were kidnapping the dragon-born, I'd be on the next ship leaving the harbor, no matter what the destination."

Giselle began walking back in the direction they'd come, Braatle by her side. Lisette followed in their wake, thinking about what Aarat had said. Someone had tried and failed to steal the egg, and someone else had taken Sunny while Aarat was too busy protecting the egg to defend the girl. This kidnapping had been well coordinated, and they had at least one mage working with them.

Lisette trotted after the others, coughing from the smoke of the still-burning cart, aware of a terrible coincidence...

Giselle had arrived just when it all happened.

CHAPTER 7

THE HARBORMASTER'S SHOES

As they hurried down the hill, Lisette stayed on the right side of the dragon, marveling at the iridescent sea foam of the scales near her spine. Braatle, she reminded herself. The dragon's name was Braatle.

"Where does the duke reside?" Braatle's voice could have been a choir, but without the force behind it that Lisette had grown used to with Aarat. The menace was the same, though. "I would pay him a visit after we recover the dragon-born."

Behind them, a cart still smoldered, casting thick smoke into the breeze, but here there was only evidence of a hurried evacuation: food stalls left untended, parcels left where they were dropped, and a single shoe in the middle of the road. A crock of basil-infused oil had shattered on the stones, leaving the area with a sweetly herbal scent.

On the other side of Braatle, Giselle strode confidently, as if this were just another day's outing. The gold coin floating above her hand — the link to the kidnapped dragon-born — never wavered. Lisette wished she could tell for sure that Giselle was trying to track the girl. For all she knew, making a coin hover in the air was a party trick every mage could do. An unexpected smile came over her face as she considered what would happen if Remy tried it. Something spectacular, she was sure.

When Giselle didn't answer the dragon's question, Lisette spoke. "The *current* duke is on the Island of Light." She paused and then added, "I think." Things had gotten chaotic when Aarat freed himself. It was possible the mages had grown tired of the duke's chicken obsession and dumped him in the ocean. The only thing Lisette really knew was that the duke was not in Harbor Crag. "But the duke you remember may be long dead."

How long had Braatle been confined? Lisette had been born and raised in Harbor Crag, and she'd never seen a dragon until she'd pitched down the hole into Aarat's cavern. Assuming the mages hadn't somehow been smuggling dragons into the warrens under cover of night, Braatle must have been chained underground for decades.

As they walked, the dragon was noticeably lagging, the leg with the chain scraping against the cobblestones. "They lured us in with talk of working together to keep the ships safe, gold coin for protection against creatures of the deep. Then one night, the duke and his mages cast a spell to make me sleep. By the time I fought it off, they had bound me and drained my magic, and cast another spell to keep me without speech." Wisps of smoke came from her nostrils. "I could not even warn the others."

Giselle raised her eyebrows at Lisette, in what was clearly a command to find another topic, one that wouldn't make the dragon so angry the city burned down.

But Lisette needed to know. "Why did they not take Aarat's speech from him?"

"He was the strongest of us all. Had they started with

Aarat, the mages would have died. But with every dragon taken, the mages grew stronger. Aarat would have been the last to be trapped." More smoke emerged between her jagged teeth.

Perhaps Giselle had a point. Lisette hastened to calm the increasingly agitated dragon. "When Aarat freed himself, he burned down Lord Hanley's residence and forced the mages and nobles to flee. We have the objects tied to the draining spells — we've been trying to figure out how to break those bonds. That's why Giselle is here."

She sincerely *hoped* that was why Giselle was here.

"Hmph." The grumpy snort sounded just like Aarat.

The closer they came to the harbor, the more people were visible. The streets were still clear — nobody wanted to get in the way of a dragon — but groups watched, ready to scatter, in the alleys and buildings. Even the street children were visible, taking the opportunity of the crowds to lighten a few purses. The citizens of Harbor Crag wouldn't be thrown off by a new dragon for long... unless Braatle set something else on fire.

Fool's Errand, the ship that had brought Giselle and Anna, was still docked, a line of stevedores unloading cargo onto two carts pulled by massive horses. The horses blew out heavy breaths and cast nervous glances toward the dragon, but the drivers had set the brakes firmly. Lisette held up a hand. "Wait here. I'll find someone."

Everyone she encountered was only too happy to direct her attention elsewhere, so it didn't take long to find the person in charge.

The harbormaster was a stout one-eyed woman of middle years who looked like she brooked no nonsense, though even she gave the dragon a wary look. She was dressed in rumpled linen and might have been mistaken for another stevedore if Lisette hadn't been told to look for a woman with a scar splitting her face. "What deep water insanity are we in for now?" she demanded when Lisette approached.

"A missing child." Lisette described Sunny. "She may be drugged or spelled."

"And the dragons are interested." With a glance around the water, the harbormaster pursed her lips. "*Fool's Errand* is still unloading and hasn't taken on any cargo yet. *Fair Lady* sent in a boat, but it hasn't gone out again. I've got four more waiting out there. The fishing boats are all in — even the mages can't change the tides. *Dancing Eel* is the only one who *might* have had a boat go out in your time-frame — the mate rowed out a while back with some crew who got caught in a brawl. I suppose they could have carried a child along with the injured sailors. Maybe too early to be your ship, maybe not."

Lisette sighed. "Someone needs to search it." And it would have to be someone Lisette trusted. Someone who couldn't be bribed. Her stomach sank. She *hated* being on the water. But she didn't trust Giselle, Remy wasn't there, and the rest of her friends were back in the freeholder quarter. Gritting her teeth, she added, "Can you get a boat and a crew to row me out?"

For the first time, a flicker of levity went over the harbormaster's features. "I'll take you out myself if you promise not to lose your breakfast on *my* shoes."

Lisette sighed again.

CHAPTER 8
DANCING EEL

Water slapped the sides of the boat with every swell, providing a counterpoint to the splash of the oars as the harbormaster's crew rowed Lisette out to *Dancing Eel*. Behind them, Harbor Crag rose from the water, a renowned scene captured in many famous paintings, but Lisette kept her eyes firmly fixed on the horizon ahead. Her fingers dug into the bench as her body tried to make everything stop *moving*.

"What I don't understand," the harbormaster said from next to her on the bench, "is how you could grow up here and never get used to being on the water. Did you never clear clogweed as a child?"

"Of course I did. That's how I know the sea is not for me." Three or four times every year, there would be a two-day bloom of clogweed in the harbor. Bright pink flowers rose above the waves, sending their spicy perfume into the air. Veteran sailors swore the fragrance called to the creatures of the depths.

Maybe that was true in deeper water, but the real problem, at least for Harbor Crag, was that if left unchecked, the clogweed would choke the harbor, fouling oars and making it nearly impossible for ships to enter.

So during each clogweed bloom, every fishing boat spent all day and night on the water picking the flowers, coming to shore only to switch crew. Volunteers from every part of Harbor Crag went out in the boats or helped build bonfires to burn the flowers on shore. Freed from their other tasks during clogweed days, children wearing floating vests went out on the boats as soon as they were old enough to help. It was a rite of passage in Harbor Crag.

Lisette had become an expert at building bonfires.

As they bounced closer to *Dancing Eel*, Lisette concentrated on the cool breeze blowing against her face, and the salty smell of the water. She just needed to stay in control of her stomach long enough to search this ship for any sign of Sunny, and then they could all go back to land, where the ground didn't sway under her feet.

Up on *Dancing Eel*, a young man in a rough canvas shirt saw them and shouted to someone else on deck. That brought another two men and a woman, all three wearing similar clothing. The oldest man leaned over and bellowed, "What're you here for, Pol? Cargo's set. We're waiting on the tide."

"Need to search the ship, Joran," the harbormaster yelled back. "Young girl's gone missing."

The rowboat bounced up and down. Lisette wiped cold sweat from her brow.

Joran drew his head back. "There's no young lass on the *Eel*. What kinda man do you take me for?"

"Still need to look, Joran." The harbor master lowered her voice and said to Lisette, "He doesn't want us searching his vessel because then we might find the spelled fire-whisky he's hiding in the hold. He sneaks the occasional bottle ashore when he thinks I'm not watching, and I pretend not to notice. But he's careful about who he sells it to, so I let it go."

Above them, Joran frowned and called down, "You've no right to board the *Eel*."

Watching Joran bob up and down relative to the rowboat was not helping Lisette's nausea. "It's us or the dragon —." The end of her sentence went into the sea with the contents of her stomach.

When she sat up, the harbormaster, the captain of *Dancing Eel*, and a dozen sailors were watching her with amusement. The harbormaster said innocently, "Was there anything else you wanted to add to that?" The two men rowing the boat guffawed. When Lisette groaned, the harbormaster huffed a laugh, looked up at the *Eel*, and yelled, "As she said, it's either us or the angry dragon comes out here for a look. You pick."

Joran threw up his hands. "Come aboard then."

Climbing up the Jacob's ladder was easier than climbing up the duke's tower, though the tower didn't move up and down. Lisette took a moment to be glad this had happened on a day with calm seas — if the waves had been any stronger, she'd never have made it this far. Two sailors hauled her up as soon as she was within reach, setting her down on the deck with a laugh.

She gave a weak wave of thanks. "Haven't quite found my sea legs yet."

"Your sea legs ran off with a man selling false gold," one said, to the amusement of the rest of the crew.

The harbormaster swung herself onto the deck with no help. "What in the watery depths is *that*?"

Lisette followed her gaze to a shining statue mounted on the mast. Made of silver, the creature had tentacles wrapping around the wood behind it, but its eyes stared forward. As Lisette watched, the tip of one tentacle moved. Magic streamed off the thing, most of it aimed toward the water.

Joran shrugged nonchalantly, though he and the rest of the crew never strayed within arm's length of the statue. "Protection against the creatures of the deep. Need it, these days. Picked up a mage from the Island of Light. He says it's making the ship look like this is one of their own."

"He should have made it also protect men from getting drunk and falling into fireplaces," one sailor joked, to the loud amusement of his fellows.

Until recently, the city's mages had been using stolen dragon magic to protect ships from Harbor Crag — and *only* Harbor Crag — against predation by the giant creatures who lived in the depths. Without that protection, ships needed to hug the coastline, so voyages took longer and were more costly. The market for shipboard mages had increased sharply.

But Aarat hadn't noticed a mage aboard *Dancing Eel*, which must have arrived days before *Fool's Errand*. Either the mage was no longer with this ship, or he had somehow hidden his magic. Lisette turned to the harbormaster, the sudden movement making her stomach lurch. She leaned over the rail and waited for her empty stomach to finish rebelling.

Luckily, the harbormaster was quick. "Your mage still aboard?"

"Scraps is down below patching him up. Turns out mages on shore leave are worse than oarsmen." Laughter and offended swearing greeted his words.

Lisette tore herself away from the railing long enough to say, "We need to see this mage after we search the ship."

They all trooped belowdecks with Lisette — the captain to be sure they didn't go anywhere they shouldn't, the harbormaster to learn what she could, and the rest of the crew because they had bets on how long Lisette would last before she heaved again.

"Sorry, flower, it's just that we have nothing else to do until the tide turns," the second mate told her as he offered his arm to steady her.

"Anything to keep you amused," she replied, and fought back another surge of nausea. "I think I'm getting better."

"Hold off another five minutes and I'll pass you half my winnings," he stage whispered, then laughed so loudly the whole ship rang.

The holds stank of rotting wood and brackish water, but Sunny wasn't there. Up one level, the crew cabin held rows of hammocks and nothing else of interest. The captain's cabin had a trunk with a false bottom large enough to hold a child, but it was full of bottles — the spelled fire-whisky the harbormaster, now conspicuously looking at the ceiling, had told her about. Farther aft, there were three passenger cabins. The first two were empty.

The third passenger cabin had an unconscious man lying on a bed, stripped to his waist, while the ship's surgeon dressed the blistered flesh of his shoulder. The unconscious man's neck and face were reddened, but those burns were less serious.

The captain gestured. "And this is our mage, though I doubt he'll be much good to us for a while."

Lisette picked up the discarded shirt and sniffed, knowing what she would find. "He didn't fall into a fire-place. He tried to steal a dragon's egg."

The dragon-born wasn't on the ship, but this mage might help them find her.

CHAPTER 9

THIS IS WHY YOU DON'T ANGER A DRAGON

S olid ground had never felt so wonderful before. Lisette stumbled off the rowboat and stood with her hands on her knees, staring at the wave-smoothed rocks while she waited for her stomach to settle. Boots crunched across the pebbles toward her, but she couldn't be bothered to look up. Even the dragon blocking the nearby road wasn't as important as making the world stop moving.

"Not a natural sailor, then?" Remy's voice accompanied his comforting hand on Lisette's shoulder. Laughter from the oarsmen hauling the boat above the tide line greeted his words.

The amused voice of the harbormaster cut through the laughter. "She did fine. Fed the fish a few times, but we won't hold that against her." Her voice took on a more serious tone. "What do you want to do with this one?"

The captain of *Dancing Eel* hadn't been able to get the mage off the boat fast enough when he found out dragons were involved.

Grabbing Remy's sleeve to pull herself upright, Lisette gestured at the unconscious figure in the boat. "He's a mage with burns from Aarat. He must have been involved." Belatedly, she realized Remy hadn't been there when she'd learned about the dragon-born's kidnapping. "Where's Giselle?"

"She's hoping maybe the tracking spell will work if she's closer, so she's gone to walk the perimeter of the city." Remy put an arm around her shoulder, his warmth welcome after the chill caused by nausea-induced sweating. "Simi and I stayed here with Braatle. Well done on removing the language nullifier. Giselle was impressed."

Remy had stayed because the blue-green dragon couldn't be left to her own devices mere hours after escaping captivity and regaining the ability to speak. When Lisette glanced over at Braatle, this time she noticed the calico cat draped over the dragon's muzzle, fast asleep. "We need to find a place for this mage, so we can question him if he survives that long. And then..." They *had* to find out where the kidnappers had taken Sunny. If she thought about it too long, she would panic — mages had used the blood of the dragon-born in their spells to subdue the dragons. "I don't know."

It seemed almost indecent that underneath her worry about Sunny and everything else, Lisette felt relief that Remy was here to help shoulder the burden. Having Giselle's magic available was helpful, but Lisette *trusted* Remy.

They walked to the rowboat and its heavily bandaged occupant. Remy winced. "*That's* why you don't anger a dragon. Among other reasons." He crouched, splayed one hand over the man's chest, and closed his eyes. When he stood up, he shook his head. "He's got a serious healing spell in place. It's going to take a day or two before he wakes up." With a glance at Lisette, he shrugged. "Move him to our apartment? My mother can keep an eye on him."

Lisette blinked. In all the excitement, she'd forgotten about Remy's mother. This was *not* how she'd planned their meeting. "Is it safe?"

Remy nodded. "When he wakes up, he'll be weak as a newborn kitten, and my mother's handy with a walking stick." He eyed the harbormaster. "Can you arrange transport to the freeholder quarter? We'll pay a fair price."

The harbormaster tilted her head at the dragon. "The sooner you make that one happy and get business back to normal, the better. I'll get some of mine to take him up the hill for you."

"My thanks." Remy turned back to Lisette. "Braatle thinks she may be able to sense if Sunny is nearby. Unless you have a better idea, I think we should make a tour of the city."

They turned to look at the blue-green dragon, who had settled on her belly. The broken chain trailing behind her reflected the sun into Lisette's eyes. "Can she make it that far? Walking down the hill took most of her strength. Going back up..."

"Her magic's still being drained by Lord Hanley and his group," Remy said. "If we could break that..." He trailed off, a speculative look in his eye.

"We still don't know how to do that," Lisette reminded him.

"No," he agreed. "But *before,* we were trying to break those spells without the dragons helping — that language nullifier explains a lot. If Braatle and I worked *together*..."

Lisette interrupted before he went too far into his thoughts. "You would need the weapon used in the spell, right?" All the weapons tied to the dragons had been in Lord Hanley's mansion before Lisette and Remy had stolen them. Now, they were stashed in Aarat's cavern to keep them safe until Remy could figure out how to break the entangled spells. At Remy's nod, Lisette rolled her shoulders to relieve the stiffness. "I'll get it."

"Are you sure?" Remy's half-smile almost hid his concern. "You're looking a little worn. Why don't you stay here and I'll go."

Huffing a laugh, Lisette touched his hand. "With the mood Aarat's in, you wouldn't stand a chance. I'll be fine. See you in a bit." She strode off, putting more energy in her step than she felt.

Halfway up the hill to the dragon warrens, her mood sank. Why couldn't the mages just leave Harbor Crag and the dragons alone? What kind of monsters used the blood of a child in their spells? And why wouldn't all the people taking up space in the stupid road either walk faster or get out of the way? That last thought made her realize that everything she'd eaten that morning was now in the harbor, so she stopped at a stall to buy a skewer of fruit chunks and a roll, which she ate while finishing the climb.

People had returned to the streets around the dragon warrens, almost as if the morning's events hadn't taken place. Even the burned cart had been removed, and another cart put up in its place, though the woman stitching the seam on a cloak in its shade watched the area nervously. It was a prime spot, at the intersection of two major roads, so she would be well rewarded for her boldness — as long as her cart didn't go up in flames.

Past the open gates of the dragon warren, nothing

moved. Lisette trudged to the hole leading to Aarat's chamber. "It's me again," she yelled before jumping onto the dirt ramp and letting momentum take her below the earth into the cavern. "Don't —"

Lisette's mouth snapped shut as a crossbow bolt sliced through the air in front of her nose.

CHAPTER 10
WORTH

The crossbow bolt bounced off the stone wall next to her ear with a metallic clang. In front of her, chaos reigned. Screams of pain followed gouts of dragon fire.

The amber and black dragon still curled around the egg, but now a score of fighters had surrounded him, each holding a shining dagger. Dressed in worn armor, the men moved like soldiers, though they wore no insignia proclaiming their allegiance. They darted in nervously, their attacks deflected by Aarat's gleaming scales.

Near the other entrance to the cavern, a knot of men stood, safely out of the way of any dragon fire. A cluster of men stepped back as one to reload their crossbows while another group stepped forward to aim. From another man came a stream of magic that splashed over the dragon.

Lisette dashed forward to get the dragon between herself and the crossbows, trying to figure out what the other brigands meant to do. No matter how skilled these fighters were, they weren't going to seriously injure an adult dragon with a dagger.

But Aarat's magic had once been bound using a spelled blade.

Another burst of dragon fire swept the cavern. One man fell to the ground, but two more rushed in. The crossbow bolts flew toward Aarat's eyes, forcing the dragon to turn his head away. But in order to shoot at the dragon, the soldiers with crossbows had to leave the safety of the passageway, and Aarat was slowly winnowing their group.

Too slowly.

If Aarat's magic was bound again, the mages would return from the Island of Light, Lord Hanley among them. Lisette couldn't let that happen.

"Slide the dagger *under* the scale," the tall man standing behind the crossbowmen in the safety of the passageway yelled, frustration in his voice. "I just need a drop!"

Lisette had no blade and no combat experience. Going up against trained fighters would get her killed and not even slow them down. But the weapon she had come to retrieve would level the playing field. Blood on the metal transferred the bonds holding the dragon's magic; non-mages couldn't hold so much power. Lisette had seen that close up, had nearly died herself when her own blood had touched the blade.

If she could get close enough to scratch the intruders, any dragon-linked weapon would kill.

Everything she and Remy had brought back from Lord Hanley's estate rested in a pile at the edge of the cavern, a jumble of spikes, daggers, pins, and other pointed objects. All had been created with the blood of a dragon-born.

She stopped just long enough to pull on her gloves, then picked up the longest weapon, a knife that wouldn't have looked out of place carving meat at a banquet.

A few of the fighters noticed movement and glanced her

direction. Then they ignored her to focus on the greater threat. Probably she was holding the knife wrong, and her inexperience would be obvious to any trained fighter. Feeling slighted was silly. She *wanted* them to ignore her. But still.

The nearest man crouched, waiting for his chance to strike while Aarat was destroying one of his colleagues. He wore heavy boots, leather breeches, and a sleeveless jerkin, but his arms were bare aside from the bracers protecting his forearms.

His arms would be the easiest target, especially if she could nick the skin while his back was turned. Without stopping to think about it, Lisette darted forward and stabbed his arm.

It was a weak blow, her natural fear of hurting anyone impossible to overcome. If the knife hadn't been bound to a dragon, the man would have killed her before she could blink.

Magic flooded the cavern, noticeable even with Aarat's power rippling over his scales. From somewhere nearby, another dragon roared. The man she'd stabbed stiffened, then threw his head back in a silent scream. He crumpled into a heap of ash and the magic drained away, snapping back to the previous bond.

Lisette stared at the ash. She'd intentionally killed a man. Hands trembling, she turned to the next fighter. But this man wasn't focused on the dragon — he advanced toward her, pulling his sword as he moved.

"I don't suppose we could all call a truce and leave," she said, voice shaking as she backed toward the pile of dragon-linked weapons. Another burst of flame and screaming told her Aarat's odds had improved again. Not enough to save *her*, maybe, but perhaps the dragon would fight them all off in the end.

The man facing Lisette cocked his head, the helm giving his face a sinister cast. "You're the woman Lord Hanley wants."

Lisette's stomach dropped. She'd *really* hoped the mage had given up his obsession. "No idea what you're talking about." Shifting the knife into her left hand, she grabbed a rusty dagger with her right and hurled it at him.

The man batted it away with his sword. "You're worth nearly as much as this dragon's blood." A quick flick of the sword knocked the knife out of her left hand, and he grabbed her arm.

Lisette let him haul her toward him. Using her momentum to her advantage, she stabbed his elbow with the pin on the back of the brooch she'd concealed in her hand. As her attacker stiffened, power flooding through him, she yanked her arm away and hissed, "I'm worth more than that man could ever pay."

Ash rained to the floor of the cavern, and the power ebbed again.

The remaining attackers suddenly realized they were fighting a battle on two fronts, which meant they couldn't concentrate entirely on Aarat. The dragon killed two more with fire and ate a third before Lisette had retrieved the long knife from where it had fallen.

A cry of triumph came from one of the last three men wielding daggers, drowned out by a snarl of rage from the dragon. The man's celebration abruptly ended when Aarat's claw pierced his chest, ripping through the boiled leather as if it wasn't there.

But the dying man's comrade picked up the dagger and

sprinted toward the cavern entrance. A torrent of flame overtook him, but the fighter with the blooded dagger reached the mage before dropping. The tall man snatched the dagger and fled into the passageway.

"Stop him!" Aarat snarled.

Lisette sprinted after the mage.

CHAPTER II

ONE DISASTER AFTER ANOTHER

Lisette ran through the dim tunnel, occasionally catching glimpses of the mage's dark cloak as she rounded corners. The corridor connected a maze of caverns and dead-ends, but the man headed unerringly toward the entrance.

Labored breathing from ahead told her that even though the mage knew the layout, he wasn't used to running; after living on the steep slope of Harbor Crag all her life, Lisette had stamina despite no particular turn of speed. As the path sloped upward, she gained ground. She could *not* allow him to get away with a dagger soaked in Aarat's blood.

As they rounded another corner, a shaft of bright light in the distance warned her they were getting close to the entrance. From there, it would be just a few steps before he would be out of the dragon warrens and able to lose himself in the crowds. Lisette gritted her teeth and ran faster.

The man in front of her glanced over his shoulder, then turned and hurled a glass bulb. "Begone!" The bulb sailed over Lisette's shoulder and shattered against the floor, releasing purple flames. The odor of decay filled the air. Remy would have created a more worthy distraction. Or, at the very least, Remy would have had better aim.

With a last burst of speed, Lisette closed the gap and snatched the back of the mage's tunic, yanking him to a halt. Then she leaped to the side as he threw another glass bulb at her. A shock wave threw them both to the side, away from where the glass had shattered on the rock wall.

Lisette tightened her hold on the mage's tunic so he couldn't face her. "Leave the dagger and I'll let you go."

"Unhand me," he wheezed. Another glass bulb sailed past her and exploded, leaving a crack that extended from the floor to the ceiling.

Lisette took three steps back, pulling the breathless mage with her. If the ceiling caved in, she wanted it to trap them on the same side as Aarat. "Drop the dagger." She still held the long knife linked to a dragon, but using it to defend herself and Aarat during battle was one thing; drawing blood on a man who seemed about to collapse from exertion was another. "I don't want to use this on you, but I will if I have to."

The mage looked over his shoulder at the knife and stopped trying to pull away. He smiled, a vicious expression that lit up his eyes. "You will, will you?"

Lisette had no time to react when he turned and grabbed the blade of the knife with his naked hand, slicing open the skin on his palm.

Magic flooded the corridor. The mage threw back his head and yelled. But instead of turning to ash, he took on a glow as the magic swirled toward him.

"Oh no." With a sick feeling, Lisette realized what she'd done. The blade had been lethal to the soldiers because they couldn't handle the inrush of magic. But a mage...

He would take over the knife's bond with its dragon and gain all the power.

The unfairness of it all made tears prick Lisette's eyes. "This *day*! One disaster after another!" In front of her, the mage arched his back as he absorbed the power.

The other dagger with Aarat's blood was in his hand. If Lisette could do nothing else, maybe she could steal it while he was distracted.

Lisette leaned forward and poked his hand with one finger, ready to jump back if the magic changed. When nothing happened, she tugged at the end of the dagger handle, but the mage's muscles were locked.

There were times to be gentle, and then there were emergencies. Lisette dropped the long knife at the edge of the passageway and twisted the mage's wrist, prying his fingers up. The metal blade held a dark, iridescent stain at the tip — Aarat's blood.

His index finger crackled as she pulled it from the blade, making Lisette shudder. How did fighters handle killing and maiming people? That sparked a memory, of Uncle Rye explaining that he hadn't been able to remain a soldier. She'd thought she understood, but now that she'd killed two people and broken another man's bone, all she wanted was to be back with Remy in her studio, fixing watches and playing with Tiffany's children.

The dagger clanged on the stone floor.

Lisette had just enough time to grab it before the mage exhaled and looked at her. Magic no longer filled the air, but she could see the power in his eyes. This mage had successfully taken over the dragon's bond.

Backing away, Lisette held the dagger with Aarat's blood behind her back and stooped to pick up the long knife. If she could get away with both weapons, Aarat wouldn't be re-bound, and they could figure out how to free the other dragon.

"Stop!" the other mage thundered. He raised his hand, one finger skewed to the side. A wave of magic slammed into her.

Expecting to be incinerated, Lisette shut her eyes and braced for the pain.

Nothing happened.

No, not nothing. She could feel the spell flowing around her. The bond with Aarat had protected her again. Cautiously opening her eyes, she saw the mage's lips purse in frustration.

He gestured again, and a section of the wall next to her exploded into dust. Lisette dodged to avoid the debris. This man had needed prepared spells and potions before, but now he could do the same thing with a gesture. She was just lucky his aim hadn't improved.

Another section of stone ignited into a ball of flame, forcing her back toward the mage. It happened again, then a third time, and she realized he was intentionally herding her. Since he couldn't harm her directly with his magic, he would get her within arm's length. She gripped the weapons tighter, trying to picture the blade of the long knife slipping between his ribs. Could she do this? She *had* to.

The mage laughed as he flicked his fingers, and another chunk of rock exploded.

A sharp crack was the only warning Lisette got. She threw herself back, not even attempting to keep her feet.

The roar of shattering stones surged and the ceiling crashed to the ground.

CHAPTER 12

FRIEND OF THE DRAGONS

With the thunder of falling rocks blotting out coherent thought, Lisette scrambled away until she pitched into a wall and fell, still scrabbling against the floor to move backward. How much of the ceiling had been weakened by the mage's blasts? Before she could regain her feet, the cave-in slowed and then stopped, the quiet broken only by pebbles sliding. She coughed as dust billowed through the passageway.

In another thirty seconds, the air cleared, giving Lisette a view of what remained. What once had been a smooth route to the surface carved through stone was now a pile of rubble, giving a clear view of the sky above.

She couldn't see the passage on the other side of the cave-in. If the mage had reached safety, he would get away.

At least he didn't have the dagger with Aarat's blood.

Lisette struggled to her feet, using the wall for support. She would go back to Aarat's chamber, give him the dagger, and retrieve the weapon that held Braatle's bond. Then Remy and Giselle would help free Braatle, and they would find and rescue Sunny.

The long knife the mage had used to slice his palm felt odd, as if her skin had gone numb. Or as if the magic... Lisette went back to the pile of rocks and looked more closely. Sure enough, the mage's boots were just visible at the edge of the rubble, an enormous boulder standing where his chest would be, removing all doubt that he was dead.

"I guess that solves that problem." If she was right, she had just found a second way to free a dragon. The first had involved Lisette nearly dying, and the second required killing a mage. Neither method was practical, considering they had dozens of dragons still bound.

Somewhere nearby was a chained, angry dragon who was gaining power again but had no speech, and Lisette had no idea which one it was. She groaned and rubbed her face. That would have to be a problem for later.

She staggered back to Aarat's cavern, bruised muscles protesting. When she reached the entrance, she hung back. "It's me."

A quick peek around the corner showed the amber and black dragon's massive head hovering an arm's length away, steam rising from his nostrils. But he retreated to curl his bulk around the egg. His musical voice lashed out. "The mage escaped?"

"No. The mage is dead." Lisette edged into the cavern, ready to leap back. Only a fool would trust an angry dragon. She held out the dagger with his blood. "This is yours."

A claw snatched the dagger from her hand before she could flinch. Flames roared, heating the opposite wall. When Aarat had finished, the dagger glowed on the ground. Any blood on the surface had turned to ash. The dragon settled more comfortably, as if a great weight had dissipated. Maybe it had — Aarat had just escaped decades of captivity. "I had not taken you for a fighter."

Since the dragon appeared calmer, Lisette moved further into the cavern. "Would it help if I told you the mage accidentally brought the ceiling down on himself while he was trying to kill me?"

Aarat's laughter rumbled through the open space.

Lisette raised the long knife. "Before he died, he took over the bond on this blade. Am I right in assuming the spell is broken?"

This time, Aarat's movements were slower and more delicate, as two razor-sharp talons took the blade from her hand. He examined the weapon and then set it aside. "Kledaag is free from the curse."

"Good." Hopefully, Remy could find a way to counter-spell the — what had he called it? — the *language nullifier* from a distance so she didn't have to get close enough to Kledaag to remove the spike first. "I came to find the weapon used to bind Braatle. Remy thinks he may be able to break the bond if they work together."

"Perhaps you should find another mage and a pile of rocks."

Lisette cocked her head, watching as delicate talons sorted through the dragon-bound weapons. Had that been a joke? She'd never noticed Aarat having a sense of humor before. Maybe she'd missed it.

The dragon dropped a wickedly sharp hatpin at her feet. "There is an entire castle of mages on the Island of Light. I'd be happy to take you there when the egg has hatched."

Or... maybe the dragon wasn't joking. Lisette busied herself with removing one glove and wrapping it around the tip of the hatpin so she didn't accidentally scratch someone during transport.

When she looked up, Aarat had uncurled, creating a gap so Lisette could see the egg with a wider crack and a chip missing. The delicate snout of a crimson dragon poked through the opening. Magic rippled over Aarat's spines. "Behold, friend of the dragons. May the luck of hatching bring strong winds to your search."

"Oh!" Lisette held her free hand over her mouth. The glow of magic pulsed from within the shell, and a shard dropped away, just enough to expose another few red scales edged in gold. "She's beautiful."

A tiny squeal of frustration came from within the egg, making Lisette smile. This was the last time this powerful creature would be no threat to her, but she couldn't wait to see the new dragon fully released. Aarat had called Lisette "friend of the dragons" — it sounded like a title, but she'd learned that even the blessings of dragons came with responsibilities. Remy would know.

Aarat closed the protective bulk of his body around his charge. "Return the dragon-born to us, Lisette." When he spoke her name, a pulse of energy came through their bond, making her skin itch. The ache of her bruises receded.

"I will." It was a stupid thing to say, nearly a promise, when promises to a dragon were a contract that dared not be broken. But Lisette meant to find Sunny if it was the last thing she did.

Holding the hatpin away from her body, she jogged up the ramp toward the open sky.

CHAPTER 13
TWINING INTERLOCK

Remy and Braatle were two streets above the harbor, the dragon stretched out on the road blocking all but the bravest foot traffic. When Remy saw Lisette, he smiled, one eyebrow quirking up, though he looked her over with concern. "Every time I see you today, you look like you've been off on another adventure."

Holding the hatpin off to the side, Lisette leaned into his hug, allowing herself to relax for a few seconds. "Remember when we were just going to excavate the magical items from the ruins of Lord Hanley's mansion and then go back home? I miss that plan." She could have been in her workshop examining what was left of Bralinost. With a sigh, she related the latest attack on Aarat and the little dragon, as well as the death of the mage who had taken over Kledaag's bond.

Remy blew out a quick breath. "Well, that's certainly one way to break the spell, but I can't say I'm excited to volunteer."

"Aarat offered to take me over to the Island of Light to

find candidates." When Remy laughed, Lisette handed over the hatpin.

Braatle lifted her head from the ground to look more closely. "Such a small thing to change my fate." Her eyes narrowed as she concentrated, and Remy stood up straighter.

"Do that again, if you please," he said, holding up the sliver of metal between them. "It pulled the spell... Ah, now *that's* interesting."

The dragon tilted her head. "A twining interlock?"

Remy and Braatle continued speaking cryptic phrases. Lisette assumed they were talking about spell constructions, because as far as she could tell, they were looking at an ordinary hatpin with no moving parts. When Simi wandered over to rub her cheeks against Lisette's boots, Lisette crouched to pet the purring cat. "I'm sure they'll start talking sense sometime soon," she whispered to the calico.

"Catalan described a technique..." Remy screwed up his face as he concentrated, then shook his head. "I need to look it up. It's in one of my books."

Feeling every bump and bruise of the day, Lisette asked, "Which book?" True, if she retrieved the book for him, she would have to walk up the hill to the freeholder quarter. But her clothes and skin had reached a level of filth that was hard to ignore, and Remy would be far better suited to help if any sighting of the dragon-born occurred.

"Which book indeed... The big brown one with the picture of a sheep on the cover. It's supposed to be Stellan the Brave's warhorse, which was spelled to repel arrows, but the artist wasn't up to the task. It's in my workspace either on my desk or in the trunk or... It's somewhere up there, anyhow."

Lisette snorted. Remy's workspace above her shop had been her bedroom until they'd moved to larger rooms across the street. In the past month, he'd crammed more stuff into the cramped space than she had in twenty years. "I'll find it."

Catching her hand, he lifted it to kiss her wrist, an intimate gesture that made her cheeks heat. "Thank you. Send it back via messenger and relax a bit."

"You mean clean up so I look less like a fire wight?"

"Wights don't exist." He shrugged one shoulder. "Or, at least, they probably don't. Geraldus has three chapters about them, but he's also terribly unreliable about dragons *and* ships, so I don't trust him at all."

Used to his diversions, Lisette smiled, nodded to the dragon, gave Simi a long stroke down her back to the tip of her tail, and strode up the hill.

THE BOOK WAS EASILY FOUND — Remy was right; it looked far more like a sheep than a horse — and dispatched with the blacksmith's oldest girl, who would be delighted to see a dragon close up.

That left Lisette free to take a few moments to recover from her morning. But it wasn't until she'd opened the door to the rooms she and Remy shared and heard her best friend gasp that she remembered she wouldn't be alone.

Tiffany got up from the table so fast the chair fell over. "What happened to *you*? Where are you hurt?"

Behind her, Remy's mother stood more gracefully, but looked concerned as well. "What can we do to help?"

"I'm fine," Lisette protested, though her breath hitched as she remembered she'd killed at least two men in Aarat's cavern. "I just need to change my clothes and wash up a bit."

Ignoring Lisette's words, Tiffany continued her inspection. "Why is there blood splashed across your neck? No, I can see it's not yours. Thank the god of the depths for small favors." She drew back so she could look at the rest of her friend. "Is that salt water dried on your boots? Did you go on a *boat*?" She clapped a hand over her mouth to muffle her burst of laughter.

Lisette's stomach turned at the memory. "It's been a horrible day." Then, realizing how that might sound to Anna, she hastily added, "Except for Remy's mother arriving, of course."

Tiffany's giggles increased, and Anna smiled. "We'll have a pot of tea for you when you're ready."

One benefit of living with a mage was instant hot water coming from the cistern on the roof, so Lisette was clean and dressed in clothing without scorch marks a few minutes later. Before she went out to the common area for the promised tea, she checked on the burned mage, who had been placed in the smallest room. He lay unmoving on a pallet that Lisette recognized from Tiffany's daughters' room, but his bandages were clean and he didn't appear to be in any pain.

"Tiffany, where's Turtle going to sleep tonight?" Lisette went out and sat down at the table, accepting the mug of tea Anna poured for her.

"She and Pot can share. It will be fine." When she saw Lisette glance behind her, she added, "They're at the bakery making designs on bread with vegetables." She frowned at Lisette. "We need to do something with your hair. It looks a bit... charred."

Anna folded her hands around her mug with a smile

that reminded Lisette of Remy when he was about to get into trouble. "You might want to wait a few days. If my son's involved, there may be more to come."

Tiffany considered that. "You have a point."

A knock on the door saved Lisette from having to defend Remy's honor, which would have been difficult since she agreed with the two women. She opened the door to see Giselle, her gray hair floating around her head like the feathers of a startled bird. The gold coin still hovered above her palm. "Remy said a mage involved in the abduction is here. Can I see him?"

"Of course." Opening the door wider, Lisette asked, "Would you like tea?"

The older woman seemed to be on the verge of refusing, but then she caught sight of Anna, still seated at the table, and her face brightened. "Thank you. That would be very welcome." Then her smile faded. "But I should see the mage first."

Lisette led her to the small room. "I don't think you'll be able to ask him anything. Remy said the healing spell will keep him from waking for a day or two."

"Even just knowing who he is will tell me who's involved with this." Giselle crouched by the bed and used his hair to turn the man's face toward the light. She hissed. "Patril, you *fool*!"

"You know him? He's from the Island of Light?"

"Worse." Giselle sat back on her heels, her face grave. "He's a professor at the Galfigon College for Magecraft."

CHAPTER 14

APOLOGIZE AND WALK AWAY

L isette watched Remy's mother prepare a mug of tea for Giselle. Anna added honey and a pinch of pepper without asking, making Lisette wonder how long they had known each other. The two women had traveled together on *Fool's Errand*, but their friendship seemed deeper than casual shipboard acquaintances. Perhaps they'd met while Remy was at the college.

The mage accepted the mug and breathed the steam deeply. "Thank you, love." She leaned back in the chair. "I suppose knowing Patril is involved makes my job here easier in some ways."

Before Lisette could ask, Tiffany did. "Why?" She nudged the plate of spiced nut bread toward Lisette and Giselle. "Eat. This will be too stale to chew by this afternoon."

Giselle dunked a slice in her tea. "Because in addition to traveling here to help free the dragons, I came to gather information on who was involved in keeping them bound." She trailed off and drank from her mug. "Remy wrote me with his suspicions, but I'd hoped he was wrong."

When it looked like Giselle had finished on the topic, Lisette touched Tiffany's arm. "The egg is finally hatching. You can tell Pot the new dragon is red." Tiffany's children had been eagerly awaiting news of the baby dragon ever since Lisette and Remy had found the egg.

Giselle's eyebrows rose. "You saw the hatching? That's a great honor."

"It wasn't so much planned as that the egg was hatching in the middle of everything." Lisette recounted her adventures of the morning, glossing over her role in the fight. Later, she would tell Tiffany what she'd done, but she didn't know Anna or Giselle well enough to talk about it with them.

When Lisette described the rockfall killing the mage and the freeing of Kledaag's bond, Giselle cocked her head. "I'll admit that I never considered that method."

"Could you not take over the bond yourself and then free them?" It seemed the easiest remedy to Lisette. Remy had been reluctant to try, claiming his magic was middling at best. Since the result of failure was instant death, Lisette didn't press. But Giselle was a professor — her magic wasn't in doubt.

"Perhaps. Certainly for some of the younger dragons. But I would imagine many of the bonds are shared between multiple mages because no person can handle that much power." She shook her head. "There must be safer ways to free them."

"Remy thinks it may help to work *with* the dragon," Lisette said. "He's trying with Braatle right now."

"And he may succeed using ways I'd never consider," Giselle said. She gave Anna a rueful grin. "Your son is obscenely clever. It got him into trouble at school."

Anna smiled. "That describes his entire life. If he hadn't

gone off to be a mage, our neighbors would have tied him up and dumped him on the next cargo ship."

They were right. Remy's twisty mind was just as likely to lead him into trouble as to provide a way out. Lisette loved him for it.

Giselle finished her bread and tea and stood. "I needed that, thank you." Turning to Lisette, she said, "If mages from the college are involved, I know some places they may be hiding, but I'll need a guide. Would you?"

"Of course." Only after she'd hastily swallowed her drink did it occur to Lisette that she'd be abandoning Remy's mother for the second time that day. "Anna, do you mind? I'd planned to show you around today, but..."

Anna waved her off. "Go find the child. We'll have plenty of time afterward."

Tiffany hugged Lisette. "If Anna gets bored, I'll bring the girls over. They'll keep her busy. Be careful out there."

"I will." Lisette followed Giselle out the door and down the steps to the street. "Where to?"

"There's a bookseller with an anchor and bell somewhere near the wharf. Do you know it?"

Lisette looked at the mage doubtfully. "The Salty Bookworm?" She had been there a few times when exploring the city with Uncle Barlow. Because the shop mainly catered to sailors looking for entertainment on long voyages, the books skewed toward lust-filled tales of adventure rather than scholarly tomes. It wasn't a place she would expect to find a professor. "It's rather..."

Giselle chuckled. "That's the place. There's a room in the back our people have used before. We may as well start there, since it's the only one for which I have a good description."

Lisette led the way out of the freeholder quarter and

they started down the main road toward the shore, weaving around carts, people, and a herd of goats. A caprine nibble on her sleeve was followed by a gentle touch at her empty coin purse. Then she heard a yelp. By the time she'd turned, a boy of about eight years was gripping his other hand and glowering at Giselle.

The child looked familiar to Lisette, but it took her a moment to recognize the boy's face. "You should have followed Remy's advice when you tried to steal from *him*." She repeated Remy's admonishment. "If you feel magic, apologize and walk away." Most of the mages in Harbor Crag had fled with Lord Hanley, but sooner or later, this child would steal from the wrong one.

"But I *want* it," the boy whined, massaging his palm. He stared at the gold coin hovering over Giselle's hand, the one that would alert them to the dragon-born.

Lisette blew out a breath, nonplussed. Street children weren't stupid enough to stay and argue when caught. This boy really *would* end up in chains if he didn't learn to control himself better.

But Giselle cocked her head. "Ah, now is it the gold you want? Or the magic?" From her tone, she might have been talking to herself. She plucked a coin — brass, not gold — from her sleeve and tossed it to him. "I'm busy at the moment, but in three days' time, ask for Giselle at the Raven's Inn. It's worth another coin for your trouble."

They continued downhill, leaving the young thief behind. Lisette checked over her shoulder to be sure he hadn't followed them. "A mage?"

"Or one attracted to magic," Giselle agreed. "Either way, he can't be left like that unsupervised."

"You think it will take us three days to find Sunny?" Lisette didn't want to imagine Aarat's mood if it took that long. And she *really* didn't want to imagine what the enemy mages might do to the dragon-born in that time.

Giselle's stride didn't slow. "No. I hope to find the child much sooner. But there's every possibility today's events are just a distraction before the main attack. We must be ready."

And with that, she collapsed.

CHAPTER 15
THE SALTY BOOKWORM

L isette reached Giselle just in time to keep her head from hitting the cobblestones. The mage's face had gone gray. For a horrible instant, Lisette thought she was dead. Then she noted two things: the slow rise and fall of the mage's chest as she breathed, and an amulet glowing beneath Giselle's tunic, the amber light pulsing rhythmically. When Lisette felt Giselle's wrist, the older woman's pulse beat in time with the amulet.

"Is she ill?" The woman roasting nuts had abandoned her stall to hurry over.

"I'm not sure what's wrong. She was fine, and then..." Lisette looked around, trying to remember where the nearest doctor would be. There was a man the sailors used to patch them up after brawls, but he dealt with knife wounds and not much else. Maybe it would be best to send for help from the freeholder quarter.

Giselle's eyes fluttered open.

Lisette leaned in. "Can I get you anything?"

The nut seller waved to the other vendors. "Claude, bring your blanket. Camille, send your boy to rouse Dr.

Algernon." Her voice dropped. "He might be sober enough by now."

"No doctor," Giselle croaked. "I just need to rest for a few hours." When she saw Lisette hesitate, the mage reached up weakly to place one hand over her amulet. "This is nothing new."

Her matter-of-factness comforted Lisette. "No doctor," she repeated to the nut seller, who looked relieved by the proclamation. The doctor's reputation had spread throughout the city. "If you could help me find a cart, I'll take her back to the freeholder quarter." She looked down at the mage. "Anna can watch over you."

Giselle grabbed Lisette's wrist. "You need to keep searching for the girl. Once they know I've seen Patril, they'll abandon anyplace I might know about. If she's not at the bookshop, there's a tea shop in the garden district."

"Which one?" There were about seventeen tea shops in the garden district. People went there for a leisurely afternoon with friends.

"There's some sort of turtle in front. Secret room, second floor." Giselle's voice was getting more faint.

Lisette put a hand on her shoulder. "If I don't find her there, I'll come by our rooms to talk to you again."

"Be careful." Giselle's eyes closed.

Lisette tensed, but the amulet continued its steady beat, and a moment later Giselle's chest rose and fell.

"You're looking for that dragon girl?" The nut seller crouched next to Lisette to tuck a blanket around the mage's legs. "We were told to look out for her."

Lisette nodded. "Who has a cart I can rent to get my friend back to the freeholder quarter? Or can you send for a carriage?"

"I'll take her there myself. You find the girl and keep the

dragons happy." She held out a hand, and they clasped wrists. "I'm Josephine."

"Lisette." Though leaving Giselle with a complete stranger felt improper, Josephine was right; finding Sunny needed to be the priority. "I have the watchmaker's shop in the freeholder quarter. If you ask anyone near there, they can help you get her to my rooms." She dug out a handful of coins. "Will this cover it? Please. For your lost trade, if nothing else," she added, when Josephine seemed about to push her hand away.

"Very well." The nut seller made the coins disappear. "Now off you go. Having the dragons angry is bad for business."

News of Braatle's destructive rage had obviously spread. "Thank you."

Lisette set off down the hill again. When she glanced over her shoulder, four people were lifting Giselle's limp form onto a handcart filled with chestnuts, walnuts, and almonds. Josephine saw her and gave an all-is-well wave. A moment later, Lisette turned the corner and they were lost to sight.

The Salty Bookworm hadn't changed since the last time Lisette had seen it, with grimy windows, a small stack of cheap, damaged folios on the pavement, and a tentacled creature holding a book, anchor, and bell on the weathered sign above the door. Rust pitted the chains holding the sign — this close to the water, everything not protected by oil or magic deteriorated quickly.

Inside, it smelled of paper and spiced cider. Bookshelves lined every wall, with well-used books crammed into every space. Three women in sailor's garb argued over which book to buy next, and a man lounged on the floor under the window next to a stack of novels.

The proprietor, a man called Screech who looked nearly as weathered as the sign out front, sat in his corner chair, feet propped on a table and book in hand. He flipped the cover closed when she entered and shook his finger as he searched his memory. Finally, his face brightened. "Ah! Barlow's lass, am I right? How's your uncle?"

"He's well, thank you." She moved closer, so the other people in the shop wouldn't catch her words. "I'm here about the missing girl. Have you heard?"

Screech let his booted feet fall to the floor and sat up. "The dragon — the new one — has gone by out front twice. Haven't found her yet, then?"

"Not yet." She lowered her voice even further. "Some of the mages involved may have been from Galfigon and..." Lisette trailed off and cast her eyes toward the back of the shop.

Worry lines appeared on Screech's leathery face. "That lot hasn't been here since early this morning. No girl, though you're welcome to check. Nothing they're paying me can make up for angering a dragon." He stood and led her to the back of the shop, pulling a large brass key from his pocket to open a door nearly hidden by stacks of books.

The door squeaked open to reveal a small room empty of people. Shelves of books lined the walls, and a table piled with more books took up the center, leaving a narrow canyon between the two. Tiny glass panes near the ceiling let in light, but there was just one door. Somewhere in the clutter was a clock that had gone too long without care. From long experience, Lisette recognized the stutter-tick of rusted gears sticking. With that cadence, it would be losing hours every day, and soon it would stop completely.

Screech was right; the dragon-born wasn't there. Lisette resigned herself to wandering the garden district in search of the correct tea shop. But first... "Did they leave anything behind?" Maybe she'd get lucky and find something labeled *Plans for taking over Harbor Crag*.

The proprietor shuffled stacks of books around on the table. "Most of these are mine. Mermaid tales, underwater cities... Chicken stories... I had a buyer for those, but he hasn't been by in a few months." He froze. "What's *that*?" he whispered.

Lisette moved around the other side of the table to see what had scared him. Between two stacks of books was a basin with a shimmering silver barrier dividing two pools of liquid, one black and the other orange. Lisette had no idea what either of them were, but they stank of magic. Clamped on the edge of the basin were the inner workings of a small clock, the cause of the uneven ticking she'd heard. "*That* looks like a problem."

CHAPTER 16

MISCALCULATED

L isette and the bookseller stared at the magic swirling in the basin on the table. Or rather, Screech stared at the uncanny fluids; Lisette's eye caught on the clock fastened to the rim. Magic could do almost anything, but no mage had ever found a reliable way to tell time using magic. Remy had told her that one morning as he watched her disassemble a pocket watch.

"I gave up a dangerous life on the waves to open a bookstore and stay *safe*," Screech hissed. He eased back.

Hoping a closer look wouldn't leave her in the middle of the spell, Lisette transferred three stacks of books to the floor. "The alarm is set to go off in five minutes," she said after examining the clock face. Remy could tell her what the spell did, but he wasn't there. "I think we probably don't want to find out what happens then."

"We need a mage," Screech said.

"We need a mage," Lisette agreed. "But in the meantime, let me stop the clock." She moved more stacks of books to the floor and opened the small pouch of tools she always carried with her.

Screech hovered near her shoulder as she examined the back of the mechanism. "Is that safe?"

"Probably safer than the alternative." Lisette selected a tiny screwdriver, hoping she wasn't about to kill them both. Her stomach churned. With a prayer for dexterity, she eased the metal among the gears. The clock ticked once more, and then made a tiny grinding noise that made Lisette's eye twitch. The second hand stopped moving and silence reigned. "There." She stood up and let out a deep breath.

"That's it?"

"No. Now we need to get Remy over here so he can look at it. I don't trust this thing." The mages who created it may have wanted the effects to happen at a certain time, but that didn't mean the barrier between the two sides wouldn't eventually degrade on its own.

"I think I'll close the shop for the day," Screech said, easing toward the door.

"Good idea." Picking her way across the room, Lisette's mind was already on her next steps. Find Remy, tell him about the mess here — tell him about Giselle's illness — and then get to the garden district as quickly as she could. Sunny could be there. And even if the dragon-born wasn't, there could be another device like this.

As they reached the main room, Screech raised his voice. "Everyone out! Take what you're reading. You can bring it back or pay me later." He clapped twice. "Now, please."

In just a few seconds, everyone was on the street with Screech closing the door behind them. He tapped Lisette on the shoulder and thrust his chin toward the harbor. "Your man Remy is the one with that dragon?"

Turning, Lisette saw blue-green dragon scales shimmering. Remy stood near Braatle's back leg, where the shackle was fastened. "That's him. I'll send him over as soon as I can."

"Appreciate it." Screech eyed his weathered shop as if it were a trusted friend. "I'd hate for anything to happen to the old girl now."

With a wave, Lisette headed toward Remy and the dragon. A crowd had gathered around them, prudently keeping out of range of the dragon's head, though Lisette thought they might not have considered the distance fire could travel. Simi sat between Braatle's shoulders, rubbing one paw over her ears, oblivious to any danger the dragon might pose.

As Lisette watched, Remy grabbed hold of the shackle in one hand and used the other to pierce the dragon's hide with the hatpin. Green sparks erupted under his fingers, and Remy grimaced. Lisette recognized that expression — it was the same one he used when his training with Simi had gone wrong and he knew the calico would extend her claws to balance but there was nothing to do other than wait for the pain.

With a boom that shattered nearby windows, the green sparks exploded, throwing Remy into the stones of the shop and knocking the onlookers to the ground. Braatle snarled with rage, her tail whipping into the shop on the opposite side of the road.

The shackle dropped to the cobblestones.

A ragged cheer went up from the crowd. Lisette sprinted to Remy and found him blinking dazedly up from the pavement where he'd fallen. "Ah, my love," he said when he saw her, voice ragged, "I may have miscalculated just a bit."

Lisette brushed the hair from his face, feeling for lumps

on his skull. Aside from a few scrapes, she couldn't find any damage. "Can't trust you on your own for five minutes. Are you hurt?"

"Let me think about that for a bit." He drew a deep breath, wiggled his fingers, and flexed his ankles. "All the parts seem in working order, which is probably more than I deserve. On the whole, I think you had the right idea. Find an excess mage and drop a boulder on him. Assuming I'm not the excess mage."

Lisette helped him sit up. "We're running low on mages at the moment."

Simi trotted over, threw herself down next to Remy, and licked her side vigorously. Remy put a hand on the cat. "I'm sorry. I should have warned you." He blinked and looked at Lisette. "Why are we running low on mages?" He cocked his head as Lisette relayed how Giselle had collapsed and been sent to the freeholder quarter. "Ah. I didn't realize... My mother will take good care of her, but I'll stop by." With an effort, he climbed to his feet.

Lisette kept a hand on his shoulder, partly to keep him upright but also to keep him from going anywhere. "Before you do that, there's something I need you to look at in the bookstore."

"Now?"

"Hm." Lisette scrunched up her face. "Sooner than later, I think."

Remy's eyebrows rose. "Sounds interesting. Let me check with Braatle first."

Magic flickered along the dragon, from her nose to the tip of her tail, as if she were relearning her shape. She turned her head to face them, and her musical voice was stronger than it had been. "I am in your debt, Remy of the Mages. It has been many years since I was unfettered."

Remy bowed, and would have pitched onto his face if Lisette hadn't grabbed his shoulder and hauled him back up. "The honor is mine. Are you able to continue the search without me for a time? I am needed elsewhere."

The dragon agreed, and Remy tasked the children in the crowd to go along and send a message if Braatle needed him.

Once the dragon and her ragtag entourage were on their way, Remy nodded to Lisette. "The bookstore, then."

Lisette held his arm as they walked to keep him from weaving. "Are you *sure* you're not injured?"

"Just a bit rattled. Now, what book is so important that you're willing to send the dragon off alone?"

"Not a book. A device in the backroom of the shop where the mages of Galfigon have been meeting."

"The Salty Bookworm?"

Of course Remy would know it. He'd originally been sent to Harbor Crag as a spy. As they walked, Lisette told him of Giselle's theory that the morning's events had merely been a distraction. Then she tried to describe what she'd seen on the table.

Remy picked up the pace. "I think you're right. Sooner than later."

The door to the Salty Bookworm was unlocked, though the shop was empty. Drawing Remy forward to keep him from the distraction of a room full of books, Lisette picked a path to the back room.

Remy stared at the swirling magic held in the basin. "Ah."

Lisette glanced back at him. "*Ah*, this is nothing to worry about? Or *ah*, we should run?"

"Mm. More of an *ah*, we should do something about this." He leaned over to look at it more closely.

"What does it do?"

"I have no idea. But one generally doesn't set up a timer unless it's important to be far away when it happens." He gestured to the screwdriver stopping the clock. "Your work, I assume?"

"It seemed like a good idea at the time." Lisette's fingers itched to take the clock apart and fix it. "I think it was supposed to go off earlier, but the salt air corroded the movement and slowed it down."

Remy stood straight and looked around. "Are there any spoons or rods? Anything I can use to get a drop of fluid?" When Lisette offered her pouch of tools, he smiled. "Thank you. The easiest way to find out what it's supposed to do is to let it happen. But just a tiny bit."

He dipped one screwdriver in the black liquid and let a drop fall to the floor. Then he dipped another screwdriver into the orange liquid. Lisette wondered if her tools would be safe to use after this. It took two tries, but the orange liquid ran off the metal to mix with the fluid on the floor. "There we are," Remy said. He stepped back.

At first, the drops did nothing but hiss and bubble. Then the head of a slimy, snake-like beast rose, its body as thick as Lisette's forearm. It opened its mouth and shrieked, the noise vibrating the floor. Remy's hand darted forward to touch the beast, and it collapsed into an ooze on the floor, the magic fading.

Lisette lowered her hands from her ears. "What was *that*?"

CHAPTER 17
TISANA'S RARE BREW

emy crouched, poking one of Lisette's screwdrivers into the darkening ooze on the floor. "*That*," he said, "was a green-striped Frisian waterbeast. They live in the ocean west of the Island of Light." He stood. "Or rather, a very realistic duplicate."

Lisette eyed the basin on the table with its two roiling sides of magical liquid, trying to imagine the scale of the resulting beast. "If these mix..."

"It would be large enough to destroy most of the buildings near the waterfront," Remy agreed.

Was this another part of the distraction or the main event? Either way, they needed to stop it. "Can you...?" She waved a hand in a suitably theatrical style.

Remy grinned. "I always love watching you try to avoid any mention of magic."

She raised her chin. "I don't have the vocabulary." Magic had never been something she'd wanted any part of. Being bound to a dragon and paired with a mage had to be some sort of cosmic jest. One reason she enjoyed living in Harbor Crag was that it hadn't attracted any new gods in the last few centuries — she'd spent two months in Rupert's Forge, which had a veritable infestation of small gods, leaving parts of the city rife with stray magic.

"Fair enough." Remy regarded the basin. "I'm a little worried that the heat released when I disable the spell will cause the liquid to boil. The energy has to go *somewhere*."

And if the boiling vapors combined before the magic was gone, Lisette understood, they could cause the very action he was trying to prevent. "Perhaps we could bail them into different buckets and you could deal with them separately?"

They regarded the basin. The silver barrier wavered, then firmed again, and Lisette sucked in her breath. "Did that just...?"

Searching between the stacks of books, Remy said, "Brilliant. Inspired. I *love* your idea of separating the liquids." His speech was so quick, the words ran together. "What containers do we have?"

Lisette dashed out to the main room and found two mugs and a brass bowl holding a dead plant. The withered sticks and dirt went onto the floor. In the meantime, Remy had found an oilskin jacket that he'd draped over the legs of an upended stool to create a depression.

Remy took a mug. "I *think* it would be best to empty both sides at roughly the same speed. So if you stand over there and empty that half, and I'm over here... Right, that's fairly obvious. Probably best not to get it on your person. Ready?"

On his signal, they each scooped up a mugful and dumped it into their respective containers. Nothing exploded, so they continued, and the level slowly dropped in the basin. The sound of their mugs scraping the basin's bottom nearly drowned out a rhythmic tapping.

Lisette stopped and leaned around the table to look at Remy's makeshift container. Orange fluid welled from the seams, then slowly dripped to the floor. "You're leaking."

"So I am." Remy sidestepped to keep his boots away from the growing puddle. "They just don't make jackets the way they used to."

Lisette grabbed the stack of chicken stories, spreading the books on the floor as a barrier to keep the pool from spreading. "Is the basin empty enough for you to do whatever you need to do without it boiling?"

"We'll find out." Remy held out a hand and concentrated. With a crackle, the basin erupted in light, and a blast of heat roared up, blackening the timbered ceiling. Then the light disappeared. Remy giggled, in the way he did when things went a little out of control. "No problem."

Lisette cleared her throat. "Is it safe for me to take this planter into the other room?"

"I'll help you carry it."

Between them, they carried the brass pot outside without the black liquid sloshing onto the ground. Remy looked over with an impish grin. "How was that again?" He waved his arm in imitation of her flourish. After she rolled her eyes, he bowed his head. The black fluid churned and gave off an oily smoke. When he opened his eyes again, he blew out a breath. "They would have leveled everything on the waterfront with that spell."

Lisette looked past him into the bookshop. As much as she wanted to stay with Remy, he needed to deal with the other half of this magical device, and she needed to get to a tea shop in the garden district. "Can you deal with the rest of this on your own?"

He pulled her in for a quick kiss. "Fly, my love. I'll follow as soon as I can. But be careful. They seem to have aimed for maximum disruption." He dropped something into her pocket. "For later."

Lisette trotted away, waiting until she had turned the corner and begun the climb uphill before checking to see what he'd given her.

It was the rusty clock that had powered the device, the one she'd been itching to fix. Even a carriage driver swearing at her to move out of his way couldn't wipe the smile from her face.

THE GARDEN DISTRICT was an oasis of calm covering three blocks. Hundreds of years ago, the area had been owned by a powerful family who had ensured their privacy by the simple means of building a wall around their adjacent estates, which blocked the streets running through. The cobblestones had been pulled up and gardens planted in their place.

That family was long gone, victim of poor shipping investments and even worse political choices, but Harbor Crag had adapted to the reconfigured streets. So the houses were gradually converted into shops and smaller living spaces, while most of the wall was left in place to muffle the noise of the busy roads beyond. The garden district had become the place to meet for tea or a light meal for those who could afford it. Those with smaller budgets could still enjoy the public gardens.

Lisette couldn't remember having seen a turtle in front of any tea shop, but she rarely went to the garden district, preferring the quiet of her shop and the serenity of her gears and springs. She counted eleven tea shops with creatures from dragons to fawns before she noticed a moss-covered granite turtle holding a delicate cup. *Tisana's Rare Brew* said the sign at the turtle's base. Unless there was another tea shop with a turtle, this was the place.

A secret room on the second floor, Giselle had said.

Warm clouds of pepper-scented air with citrus undertones billowed out when Lisette opened the door. Inside, a rug with cavorting turtles cushioned the floor, and silk curtains hung from the ceiling to form a maze. From the way the fabric moved, plaster walls lay behind some of the drapes, but she got a better idea of the layout by listening to unseen people talking and the occasional clink of porcelain saucers.

Presumably, someone usually stayed near the door to greet and guide customers, but since nobody was there, Lisette took the opportunity to wander.

Some tea shops existed to sell their beverages, others to give friends a comfortable place to meet. Tisana's Rare Brew allowed people to meet secretly — which meant, Lisette realized, there would be other entrances.

She ducked between a curtain and a wall to avoid someone carrying a clattering tray, then stilled as she heard a man speak from somewhere nearby.

"We had not expected the second dragon to interfere." The man's step grew closer, as if he came down a set of stairs.

"Did I ask for excuses?" The venom in the second man's speech made Lisette's blood freeze. She recognized that voice. "Gather your people and prepare our departure."

Lord Hanley was here.

CHAPTER 18

MORE CULINARY THAN AMOROUS

Hiding behind the curtain in the tea shop, Lisette struggled to breathe. Lord Hanley. Almost close enough to touch. The last time she'd seen him, he'd held a blade to her niece's throat, and it had only been the combined efforts of Remy, Aarat, and the free-holders that had made him flee the city. She'd hoped never to see him again. If he caught her...

No. She couldn't think like that.

If Lord Hanley was here, that meant she was in the right place, and Sunny was nearby. All she needed to do was sneak out, find Remy, and then let someone whose mind *wasn't* spinning in panicked circles figure out how to rescue the dragon-born.

Except... from the bit of conversation she'd overheard, Lord Hanley was preparing to leave. By the time she ran to The Salty Bookworm, he could be gone, and she would never find Sunny again.

No problem. Lisette would just sneak upstairs and get Sunny out on her own before the girl was taken away.

A woman's voice coming from a curtained alcove rose

above the pounding of Lisette's pulse. "He's a bricklayer! How exciting can he be?"

"Oh, Freya," her friend drawled, "he knows how to work with his hands. It doesn't get much more exciting than that."

The first woman's voice was drowned out by the laughter of her friends.

Lisette tried to think about this logically. The two men had been talking as they walked down the stairs. They wouldn't have done that unless they were both leaving. Therefore, this was the perfect opportunity.

Biting her lip, Lisette forced herself to tug the curtain to the side. A young man walked by holding a tray piled high with empty cups and plates, humming the latest song that had captured the city's interest. It told of a romantic liaison between a possessive sailor and various sea monsters. The server reached the chorus and quietly sang, "Up the anchor, drop your blade, avert your eyes, she's *my* mermaid!"

Lisette favored the version told from the point of view of the object of his affection, in which the sailor was described in terms distinctly more culinary than amorous. When they'd heard it the first time during a night out with Tiffany and her baker, Remy had offered that this new version was more consistent with the books he'd read, and then pulled a giggling Lisette to her feet so they could join the dancers.

The memory of that evening steadied her. Lisette waited until the server had passed, then slid out from cover, gliding along the carpet as she searched for the stairs she'd heard. They weren't visible, but since she had a rough idea of how far away the men had been when they were talking, she felt her way along the wall. Her first glimpse behind a curtain showed her a room with a solitary woman eating a cake drowned in orange syrup. Making a mental note to bring Tiffany here someday, Lisette left the woman to her sweets and felt her way along the wall another two steps.

This time, she found a dark opening, with carpeted stairs rising in a tight curve. It had to be the way to get to the secret room on the second floor, but from the increasing gloom on the upper stairs, there was no light beyond what leaked from where she stood. A peal of nearby laughter startled her.

"But we can't *possibly* use that theater. Isn't that where they pay actors to stand in for props?" Two young men came into view, arm in arm. Lisette hurried into the stairwell before they noticed her.

As she climbed the stairs, Lisette kept one hand in front of her and another on the wall. Then she turned the corner and saw a sliver of light leaking out under the door at the top of the staircase. She put an ear to the door and heard nothing. The knob turned freely, but the door didn't move, even when she bumped it with her shoulder. Bolted.

With shaking hands, she opened her tool bag and extracted the lock picks. There was nowhere to hide up here — if Lord Hanley came back before she left, she'd be trapped.

Lisette planned her moves as she let her fingers probe the lock. The color of the light coming under the door told her there was at least one window in the room. That would give her an alternate exit, if necessary.

Voices filtered up from below. "We'll need food suitable for travel." That was the man Lord Hanley had been talking to.

A woman replied. "Of course. I'll have the kitchen prepare something."

Lisette prayed for them to have other business to

discuss: food, carriages, tea, *anything* to keep that man from climbing the stairs. With a final click, the bolt slid free. Lisette automatically stowed her lock picks — Uncle Rye had once pointed out that it was hard to pretend to have entered a room by accident when holding a thief's tools in one's hand — and opened the door to reveal a small vacant room.

As with everywhere else in the tea shop, the room had thick carpeting and heavy hangings on the walls. Opposite the door, a row of windows overlooked the block's communal gardens. A large map of Harbor Crag had been pinned to the curtains on one wall. Most of the space was taken up by a round wooden table and four chairs. Bags and trunks were heaped against the wall near the door.

For a moment, Lisette thought the risk had been for naught. Then she saw a lock of brown hair spilling over the edge of the bags. Lisette locked the door behind her and crossed the room in two steps.

A small girl with a scar bisecting her left eyebrow was draped over the mound of luggage, as if she were just another item to be hauled around. Her cheeks were pale and her eyes closed, but other than a bandage around her wrist, the dragon-born seemed unharmed.

"Sunny! Wake up!" Lisette shook the girl, who flopped without waking. Drugged or spelled, Lisette didn't know, but it didn't really matter now. The dragon-born would have to be carried out.

Behind her, a metal key scraped in the lock.

CHAPTER 19
ARCHITECTURAL MODIFICATIONS

With Lord Hanley's man at the door, stealth no longer mattered. Lisette sprang across the room to wedge a chair under the handle. The knob rattled as she moved the pile of luggage to further block the threshold.

The door rattled again, and the man grunted. "Who's there? Open this door," he hissed. Lisette could hear him pushing against the door, but the lack of a landing meant he couldn't throw his weight against it.

Hoping the door held, Lisette rushed to the opposite wall and opened the largest window, which overlooked the communal gardens. The stone patio directly below worried her — climbing down with the unconscious Sunny would be tricky, and if they fell, that substrate wouldn't be forgiving. But since that was the only way out, she'd have to take that chance.

A breeze from the open window rippled against the wall hangings, giving Lisette pause. Downstairs in the main tea room, the curtains had hidden doorways and alcoves. There were no windows on the side walls, which suggested rooms on either side. Could she get into them from here?

Dust tickled her nose as she slipped behind the fabric on the left wall, and the ripping of cloth made her wince. If she got out of this alive, she would owe the teashop proprietor recompense. Halfway along the wall, a change in the plaster told her there *had* been a doorway at one time, but it had been covered over.

When she backed out of the wall hangings, the door to the stairs was open a finger's width, the chair bending under the strain. Lisette slammed the door closed and turned the bolt. Then she sacrificed one of her remaining screwdrivers, jamming it into the wood to keep the lock's thumb turn from moving. It wouldn't last long, but it might buy her a minute.

Two hushed voices on the other side of the door told her another man had arrived. Even as she forged a path behind the hangings on the righthand wall, Lisette noted they were trying not to raise attention among the tea shop patrons. Perhaps she could figure out a way to use that against them.

This wall, too, showed signs of a previous door opening being covered over. But at some point, something heavy had hit the wall and cracked the plaster. Chunks had fallen away. Living in the freeholder quarter, Lisette had seen many architectural modifications, and recognized this one as being done for privacy, not security. The door was still there — the handle had been removed and a layer of plaster and paint smoothed over the whole thing. The hinges were on the opposite side.

One well-placed blow with the heel of her hand removed the plaster over the deadbolt's keyhole. Plaster had dried in the lock, and for a long moment, she thought she wouldn't be able to turn the bolt, but it finally slid open with a grinding that made her grit her teeth.

The door swung open, and Lisette pushed through the remaining plaster, revealing a — thankfully uninhabited — lush bedchamber, with silk sheets and a vase of orange roses on a low table. No personal possessions waited, but charcoal portraits of men and women in seductive poses covered every inch of the walls. Clearly, this was where wealthy people conducted their liaisons. Lisette had always wondered what these sorts of places were like, but not enough to pay to find out. Finding this here was good luck — not only was her curiosity satisfied, but this sort of business would have multiple exits.

Lisette burrowed under the wall hanging, grabbed Sunny under the arms, and hauled the dragon-born into the next room. "Give me a second," she whispered to the unconscious girl. Back in Lord Hanley's room, she opened one of the cases and tossed it out the window, smiling as books and papers scattered on the patio. The stairwell door had been unlocked and opened a finger's width, so she slammed it shut and locked it again. Then she ducked under the wall hanging, and quietly closed the door behind her and turned the lock.

Wood splintered in the room next door — Lord Hanley's men had given up on stealth. Lisette strained to shove the brass bed frame against the connecting door. It would have been easier to move without the plush carpet, but at least that muffled the sound.

Hoisting Sunny over her shoulder, Lisette staggered out of the room and into a hallway connected to a sunlit spiral staircase. A startled attendant carrying a basket of folded sheets stood on the top step. "Where did you come from?" Then she caught sight of the girl over Lisette's shoulder and her look went from surprise to anger. "No. We don't allow that —"

Lisette cut her off. "I need the fastest way out of here where nobody will see us. The men behind us will kill her."

Faced with the choice of getting her questions answered or having the whole situation go away, the attendant dropped her basket on the landing. "This way!"

Lisette followed her to the other end of the hallway, but instead of opening one of the bedroom doors, the attendant swung open a section of wood paneling at waist height, just large enough for Lisette to crawl into. Beyond was a metal-lined slide heading into the darkness below.

"Laundry chute," the attendant whispered. "It's safe. We've had to hide clients this way before. From the basement, there's a half-door that goes into the coal tunnels under the gardens. It's impossible to get lost."

A nearby explosion rattled the walls. Taking that as a sign that Lord Hanley had discovered their path, Lisette leaned forward to ease the unconscious dragon-born into the chute and then listened to her slide away. Something metallic clanged against the side of the chute on the way down.

Hoping she wasn't going to land on top of the girl, Lisette climbed in, bracing her legs on either side. "You might want to come with us," she suggested to the attendant.

The woman shook her head, ready to close the panel. "I'll slow them down by taking them to the owner."

"Thank you." Lisette relaxed her legs.

As she slid, the panel closed, cutting off all light, and Lisette dropped into the void.

CHAPTER 20
STATUES OF BIG FISH

The laundry chute had never been meant for people, but it wouldn't have been too terrible if only she'd been able to see. As it was, Lisette's head banged against the side with every change of direction. Once she'd estimated she was close to the basement, she pushed harder against the sides to slow her fall. A faint glow from below gave her a second to get her bearings before somebody dumped a load of sheets into the chute. But she had seen enough for her to swing her weight to the side and avoid landing directly on Sunny.

The basement had a narrow strip of windows near the ceiling, letting in a weak beam of light and displaying the shoes of people strolling by outside. Heated dust warred with the odor of moldy plaster. An old iron boiler in the corner provided heated water for the building, but even from across the room Lisette could feel it had been converted from coal to magic.

She wondered how long it would work now that most of the mages of Harbor Crag had decamped to the Island of Light. Then again, a place like this could afford to hire a mage to recharge the spell a few times during the year. Not having to deal with shoveling coal into the boiler would be worth it. The only real drawback of using magic to heat water was that heating large quantities took time, which explained why there were no tubs or drying racks — the laundry was done elsewhere.

The opposite wall held stairs rising to the ground floor. Taking Sunny out that way would risk running into Lord Hanley's men. But the attendant had said there was a door leading to the coal tunnels under the gardens, so Lisette kept looking. There. A smaller metal door was hidden behind a tower of cleaning supplies. After moving the mops and brooms to the side, Lisette opened the heavy door, revealing a dim, musty tunnel with metal tracks running along the floor.

She considered the tunnel with a sigh. "At least it's not a boat," she said in the direction of Sunny's inert form.

When Lisette hoisted the girl over her shoulder, a hollow silver ball formed of filigree rolled across the floor, magic radiating in all directions. Lisette nearly left it there, figuring one of the wealthy patrons of the house had forgotten it in the sheets, but then she remembered the clanking sound as the dragon-born slid down the chute. If this was something Lord Hanley had created, that was even more reason to leave it behind, except... What if it held the key to waking Sunny?

With a muttered curse against mages who weren't Remy, Lisette shoved the ball into her pocket and stumbled into the tunnel.

∾

TWENTY MINUTES LATER, Lisette finally emerged into the sunlight. Her back hurt, her head ached from where she'd bumped it on the tunnel's ceiling, and her legs reminded her of all the walking she'd done that day. In the darkness, she'd lost all sense of direction, so it was a shock when she found herself in a sunken courtyard with marble columns surrounding the center.

The green algae-stained statues told her where she was — the ruins of the sea serpent temple a few streets over from the house of Jasque the Mad, where she and Remy had found the dragon's egg. The area was safe enough in the daytime, but she probably wouldn't be able to find help until she'd walked a bit. Setting Sunny down next to a stone plinth, Lisette groaned as she rolled her shoulders. She'd heard no sound of pursuit in the tunnel — a brief rest should be safe enough, though the temple buzzed with the uncanny, making her want to leave. The small god who had rested here was gone — mostly — but Lisette didn't want it to mistake her for an acolyte.

Ten minutes, she thought. Ten minutes and she would pick up Sunny and find help. As she stretched her legs, a familiar meow cut into her thoughts. She stood. "Simi?"

The calico trotted down the stairs and jumped onto her shoulder, purring and rubbing her cheeks against Lisette's hair.

"Is Remy around?" If the cat was here, Remy was nearby. Probably the dragon as well. Shielding the cat's ears with her hand, Lisette leaned her head back and yelled up to the sky. "Remy!"

The cat jumped off her shoulder and raced away. Lisette crouched to pick up Sunny, but before she could stand, the calico returned more slowly, tail held straight up, occasionally glancing over her shoulder. Remy's exasperated voice came from behind the temple's outer walls. "Simi, you better not have dragged me over here to look at statues of big fish. This isn't the time —"

"Remy!" Leaving the dragon-born, Lisette ran up the steps. "I've got Sunny here."

Remy rounded the corner, a smile lighting up his face as he saw her. "I thought you were going to the tea shop...?" He followed her down the steps to the sunken courtyard where Sunny lay sleeping.

Lisette quickly told him what had happened at the tea shop. "I can't get her to wake up. As far as I know, they didn't follow me, but we should probably leave."

Remy crouched by the sleeping girl, laying a hand on her brow. After a moment, he nodded. "There's a spell. Giselle will have a better idea of how to safely break it." He lifted the girl in his arms and they began climbing out of the courtyard. "Maybe it's wearing off on its own. Braatle and I were on our way to the tea shop when she told me she sensed Sunny again." He stopped and frowned. "Did Lord Hanley set a spell on *you*? Something feels different."

Lisette's stomach sank. The idea of Lord Hanley controlling her was a nightmare that still occasionally plagued her. "He never saw me, but..." Then she remembered the silver ball she'd shoved in her pocket. She held it up. "Could it be this? Sunny had it with her, I think, and I didn't know if you would need it to wake her."

Remy shifted Sunny onto his shoulder to free up one hand. He took the ball from her and examined it.

On the street, Braatle roared.

Glancing toward the dragon, Remy nodded. "That explains it." He stowed the ball in his satchel and began climbing the steps again. "Let's get out there before Braatle charges in and destroys what's left of the temple. There's too much magic here for that to end well."

Lisette scrambled to keep up. "I don't understand."

"This little trinket is what has been hiding Sunny. When you put her down and walked away, she was no longer concealed from us. Now she's hidden again."

Which was why Braatle had called in alarm, Lisette realized. But if Remy and Braatle had detected Sunny when Lisette walked away with the silver ball... "So Lord Hanley knows where she is now, too."

"Indeed." Once he'd climbed the steps, Remy's speed increased until he was nearly trotting, the dragon-born bouncing on his shoulder. "Now would be a great time to leave."

CHAPTER 21
EXTRA-SPECIAL MANNERS

Aside from a vague itch between her shoulder blades, Lisette felt no hint of Lord Hanley as they climbed the hill to the freeholder quarter.

Braatle had wanted to bring Sunny back to the dragon warrens, but Remy persuaded the dragon that the girl would do better in their rooms. "My professor is there, and she has more experience than I do," he said. "Besides, the dragon-born is going to need nursing care until she's awake, and we can't very well bring other people into the warrens. You can stay nearby, if you want," he added.

Lisette raised one eyebrow at him, but kept her mouth shut. Uncle Barlow would be delighted to have a dragon lounging in the street in front of the shop. If anyone else complained, she'd send them to Remy.

Though the dragon didn't argue further, a plume of smoke rose from Braatle's nostrils, dissipating as it climbed into the late afternoon sky.

With that resolved, Remy shifted his grip on the girl he carried. "I wonder how long it will take for the horses to become accustomed to dragons."

Lisette had more practical questions, mostly centered on how many people were staying in their rooms and whether she and Remy could stay in Rye and Barlow's shop overnight. They'd planned for Remy's mother, Anna, to stay in the spare room, but now they also had Sunny, Giselle, and the burned mage from the ship. "Your mother is probably wishing she'd kept sailing past Harbor Crag."

Remy chuckled. "My mother is thanking the stars we've handed her a crisis so she has something to do," he corrected. "If I had promised she'd be in the middle of all this, she would have been here ages ago."

It was true that Remy must have inherited his love of chaotic situations from *somewhere*. "You know I had big plans to impress her with how well we were getting along here, right?"

"Trust me, this is far better." Then he sighed. "Though I could have done without Lord Hanley in the city again. He came back faster than I'd hoped."

Lisette couldn't disagree. She'd been hoping Lord Hanley would stay on the Island of Light for the rest of his life. Or be eaten by a sea monster on his journey there. She wasn't picky.

Traveling behind Braatle meant the roads were clear of people, but the air was rich with the scents of spices, roasted meat, and grilled vegetables. This was the time of day when most people bought their evening meal, either to eat while visiting with friends or to bring home to their families.

When they arrived in the freeholder quarter, Lisette glanced up at their rooms just in time to see Tiffany keeping Ziggy, Turtle, and Pot from falling to the street as the girls leaned out the window to get a better look at the dragon.

Still hanging out the window, Turtle turned her head to

yell to someone in the room. "They're here! And they have Sunny with them!" Then all three girls disappeared inside, presumably to spread the word.

Tiffany waved and called. "Do you want me to bring a doctor?" When Lisette shook her head, Tiffany turned her attention to Braatle. "Welcome to the freeholder quarter." Then she ducked inside.

Lisette realized she needed to gather Rye, Barlow, Tiffany, and anyone else who might be brave enough to come speak to Braatle, and make sure they were aware that they should never explicitly give their name to any dragon.

Generations ago, that had been common knowledge. Aarat had been shocked that Lisette hadn't known. "Are the children no longer taught? Your name gives me power over you." Her ignorance hadn't stopped him from binding Lisette to him by her name, though. He'd been chained and desperate. And even though her bond with Aarat had saved her life multiple times, having a permanent tie to the dragon still chafed. She didn't want any of the other free-holders to risk the same fate.

The girls ran out of the building ten seconds later. Pot was first out the door. She raised a fist to the sky and yelled, "I win!" Turtle was right behind her, with Ziggy only a few seconds after that, which meant the older girls had helped her down the steps before racing for the door.

Lisette darted past Braatle to intercept them, scooping up Ziggy before the toddler could throw herself at the dragon. "We use our extra-special manners with dragons, remember? No yelling, no hitting, and?" She raised her eyebrows and waited.

"No touching unless we ask permission first," Turtle and Pot chorused. These were the rules they followed —

mostly — when spending time in Lisette's shop among all the clocks and other easily broken items.

"Promise?"

Turtle and Pot nodded, their eyes wide with excitement. Ziggy used Lisette's moment of inattention to throw her weight toward the dragon, making Lisette lurch sideways to keep from falling. Ziggy laughed and Lisette moved the girl onto her hip. "You're getting too big for that. Or maybe I'm getting too old."

At Lisette's side, Pot patted her arm and said solemnly, "It's okay to get old, Auntie Lisette. We can take care of you just like we take care of Nana." Turtle was on her other side, still staring at the blue dragon.

"Thank you, Pot. That's very nice of you." Lisette walked toward the door, the girls keeping pace. "Maybe you can help now. We're going to need to make a space for Sunny to lie down until she's better."

"The bad man already has Turtle's bed, but maybe Sunny can have Ziggy's cot."

Lisette suppressed a smile at Pot's generous gift of a sibling's belongings. "And where is Ziggy going to sleep?" Behind her, she could hear Remy telling Braatle they would be going to their rooms above the shops and the dragon could stand on her hind legs and look through the window if she wanted to see the space, but she wouldn't fit up the stairs and the building would probably come down if she tried.

Pot answered, "With Mama and Papa. Ziggy won't care if Papa snores."

Lisette worked to keep a straight face. "Good thinking." She pulled the door to the stairs open and waited for Remy to go ahead of her, the dragon-born still limp in his arms.

Then her blood froze as she heard Turtle say to Braatle in her most polite tones, "My name is Clara, but everyone calls me Turtle, and this is Pot and the baby is Ziggy. What's your name?"

CHAPTER 22

NORMAL

L isette crouched to set Ziggy on the ground. "Pot, take your little sister upstairs. No arguments!" she added, when Pot drew breath to protest. "Tell Remy I need him down here right now."

The children of the freeholder quarter gained responsibilities as they grew, so Pot recognized Lisette's serious tone. She took Ziggy's hand and dragged the toddler inside. "Uncle Remy," she yelled, her voice carrying clearly from the stairwell, "Auntie Lisette wants you down there *right now*!"

Though she'd been hoping for a little more discretion, Lisette put that out of her mind. She turned back to the dragon in time to hear Braatle hiss. Turtle giggled. "My head *tickles*."

"Braatle," Lisette said carefully, "she's just a child. She didn't know what she was saying."

The dragon lowered her head, so Lisette could see each tiny blue and green scale embedded in the skin around her eyes. "I can no more forget what I have learned than you can unsee what has happened." She rubbed her cheek on her forearm, the movement causing one shimmering scale to drop to the road. "But I am not such a monster as to use a child's innocence against her. At least not without great need."

It was that last part that worried Lisette. The needs of dragons did not always align with those of the humans who lived near them. But short of killing the dragon, she didn't see that there was anything she could do. Maybe Remy would know some way to remove Turtle from the dragon's bond.

Remy jogged out of the building, Simi at his heels. "What did I miss?" The cat leaped onto the dragon's head and sprawled between her ears.

Braatle cast him a baleful gaze. "The child offered me her name. So *much* have the humans forgotten while my people have been in chains."

"Ah." Remy lifted Turtle onto his shoulder, his cheerful demeanor unchanged. "Turtle, my love, your mother may send me off to the sea monsters for this. But what's done is done."

"Braatle's a *nice* dragon," Turtle insisted. "She's my friend. She can make my head tickle."

The dragon blinked.

Remy patted the girl's boots absently, the same way he often patted Simi. "Having a dragon friend might not be a terrible thing." He turned back to the dragon. "Giselle is examining the dragon-born now. Do you require anything?"

"I do not."

"Let me know if that changes." He glanced at Lisette. With the hand not anchoring Turtle on his shoulder, Remy gestured to the shop across the street. "We should perhaps talk to Rye and Barlow before the error compounds."

As LISETTE HAD EXPECTED, Uncle Barlow was delighted to have a dragon taking up most of the road in front of the shop. He leaned his stout figure to the side so he could watch the street. "Would she like a blanket, do you think? Or pillows to rest her head on?"

Uncle Rye was more practical. "If we made the street one-way while she's here, we'll have fewer carts stuck trying to turn around. That's if the horses will even go near a dragon." He shook out the rag he'd been using to apply linseed oil to a frame and refolded it before shoving it into a pocket of his smock. "Was that Sunny I saw Remy carrying?"

"Yes."

While Remy impressed upon Barlow the rules for dealing with a dragon, Lisette told Rye what had happened during the day. When she reached the part about Lord Hanley being in Harbor Crag, Rye growled in disgust. "We should have killed him before he could run away."

"I'm fairly certain the dragons will take care of that for us if we give them a chance."

Rye considered that. "I suppose that's one good thing about having a dragon blocking the street, even given the danger of Barlow irritating it enough to burn down the quarter. What else do you need?"

"An empty bed or two?"

Rye nodded. "We'll take care of your burned mage. Though I'll warn you, if he wakes up and tries something, he'll be sorry."

"We need information from him," Lisette warned.

"Understood."

Lisette wondered how she'd grown up around her

Uncle Rye without realizing he'd been a soldier in his youth. Now that she knew, she saw the signs everywhere. "Thank you. Hopefully, we'll be able to get things back to normal soon."

Rye's bark of laughter made the other two men look up in alarm, and he waved one hand in reassurance. "We have dragons and mages going to war in the city. I don't think normal is coming back anytime soon." With a shake of his head, he took her arm. "Let's go meet the dragon, and then Barlow and I will collect our patient."

THERE WAS a formula for introducing a dragon to a human, one that didn't leave the possibility of a bond. Remy took the uncles into the street. "Braatle, may I introduce these men to you? They are known as Barlow and Rye."

And that was all that was necessary. "You can introduce yourself that way as well," Remy said as they climbed the stairs to their rooms. "Saying 'I am known as' has a much different meaning than 'My name is,' though I couldn't tell you why."

"Tiffany's going to kill me," Lisette said, with a glance at Turtle, who was riding on Remy's back. She remembered her first glimpse of Turtle as a newborn, when she'd sworn to keep the girl safe. And now... this.

But Tiffany only blamed herself. "I knew there was a risk sending them downstairs to see the dragon," she said with a sigh as she made space for Turtle on her lap. "I didn't even think to warn them about giving their names."

Somehow, that made Lisette feel even worse. "I was *right there*. I should have..."

Tiffany raised her brows. "Should have what? There's

no way to keep them safe from everything. You know that. We'll just have to see how this settles out."

"Turtle's protected from certain kinds of magic," Remy offered. "The freeholder quarter may find that useful in the future."

Tiffany nodded. "We'll just have to see." Then she frowned at the girls. "Though you'll let *me* be the one to tell your father." She stood, helping all three girls to their feet. "Now it's time for us to go home. Say goodnight, Turtle and Pot. Ziggy, no pulling Auntie Lisette's hair when she gives you a hug, or she'll never want to hug you again."

After Tiffany and her daughters had left, and Rye and Barlow had carried the sleeping mage away with Anna going along to show them what nursing needed to be done, Remy put his arms around Lisette. "It wasn't your fault. Tiffany knows her daughters better than anyone and *she* didn't see it coming." He tightened his arms briefly, then stepped back. "Let's get Sunny into the sickroom so we're not tripping over her all night, and I'll see what I can do to wake her."

Before they'd finished moving the dragon-born, Giselle came out of the guest room, her gray hair even wilder than usual. The professor looked tired, but far better than she had when she'd collapsed in the street. "Nothing to worry about," she told Lisette, settling herself on the floor next to the mattress in the spare room. "Just a little heart problem I've had my entire life. Every once in a while, it kicks up a fuss, and I was due for an episode. I'll be fine by tomorrow."

Remy sat down on the other side of the mattress, with the dragon-born between them, and Lisette left them to their consultation.

She was half-asleep by the window when Anna returned.

"Braatle's quite a nice dragon, isn't she?" Remy's mother said. When Lisette started and nearly fell off the chair, Anna smiled reassurance. "Don't worry. Rye introduced me to her properly." She sat down across the table with a fresh pot of tea and lowered her voice. "Now tell me how worried I should be about the mages attacking Harbor Crag. And more importantly, can I trust Giselle?"

CHAPTER 23

COINCIDENCE

As the setting sun gilded the buildings of the freeholder quarter, Lisette poured herself a mug of tea and considered Anna's question. The first sip made her stomach ache. She pushed the mug away. Too much tea and stress were a bad combination. "Some of the mages attacking Harbor Crag today used to live here. But others are from Giselle's college." Then she told Anna about Braatle, the baby dragon, the magical device in the bookshop, and Sunny's rescue. The facts were important, naturally, but it also gave her an excuse to avoid speculating about Giselle. Across the table, Remy's mother listened intently, though Lisette thought Anna wasn't fooled by her delay.

A flash of light from the sickroom briefly made the apartment brighter than it ever was at noon. That was followed by Remy's apologetic laugh and Giselle's, "Perhaps *not*." They were trying to wake the dragon-born. Lisette hoped the two mages didn't bring down the building during their attempts — Remy's magic wasn't always well behaved.

When the laughter from the other room had faded, Lisette said, "I don't *think* all the mages at the college have joined with Lord Hanley. I'm fairly sure that Giselle had nothing to do with the attacks on the dragons and Harbor Crag." Honesty compelled her to add, "But it's an odd coincidence, her showing up on the very day the mages attacked."

Anna had her fingers wrapped around her own mug, as if letting it warm her, though the room was a comfortable temperature. Living with a mage, even one whose magic was occasionally temperamental, had some benefits. Of course, the window had recently been replaced after a magical miscalculation, so it wasn't always perfect.

A wistful smile pulled at Anna's face. "I'm... *fond* of Giselle. We met on the voyage here, but I feel like I've known her for years. It makes it difficult for me to trust my judgment."

"Yes, I know the feeling," Lisette said. Remy had been a mystery when they'd first met, and later she'd learned he was a spy. Then her mind suggested a twist on the words she'd just used. "But it's possible the attack happened now *because* Giselle arrived, even though she wasn't involved."

Another flash of light and the pure hum of a wind chime came from the sickroom. Lisette and Anna waited, but there were just the indistinct murmurs of Remy and Giselle talking.

"Aarat," Lisette started, then explained, "the other free dragon." When Anna nodded, she continued. "Aarat knew there was a mage on your ship. It was why we were waiting when you arrived... looking like we'd been cleaning chimneys all morning."

"Which you had not," Anna suggested.

"No. We were trying to remove artifacts from the ashes

of Lord Hanley's house before someone else got hurt." Saying that reminded her they needed to go back. It would have to wait until the current crisis was resolved and Lord Hanley had been removed from the city. "But my point was that if Aarat knew there was a mage on the ship, maybe the other mages knew, too."

Anna cocked her head to the side, looking so much like Remy that Lisette nearly smiled. "Ah. I think I see."

Lisette continued. "They seemed less prepared than I would have expected. Lord Hanley was telling someone to gather supplies for their escape. If *I'd* been planning on stealing the dragon-born, I'd have had multiple escape routes planned."

Anna thought about this for a moment. "From what you've said, they meant to use Sunny's blood to re-chain Aarat. If it had gone as intended, they wouldn't have *needed* to leave Harbor Crag afterward."

"Agreed, but the attack on the waterfront really only makes sense as a diversion. If that had happened *first*, Remy would have been too busy dealing with a sea monster to respond immediately when Sunny was taken. Maybe Aarat as well. So why go ahead even after the device didn't activate?"

Anna considered this silently.

Lisette blew out a breath in a quiet laugh. "Can you imagine how angry Lord Hanley must be about it all? The diversion never happened, Braatle broke free and raised the alarm before they could get on a ship with Sunny, and now they've lost her as well." She dug the rusted clock out of her pocket and placed it on the table. "I don't think they originally intended to attack the dragons today. If Giselle hadn't arrived, they could have just waited another day and found a clock that hadn't rusted into unreliability."

But Giselle *had* arrived, and the hastily rescheduled attacks had to go forward no matter what. Because the college mages might be willing to face Remy, who had just barely graduated, but they wouldn't want to go up against Giselle.

A rumble accompanied the next blast of light from the sickroom. After a glance in that direction, Anna leaned forward. "Would you show me your shop? Remy's letters made me curious."

"It might be safer than staying here," Lisette agreed. She stood, scooping up the rusty clock, and then went to the doorway of the sickroom. Sunny still slept, and Remy and Giselle were considering a point in the air above the girl's head. Hoping she wasn't interrupting, Lisette said, "Anna and I are going across the street for a bit. Yell if you need anything."

Remy smiled, though he didn't look over at her. "I'll try not to knock down the building."

"The freeholder quarter thanks you."

On their way across the street, they stopped so Lisette could properly introduce Anna to the dragon. A group of freeholders had taken up guard duty in the area, probably organized by Rye. Whether the guards were to protect the dragon or to protect people *from* the dragon, Lisette didn't ask. Simi was asleep, draped upside-down over Braatle's left foreleg.

Once they were inside her shop, Lisette took a deep breath, the smell of metal and oil and Barlow's lemon furniture polish instantly relaxing her. "This is it," she said, moving to light the lamps. The front of the narrow shop was filled with displays of clocks and other mechanical curiosities, some of which were for sale. On the right side, stairs just barely wide enough for one person led to the upper story, where Remy studied and experimented on the artifacts they'd found.

In front of the stairs was an opening to the uncles' shop next door. Lisette waved one hand at it. "This gives my uncles the best acoustics to listen in when I'm talking to customers."

She'd intentionally said it loudly enough to be heard, and smiled when Barlow called, "Where else would I get my drama?" Three seconds later, he ducked through the opening and pointed to his left. "Anna, we have a lovely settee right here if you ever want to listen to our Lisette yelling at her customers for abusing their watches."

"I don't yell."

Barlow ignored her protest and nodded at Anna. "She has *quite* the reputation." He waved. "Come by anytime." Then he disappeared back onto his side of the wall.

"I don't yell much, anyhow," Lisette clarified. After opening the pass-through in the counter, she led Anna to the back. "And this is where I do my work."

Anna wandered around her workbench, examining her tools and the cabinets filled with jars of small screws and other bits of metal, though she was careful not to touch anything. "It's all so intricate. How did you learn to do this?"

"I grew up in here. My mother taught me." Lisette set the rusty clock on the workbench.

"Will you show me?" Anna gestured at the clock Lisette had just put down.

And so Lisette stripped the movement, showing Anna the rusted gears that were catching, and giving her a general overview of how it all worked. Her fingers moved steadily, separating the tiny gears of the wheel train. Anna asked a few questions, but seemed content to watch and learn.

This was Lisette's element, the one place where she'd always felt sure of what she was doing. Everything in her shop was precise and fixable, and even a rusty clock with no real value could be functional again if she expended a little effort. It was all springs and levers and things that could be understood and required no magic.

By the time she had everything disassembled and put into the cleaner, her mind had cleared. She was no longer jumpy from knowing Lord Hanley was in Harbor Crag. Even the guilt from allowing Turtle to give her name to the dragon had faded. Lisette put all her tools in their places and wiped down the bench top. "I may have to sand a few things, but the cleaner gets rid of more rust than you would think."

"Then you have to put it all back together."

"Yes. But it's not hard." She paused. "As long as you haven't lost any pieces," she qualified.

That made Anna laugh.

Lisette glanced through the front window of the shop where the dragon could be seen lying in the road. Then she looked back at Anna. "I'm glad you came. Remy wanted to take me to meet you, but even before today, we couldn't really leave."

They were both bound to the city: Remy, because of the artifacts abandoned when the mages fled to the Island of Light, and Lisette, because she had made deals with Aarat. And both of them had been trying to free the other dragons.

Anna smiled and opened her mouth to reply, but she was cut off by a roar from Braatle.

Outside, the street erupted in magic.

CHAPTER 24
NOT A CHANCE

Green sparks showered down, landing on the street where Braatle had been resting. Lisette saw Simi dash into the building opposite. The calico would be running to Remy, her safe harbor in any storm.

Anna stood at the counter by Lisette's side. "Can you see anything?"

"No. But I can't imagine they'll try anything that might harm Sunny." Because the dragon-born *had* to be the object of this attack. Without Sunny's blood, the mages couldn't re-capture Aarat. And without stealing the magic of the dragons, the Harbor Crag mages could not retake the city.

A glow of dragon fire further up the street was followed by people yelling in fear and anger. Lisette bit her lip. Instead of retreating as soon as magic erupted, the free-holders had held their ground.

That meant the attackers were approaching from the east.

But if the dragon had been drawn away, that left the street open in the other direction. Lisette levered up the pass-through and grabbed her broom, the one with a stout wooden handle. "Lock the door behind me and blow out the lanterns. The shop should be safe enough."

"Not a chance," Anna said firmly. She removed a glowing dagger from her vest and smiled at Lisette's stare. "It was a present from Remy the first year he was at the college. He was so proud of adding a light spell to the blade that I never had the heart to tell him most people don't use daggers in the dark. Still, it's harder to lose." She hid the dagger in her vest again and nodded to the door. "Shall we?"

The two women crept out, turned right, and stopped in a shadowed doorway. Behind them, dragon fire briefly illuminated their surroundings, but even without it, enough light spilled from the windows lining the street to pick out objects. "Do you see anything?"

Anna's voice sounded calmer than Lisette felt. "No. Is there any way for them to get into your rooms from the other side of the building?"

"No." No doorways had been cut through to the back-facing building. Lisette considered how she would approach if she were trying to sneak into their rooms. "Not unless they go in through the roof."

Which the attackers could do, she realized. Most of the living quarters had a hatch in the ceiling so the occupants could climb out to fix leaks or clear snow before the weight caused the building to buckle. If the attackers had a ladder and no fear of heights, it wouldn't be hard to get onto the roof.

"Can we get up —" Anna fell silent as two figures approached. She shifted her weight, as if ready to attack, but Lisette stopped her with one hand.

"Who's there?" Uncle Rye called.

"It's us," Lisette said. She moved out of the alcove. "You have *another* sword?" Remy had accidentally destroyed the last one, and Rye hadn't seemed too bothered by the loss.

"Your man found one in the rubble of a building and thought I might as well keep it. Just in case."

Barlow stepped out from behind his partner, a marble jug dangling from one hand. "If I'd known Remy was taking orders, I would have asked for one of my own."

Lisette winced at the idea of her Uncle Barlow with anything larger than a paring knife, but Rye was more direct. "To give to your attacker in case his was broken?" He shook his head. "Never mind." He looked at Lisette and Anna. "Have you seen anyone?"

"No. We were discussing the roof."

Rye nodded. "It looks like Turtle's friend may yet take care of everything on her own, but we should have someone up there."

She could see him trying to calculate which location would be safer, so he could send the two women there. But she also knew how much he hated heights, so she spoke again before he could decide. "We'll take the roof. You two stay down here to sound the alarm if anyone comes this way." She frowned at Barlow. "Remy and Giselle and Braatle can handle the magic." She trusted Rye's training and sense of self-preservation. Barlow, on the other hand, got excited and forgot about everything that could go wrong.

Rye nodded. "Stay safe."

"You as well."

By now, Remy would have set traps on the stairs going up to the apartment. They would have to access the roof farther down the block. Taking Anna's arm, Lisette ran across the street to the weaver's shop. Coralie waited near the door wielding giant scissors. Her back might have been stooped from age, but there was a murderous gleam in her eyes.

The weaver ushered them in, then closed and locked the door. "You here to get onto the roof?"

"Yes."

Coralie nodded. "Up the stairs, then left. The racks swing away from the wall. Ladder's behind 'em." She pointed her scissors beyond the giant loom where threads of purple, blue, gold, and green shimmered. "Do the free-holders proud. I'll hold the door."

Lisette and Anna ran up the stairs, which had been built to avoid taking up space in the weaving room below. On the floor above, the hallway was packed with bolts of cloth, some wound around sanded and varnished planks and others hanging from rods. All the fabric in the enclosed space muffled any noise, including the roaring of the dragon. The rack mounted on the wall to the left was hinged; swinging it to the side revealed a ladder built into the wall.

Handing Anna the broom, Lisette climbed to the ceiling. As she worked the stiff latch, she looked down. "You're not bothered by heights, are you?" She should have asked before. No, she *should* have found some reason to send Remy's mother as far away from danger as possible.

Anna smiled, as if reading her thoughts. "Not at all."

"I tried," Lisette muttered. The latch clicked, but the cover didn't move until she banged it with the heel of one hand. The hatch flew open, and suddenly Braatle's screams of rage were no longer muffled. Lisette boosted herself onto the roof tiles, leaned down to take the broom, and then rolled to the side to make room for Anna.

Up on the roof, it was darker, with only the crescent

moon for light. But after her eyes adjusted, Lisette could see well enough to pick out a few broken tiles. When all this was over, she'd have to remember to come back to replace them. She'd have to be careful about how she phrased it, though, or Coralie would climb up here herself.

Anna pulled herself onto the gently sloping roof and swung the hatch closed. "If I'd known how exciting Harbor Crag was, I would have moved here years ago," she whispered. She looked around as if getting her bearings, then pointed. "That should be the one going down to your rooms, correct?"

"Yes." On their way across the tiles slick from the damp sea air, Lisette detoured to the crest of the roof so she could see the other side. There was no sign of anyone else on the roof. With any luck, it would stay that way until Braatle drove the intruders away.

They settled on the tiles above the guest bedroom, listening as the shouting and roars from the street below slowly quieted. So much could happen in just a few minutes. Lisette wanted to be down there helping to defend her home, but she knew guarding the roof was necessary. Children growing up in the freeholder quarter quickly learned that even the smallest jobs were important. She and Anna would stay here until they were sure the danger was past.

"It's hard to wait," Anna murmured.

Lisette nodded. But before she could reply, the cover rattled, as if someone had flipped the catch to open it. Probably Remy coming to tell them the intruders had gone, but she still readied herself.

Then the hatch flew open, and a strange man appeared.

CHAPTER 25
SLIPPERY

Crouched on the roof, Lisette stared at the stranger coming through the hatch. From her *home*, her mind insisted. The man seemed just as surprised to see Anna and Lisette as they were to see him.

Remy's mother was the first to recover. With one hand, she grabbed the man's hair. The other held the shining dagger to his throat. "Stay right where you are," she hissed. "Otherwise, my son down there will have one less intruder to deal with."

The man moved just enough to see the dagger, then froze. Not a trained fighter, Lisette realized. And just when she worked out the obvious corollary — if he wasn't a fighter, then he must be a mage — a wave of tiredness passed over her.

Next to her, Anna slumped to the roof tiles, the shining dagger falling from her grip. Lisette's eyelids drooped and her thoughts grew woolly, as she watched the strange man scramble onto the roof and lean back through the hatch to grasp something. Sunny, she realized slowly, as if watching from a distance. They were stealing the dragon-born.

Suddenly, Aarat's magic burned through Lisette, and she couldn't stifle her gasp of pain. But the spell on her dropped away.

Lisette tightened her grip on the broom she'd nearly dropped. "Remy! Giselle!" she yelled. With all her strength, she swung the stick, striking the stranger's ribs. He narrowly avoided falling down the ladder, then rolled away from her second blow. "They're up here. On the roof!"

Moss on the tiles made her footing uncertain. Wobbling, Lisette swung the broom at the strange mage again, hoping that if he was busy avoiding her, he wouldn't be able to launch the next spell.

From the still open hatch, a blast of magic lit up the night. Good. Remy or Giselle had entered the fray. Lisette hoped that meant Sunny was safe.

The mage on the roof rolled to the side, and Lisette's blow cracked a tile.

The absurdity of the situation struck her. This was like the time she'd seen Tiffany's mother trying to kill a rat in the bakery. By the time she'd been done, flour and spices covered every surface and the rodent had escaped out the window, unharmed.

She wished she'd grabbed Anna's dagger, but it was too late now.

This time the man rolled far enough that she had to take two careful steps toward him. Once again, a wave of tiredness rolled through her, to be burned off nearly immediately by the dragon magic. "That won't *work* on me," Lisette growled. Her next swing glanced off his ear and the man yelped. Another blow like that would daze him long enough for Remy to get up here and deal with him properly.

Except her feet suddenly flew out from under her and Lisette was sliding toward the edge of the roof, fingers scrabbling on the slippery tiles. Realizing he couldn't control her with magic, the mage had done the next best thing — he'd given her a magical push and let momentum take care of the rest.

Lisette couldn't help the panicked scream that emerged as her feet encountered empty air. Dirt and moss clung to her fingers, preventing her from holding on. And she was still sliding.

The skid came to a halt when her hips hit the roof's edge. Her legs dangled above the street, but her upper body was plastered to the tiles above. "Remy?" The quaver in her voice couldn't be helped, but she thought her cry had been loud enough to be heard.

Another blast of magic came from somewhere nearby. No, Remy wouldn't be free to help her right away. Lisette tried not to move, tried to almost not breathe. She just had to stay here long enough for someone to throw her a line. She could do that.

The roof edge crumbled beneath her, and she fell.

"Aaaahhh —" Her breath was propelled out of her with a grunt when she hit something solid. But it wasn't the pavement.

Scales scraped against her arm as she slid — slowly this time — to the ground. Braatle tilted her head so she could look down, and her eyes glowed in the darkness. "Friend of dragons," she said, her voice so beautiful that it hurt to listen, "you lack the wings to fly."

Lisette slowly climbed to her feet, feeling every strained muscle. Even though she was on solid ground, her body still insisted she might fall again at any second. "Thank you, Braatle."

The blasts of magic coming from the upper story of the building had stopped. Lisette hoped that meant Remy and Giselle had defeated the mages, but she needed to go up and check.

Once again, the safest way upstairs was through the weaver's shop. Coralie unlocked the door for her and offered the scissors she'd been holding as a weapon. "Careful on the roof," the old woman admonished with an overly serious gaze, "the moss gets slippery." She had obviously seen Lisette's landing. Or she'd figured it out from the state of her tunic.

"That's the truth." Lisette tucked the scissors in her belt and kept moving. If she held still too long, her muscles would stiffen and she'd probably slide off the roof again. Hopefully, Anna was already awake and dealing with the man on the roof. Otherwise, Lisette would see to it that the mage ended up with scissors in some vital part of his anatomy.

The hatch to the roof was still open. Lisette boosted herself onto the tiles, careful about where she put her weight. She couldn't depend on Braatle breaking her fall twice in one evening.

When her eyes had adjusted to the starlight, Lisette sighed in relief. No one else was in sight. If Sunny had been pulled up through the hatch, Remy and probably even Giselle would be up here fighting to get her back. Once again, Lisette made a detour so she could look over the crest to the other side of the building, but she was the only one there. Anna had already gone back into their rooms to join the battle against the other mage.

Broken tiles littered the rooftop and a section of the edge was missing, making it look as if some giant beast had taken a bite. She and Remy needed to repair that before it next rained. For now, Lisette crept to the hatch and leaned in. "Is it safe to come down?"

Remy called up, "Yes. One got away, but we've added another mage to our collection. And Sunny is fine."

Lisette wasted no time in getting off the roof. She found Giselle and Remy standing over another stranger who was bound and blindfolded. Giselle's hair stuck straight out, and there were scorch marks on the ceiling. The dragon-born, still asleep, lay next to the wall.

Ignoring the slimy mess on her clothing, Remy pulled Lisette into a long hug. "You're not hurt? I heard you call..."

"I'm fine. Braatle caught me." She leaned back so she could see around him. "Where's your mother?"

The blood drained from Remy's face. "She was with you."

Lisette's stomach lurched.

Ten minutes of searching told them the awful truth: Anna had disappeared.

CHAPTER 26

THE MESSAGE

As soon as Giselle saw the glowing dagger Lisette had found on the roof during the search, her jaw tightened. "Anna would never leave that behind." In the next instant, she was rooting through her bag for the supplies she needed to cast the tracking spell, the same one she'd cast to find the dragon-born, though this time she had Lisette hold the token.

The dagger rose above Lisette's hand and then rotated until the blade pointed down the hill and to the north.

Giselle sat back heavily in her chair. "Go. Braatle and I will keep watch over the child in case they return. And hurry — they'll cloak her presence sooner rather than later."

Lisette didn't need to be told twice. Grabbing Remy's arm with her free hand, she pulled him along with her as she ran down the stairs. The dagger moved with her, its angle unchanged.

When they reached the street, Lisette stole a glance at Remy's face. For once, there was no sign of humor. He just looked lost. She interlaced her fingers with his and squeezed. "The spell wouldn't have worked if she were dead, right?"

He gave the tiniest of nods as they hurried to the edge of the freeholder quarter.

"They wouldn't have taken her without a purpose. So they'll keep her safe." Lisette assumed Anna would be kept as a bargaining chip to force Remy and possibly Giselle away from the fight for Harbor Crag. But for now, Remy needed to believe they could get his mother back safely.

Tiffany caught up to them as they turned onto the broad street leading down to the harbor. After two steps to catch her breath, she asked, "Where are you going?"

"Anna's been taken." Lisette explained quickly, keeping one eye on the dagger as they trotted downhill. This early in the evening, there should have been more people on the street, returning from work or time with friends. But the evening vendors had shuttered their carts, and the few pedestrians moved with purpose. Everyone near the freeholder quarter had heard Braatle's roars.

The tip of the glowing blade had migrated, pointing slightly more north than before, at a speed that would have been impossible on foot unless Anna was within sight. That alone told her their quarry had used a carriage to get away from the freeholder quarter. "They aren't taking her to the harbor."

Suddenly, the dagger wobbled and rotated freely, just as the coin had done above Giselle's hand. Remy pulled Lisette to a stop and held his forearm along the line where it had last pointed. "They've cloaked her. Assuming they haven't moved since then, where would she be?"

Lisette's eyes followed the line, and she frowned. "The perfume district?"

Tiffany nodded. "Or maybe the theater on the green?"

The perfume district had originally been the home of a family of skilled perfumers. For a hundred years, the two blocks had been famous for scents and other luxury goods, including silks, jewelry, and imported magical baubles. But after a very public argument about taxes with the then-duke fifty years before, the perfumers had sold everything and moved to the Island of Light.

When the infamous courtesan Lady Velvet had moved into the largest residence, the name of the district had taken on a slightly different meaning, but the rest of the businesses had stayed. These days, to be a courtesan in the perfume district was a mark of distinction, and many of those who retired from the profession were sought by other businesses for their skill in negotiations and manners.

Beyond the small perfume district was the open-air theater used by the city's troupe during the summer. Stone benches had been crafted and placed on the hill in a semi-circle facing a plateau that provided a natural stage. With some minor magic for sound enhancement and backdrops, plays could be performed for up to six hundred patrons.

While the city's rulers claimed the theater as one of their shining achievements, in truth, the area would have been built over in a heartbeat if it hadn't been for the dens of white-throated badgers living at the site, constrained to this small portion of the city by spells attributed to Luella the Difficult nearly five hundred years before. During the summer, the badgers roamed the cliffs to the north, plundering bird nests and catching the rodents who also preyed upon the birds. When the weather cooled, the badgers hibernated — unless anyone was foolish enough to put a heated structure on the site.

Every generation, the duke would offer a bounty for anyone who could successfully drive out the badgers, but the mages kept excellent records, and Luella was known as *the Difficult* for reasons beyond her personality. Lisette had taken Remy there once and when they had come close, he had laughed in astonishment and refused to set foot on the grass. "If you could see what I see... It might not be just badgers who get trapped here."

Now, faced with the choice between blocks full of people and an open field that repelled mages, Lisette pulled them through a narrow alley that would bring them closer to the perfume district. "Probably not the green if it affects all mages like it does Remy." She considered the little she knew about where they were going. It wasn't a place she'd often been. "Perhaps they've rented a room there?"

When they turned the corner into the perfume district, the air was heavy with lilac and rose, courtesy of a vendor waving a scented fan over thousands of tiny glass bulbs in the cart before him. "Souvenir of the evening, ladies and gents?" He winked. "And this souvenir won't require a medical mage before you can go home again!"

Ignoring the vendor, Lisette looked at the street crowded with carriages and people. Here, there was no sign of the quiet brought on by a dragon fighting mages in the street. Women and men lounged in the open windows above, calling down to passersby. If Anna had been brought here, *someone* had to have seen something. "Let's split up and talk to people. I'll take the left. Tiff, you take the right, and Remy can talk to people on the street. Meet back here in fifteen minutes."

On a night when she wasn't worried about Anna, Lisette would have found the experience amusing. The perfume district hired its own guards, whose purpose was to keep the residents safe and the businesses unharmed. Within two minutes, Lisette had been propositioned twice and shown ruby earrings worth more than her entire shop, but her refusals to all the offers were received with good-natured shrugs. Everyone was perfectly willing to answer her questions, especially when she mentioned the dragons, but nobody had seen anything.

"It's the night crowd, love," said the man selling candied rose petals on a second-floor landing overlooking the street, his fingers busy counting out change even as he spoke. "We're so busy you could bring a sea serpent through and we might miss it. But I'll keep an eye out."

Lisette thanked him and moved on. A man on the next balcony told her the same thing. "When I'm not working in there," he said, tilting his head at the rooms behind him, "I'm trying to catch someone's eye. I don't even see the carriages anymore, not unless I'm escorting someone to another part of town."

The guards were slightly more observant, but without a description of the conveyance, they couldn't help. "But I know we didn't see a sleeping woman being carried into a building," one added. "That sort of thing would be stopped." His partner nodded emphatically.

At the end of the row, Lisette slipped down the stairs and found Remy and Tiffany outside a raucous bar. "No luck," she told them. From their worried looks, she didn't need to ask if they'd learned anything. "We'll keep looking."

A young boy in ragged clothing, his face strangely slack, ran up and tugged on Remy's sleeve. "Lord Hanley has a message for you."

Before Lisette could react, Remy had a coin out and had dropped to one knee so he was at eye level with the boy. "The message?"

The child's voice deepened, as if he were imitating not just the words, but the tone. "You have six hours until the fire takes her from the green." The boy sagged once he'd finished the sentence, the compulsion satisfied.

Remy held out one arm to steady the child and peered into his eyes. Then he handed over the coin. Lisette saw a spark of magic, and the boy's eyes focused again. With a suspicious glare, the child leaped to his feet and disappeared into the crowd.

As he stood, Remy wiped his hands on his tunic. "Once this is over, we need to make sure Lord Hanley hasn't left his mark on anyone else." He straightened his shoulders. "Let's find out what awaits us at the green."

CHAPTER 27
ALL THE MAGIC OF AN OLD BOOT

After the lights and bustle of the perfume district, the eerie quiet of the unlit green made Lisette shiver. When they reached the edge, Remy reached out to hold Lisette and Tiffany back. "Wait."

Mist drifted above the grass, and there was just enough light to pick out the stone benches set in semicircles on the terraced slope. At the lowest level, a cage made of solid bars with a sparkle of magic rested in the middle of the stage. Anna stood within, apparently unharmed, examining each bar from top to bottom.

Remy's mother might be the center of some sort of trap for mages, but she wasn't planning on sitting around while she waited to be rescued. For some reason that buoyed Lisette's spirits, making the night feel real in a way it hadn't since they'd realized Anna had been taken.

Tiffany rubbed her arms. "Is it my imagination, or is it colder here? Colder than it should be."

"It's real," Remy said. He crouched to look at the ground, carefully staying outside the stone boundary of the green. "There's a new spell woven into Luella the Difficult's original working. It's pulling heat from the area and concentrating it under the stage."

Six hours until the fire takes her from the green, the boy had said. If Lord Hanley had wanted Anna dead, he would have killed her. This display was intended to keep Remy out of the fight to protect the dragon-born.

But what else could they do? Even if Remy chose the dragon-born, his concentration would be destroyed. No, Remy needed to stay and free his mother. "What do you need us to do?"

He stood, narrowing his eyes as he looked at the mist swirling around the green. "Somehow, I have to get down to the plateau so I can untangle the spell holding my mother. How did he...? Never mind, that's not important now. But Luella's spell senses magic, and he's tapped into that. If I step foot on the green, bad things will happen."

Visiting mages had never been able to alter Luella the Difficult's spell, but Lord Hanley had lived in Harbor Crag his entire life. He'd been able to study it for years, and Remy was seeing the results.

All three stared at the stage, where Anna now examined the ground beneath her, prodding at it experimentally with the toe of her boot.

"A cart?" Tiffany suggested. "Lisette and I could pull you where you need to go."

"Or a horse," Lisette said.

Tiffany made a face. "Would you trust a horse not to panic and run off the cliff?"

"No horses," Remy said firmly. "They make me break out in hives and that's very distracting." He frowned at Lisette. "You should stay off the green as well. I suspect your bond with Aarat will be a problem."

"Whereas I," Tiffany said, waving one hand along her

curvy body from head to toe, "have all the magic of an old boot. I'm going to let Anna know we're here."

Before the others could stop her, she walked onto the green.

Lisette clapped both hands over her mouth and watched her best friend confidently descend the slope toward the stage. Tiffany stopped on the lowest level, not touching the plateau, where she and Anna had a brief conversation. Remy's mother looked up and waved at them, and they waved back. A few minutes later, Tiffany returned to their position.

"She's fine for the moment. It's definitely warmer near the stage, but not bad. Though she says it was cooler when she woke there." Tiffany gave the ground a worried look. "If this keeps up, we may have a problem with the badgers."

The badgers would be drawn to the warmth of the stage. While they weren't particularly aggressive, grumpy badgers would make everything more difficult.

To save Anna, they needed more people who could walk on the grass. Lisette could do nothing here to help. As much as she wanted to stay, logic dictated otherwise. "I'll go back, send more people, and tell Giselle what is going on." She kissed Tiffany on the cheek, and then Remy. "Please be careful."

"I'm always careful," Remy argued, sounding hurt.

Tiffany shook her head at him and then looked at Lisette. "Can you make sure Turtle stays in the quarter? She'll want to come here and if a dragon bond is a problem..."

Lisette nodded, not trusting herself to speak. Somehow, everything had gone wrong in the space of one day, and she didn't know how to fix it.

～

Uncle Rye met Lisette at the edge of the freeholder district. "Did you find Remy's mother?"

"Yes, but..." She explained the situation on the green. "They need a small cart, something to fend off badgers, and some people who have absolutely no magic at all."

Rye nodded. "I'll take care of that while you tell the professor. She's still trying to wake the girl." He put a hand on her shoulder to keep her in place. "See if you can convince her to rest. Her working herself into an early grave is the last thing we need." He squeezed her shoulder and dropped his hand.

"I'll try."

Seeing the empty street in front of her shop, Lisette thought Braatle must have been patrolling elsewhere, but then she saw the dragon's bulk crouched on the roof. Tactically, it was an excellent spot. But Lisette and Remy would *definitely* need to check the roof tiles before the next rain.

When Lisette climbed the stairs to the rooms she shared with Remy, everything felt strangely quiet after the earlier commotion. "Giselle?"

"In here." The mage's exhausted voice came from the room where Sunny lay on the thin mattress. "Have you found Anna?" Her words danced a perilous line between hope and despair.

Lisette went into the room to find Giselle seated on the floor next to the still-sleeping dragon-born. "Anna is fine for the moment." For an instant, she thought Giselle would collapse in relief, but as Lisette explained the circumstances, the mage recovered her equilibrium.

"Six hours?" Giselle pushed herself to her feet. "Then they're planning another assault to steal the dragon-born tonight. They know she's here. We need to move the girl while Remy's dealing with Hanley's little trap."

Lisette must have made a noise because Giselle looked directly at her, a tiny smile showing on her tired face. "For most purposes, Remy isn't the first mage I would call on. His magic is too unpredictable and he's easily distracted, especially when he's bored. But for a trap like that? Harbor Crag might need a new theater afterward, but Remy is the mage most capable of keeping Anna safe. Have him tell you of the Finnigan's Mage Society mystery coins he amassed when he was at the college."

The knotted muscles in Lisette's shoulders relaxed. Giselle was right, of course.

The professor continued. "So while he handles that, we need to move quickly. I know why nothing we've tried has woken the dragon-born, even if I don't know how to fix it. We need allies." Her face was serious again. "We need to free more dragons."

CHAPTER 28
PARADE

In the hours after midnight, the streets of the freeholder quarter should have been quiet and dark. Tonight, they were not. Somehow Lisette had become part of what could only be termed a parade.

Giselle had decided to bring the unconscious girl to the dragon warrens, where she would be better protected against magical attacks. Naturally, half the denizens of the freeholder quarter had elected to come along. Some wanted a second chance against the mages who had taken Remy's mother, and the others had missed the first battle and didn't want to be left out of a second. Freeholders carrying lanterns and makeshift cudgels patrolled the edges of the group, calling to each other and passing a bottle around.

Uncle Rye had sent Barlow with the group to help Remy at the green, but Rye had stayed behind to protect Sunny, being one of the few freeholders with any combat experience.

In the middle of the group was Braatle, weary but fierce. Lisette walked at the dragon's shoulder with the unconscious Sunny in her arms — her shoulders ached under the burden, but the dragon trusted few people. On Lisette's other side, Giselle talked to the dragon of changes in the magic schools. "... which led to the expansion of Galfigon College, as many mages leaving the Island of Light settled there."

And somehow they had also picked up a black cat, nearly full-grown but still in that lanky stage, who wove between Braatle's feet, constantly in danger of being crushed but always safe by a hair.

"But the Island of Light didn't continue their expansion?" The blue-green dragon cocked her head, eyeing an orange cat sitting on the edge of the roof and grooming himself with no concern for all the activity below. The young black cat trotting along the pavement didn't acknowledge his compatriot.

"No. I think they would have, but they took heavy losses in shipping and mages were forced to go along on sea voyages to keep the creatures of the deep away." Giselle reached out a hand toward Lisette to steady herself on the uneven road as the freeholder quarter gave way to the upper limits of the city. "Only recently did we realize the duke's people in Harbor Crag were tipping the scales by using magic stolen from the dragons. Until then, we believed you had all left."

They had reached the outer walls of the dragon warrens and turned to follow the road to the gates. Aside from a lingering smell of smoke, there was no sign that Braatle had torched a cart.

Lisette suddenly realized this entire band of people would happily walk straight through the gates into the warrens if she didn't stop them. "Uncle Rye, everyone needs to stay at the gates. The entrances to the caverns are easy to miss, especially in the dark."

He nodded and strode to the front of the column to warn the others. In the end, only Lisette, Giselle, and Rye — and the cat — escorted Braatle through the crumbling outer walls to the main tunnel, where they passed the mostly buried body of the mage who had flung magic so unwisely earlier in the day.

Rye paused at the cave-in and held his torch closer. "We should dig him out and rebury him properly when it's light, or it will smell like there's a dead rat in the walls by next week."

Lisette suspected the two unchained dragons would take care of the problem on their own, but decided not to say anything.

When they came close to the opening of Aarat's cavern, Lisette called ahead. "It's Lisette," she said, not wanting to startle the broody dragon. "And I'm with the dragon-born, plus a couple of people who are here to help. And Braatle."

The black cat dashed around the corner into Aarat's cavern.

"And a cat!" Lisette yelled belatedly. She knew the dragon loved cats, but sudden movements seemed like a terrible idea. She peeked around the entrance cautiously.

The huge amber dragon crouched facing her, his back to one wall. "Lisette." From that position, he could turn his head to spit fire at either entrance to his cavern. In the corner protected by his bulk, the tiny red dragon — free of her shell and just barely larger than the cat — slept on a scattering of gold coins, her tail tip curled around to rest on her snout. The black cat sniffed a few times and then hopped over the tail to settle in the hollow, purring so loudly that Lisette could hear him all the way across the chamber. Despite the chaos of the day, the sight made her smile.

Braatle slid past Lisette, entering the chamber to crouch opposite Aarat in a position that also allowed her to defend both entrances. Aarat sang a chord, and Braatle added tones, the harmonics vibrating the wall near Lisette's shoulder. Wordless greeting? Dragon speech? Remy would know. After two long breaths, the music died away.

A hand touched her back, reminding Lisette that she had other responsibilities. She moved forward and waited for the others to follow. "Aarat, this is Remy's teacher, Giselle. And this is my uncle, Rye." There was no danger in her identifying her friends. Only a name freely offered by the person would give the dragon power over them. "Giselle has an idea for waking up Sunny. Rye's here to help guard her."

Rye moved into view and bowed at the waist. "Pleased to meet you." His voice sounded only a little strangled.

Giselle bowed her head. "I'm honored to meet the dragon Aarat," she said, her words spoken with formal precision. Then she looked at Lisette and returned to her usual bearing. "You should probably put the child down before you drop her."

Since Aarat didn't *seem* to be in a mood to roast any of them, Lisette walked closer.

"Place her next to Dinaat," Aarat said. His head snaked forward to sniff at the child's sleeping form, and then he sneezed. "They have used *dragon* magic to bind her." A hint of smoke and fire came from his nostrils, but he turned his head away before Sunny or Lisette could be harmed.

Figuring Dinaat had to be the baby dragon, Lisette carried her burden to the corner, very aware of Aarat's attention on her. She was bound to him and he trusted her, yet his protective instincts around the baby dragon overrode everything. Rye and Giselle would need to keep their distance. Lisette crouched and placed the dragon-born between Dinaat and the rock wall. Without waking, Dinnat shifted her head to rest against Sunny's hip, as if the sleeping dragon was reassuring herself that the dragon-born was nearby. The black cat yawned, stretched, and filled the space between the two.

Lisette sighed in relief and rubbed her left shoulder. It had been a long day. But now they were here, she'd have a chance to sit down and relax while Giselle worked.

Across the chamber, Giselle met Aarat's gaze. "The stronger my attempts to free the dragon-born, the stronger the response of the dragon magic. I don't have the power needed to destroy the spell. And we haven't yet captured the mage responsible."

Aarat growled, smoke rising from his nostrils.

Giselle ignored the signs of irritation. "I think our best hope is to keep them from using the dragons as a source of power." She turned to face Lisette. "Which is going to require your help."

Lisette sighed as she found herself the center of attention once again.

CHAPTER 29
VITAL COG

Having a powerful mage *and* a dangerous dragon staring at her expectantly did not reassure Lisette. She cleared her throat. "Don't get me wrong, I think keeping dragon magic away from Lord Hanley is an excellent idea. I just don't see how I'm a vital cog in this plan." After all, the only reason she'd become involved with dragons in the first place was because she'd literally fallen into Aarat's cavern. As qualifications went, that seemed like a *very* low bar.

Giselle shook her head, her wild hair forming a gray halo around her face. "So modest. Or do you really not...?" Her head tilted as she regarded Lisette. "How did you remove the spell that stole Braatle's speech?"

"You were there." Lisette glanced at Rye, wondering if he'd noticed mental lapses from Giselle, but he was getting familiar with the cavern, eyeing the ramp to the surface as if wondering how to block it.

"Humor me." Giselle smiled. "Tell me how *you* think it happened."

"Um..." Lisette thought back to the morning. "Once I

touched the metal and realized what was going on, I took out the cotter pin and pulled out the spike." In her mind's eye, she remembered the scale crumbling as she'd yanked, and she rubbed her still healing hand. "Or that's what I tried to do, anyway. It got stuck and I damaged Braatle's scales a little."

Magic flared and rippled over Braatle's blue and green scales from nose to tail, but the dragon didn't comment.

Giselle nodded, looking like a teacher proud of a student who has successfully completed the first part of a problem. "Yes, but how did you get close for long enough to remove the cotter pin?"

"Luck?" Lisette looked at the other woman doubtfully. "I seem to remember being knocked down a few times."

Braatle snorted. "You feel like Aarat. I was not trying to harm you, even when I couldn't understand your speech."

"Ah." The point of Giselle's questions suddenly hit Lisette. "You need me to remove the language spells from the other dragons."

Halfway up the ramp, Rye turned. "What? No. Absolutely not. That's too dangerous."

Giselle ignored him. "We can't break the hold Lord Hanley has over the other dragons without their help. And we can't gain their trust if we can't communicate."

The professor was right. Lisette could feel it in her bones. If her bond with Aarat made it possible for her to approach the other dragons, she had to do it. The only other choice in Harbor Crag was Turtle, who now had a bond with Braatle, and Lisette would wrestle a thousand dragons before putting her niece in harm's way.

That didn't make her bruised and battered body feel any stronger.

Lisette inhaled deeply and blew out her breath as she

gathered her willpower. The task wouldn't get any smaller by waiting. And how long could Sunny go without food and drink?

"Alright then. Let's do this."

LISETTE CHEWED on her lower lip as she stared into the cavern where a pale yellow dragon with brown legs and tail glared at her balefully. Steam rose from his nostrils. At the far corner of the room, a thick chain connected him to the wall.

They had decided the smaller the dragon, the better, at least to begin with, and this was the smallest in the first five caves. But smaller didn't mean *small*. One good swing of that tail and Lisette would go flying. And that didn't even address the fire.

"Maybe a bigger dragon would be slower," she said, her voice sounding tinny in her ears.

Giselle patted her on the shoulder. "You'll do fine. Braatle was bigger and faster and this time she'll be helping you."

Lisette had her doubts about that, too. Avoiding damage from the dragon helping her would be key. Suddenly, she was glad they had left Aarat and Rye defending the dragon-born and baby dragon; Uncle Rye wouldn't be around to see her get crushed or roasted. She hoped Remy was having better luck freeing his mother on the green.

"Off you go," Giselle said cheerfully. "I'll do my best to keep him distracted."

Before Lisette could come up with another excuse to

delay this folly, Braatle slid past her into the yellow dragon's cavern.

When the dragons bellowed at each other, fear locked Lisette's joints. No, she absolutely could *not* go in there. This was *madness*.

Braatle threw herself against the yellow dragon's front end, trapping her opponent's neck against the floor. Flames erupted from the smaller dragon's mouth, but Braatle was out of the way and the yellow dragon couldn't turn his head with his neck pinned to the ground.

"Well done, Braatle," Giselle yelled approvingly. She pushed Lisette forward. "Your turn!"

Without the protection of the wall next to her, Lisette realized she *could* move. She sprinted across the rough floor.

Even though he couldn't see past Braatle's bulk, the yellow dragon sensed her coming. His tail swept out, catching Lisette in the thigh and sending her tumbling. But when she rolled to her feet, she was behind the dragon's right shoulder, exactly where she'd planned to go. The two struggling dragons felt *awfully* close.

When she'd been planning her approach, Lisette had decided to keep her left hand gloved and her right hand bare as a compromise between protection and dexterity. Now she felt along the razor sharp scales with her left hand, searching for anything that felt like it didn't belong.

Nothing. "It's not here!"

No need to panic yet. She'd found the one on Braatle behind the dragon's *left* elbow — maybe whoever had done this had been consistent. But it meant she needed to get to the other side.

Going around the front end was absolutely out. The other direction left her exposed to another sweep of the tail, and she was lucky she hadn't broken bones with the last hit. That left one path — over the top.

Braatle slid toward her as Lisette was pulling on her second glove, the yellow dragon thrashing wildly. Then a spell detonated and the yellow dragon quieted. Lisette scrambled up and over to the dragon's left side. The wall was right behind her, protecting her from the dragon's tail. She ran her hands under razor-sharp scales.

There! Her left hand had snagged on the chain looping around the scale. Raising her right hand to her mouth, she used her teeth to pull off the glove. The metal construct was the same — she just needed to remove the cotter pin, and then she'd be able to yank the spike out.

"Almost there," she called to Braatle.

With a roar, the yellow dragon rolled toward her.

Dragon scales crunched against leather, and Lisette was crushed against the stone wall, unable to breathe.

CHAPTER 30
YOU STINK OF AARAT

B lack spots formed in Lisette's vision as she struggled for air. Her right hand was free, but the left was trapped in the chain attached to the spike going through the dragon's scale. If she could just get the spike out, they could *explain*.

The yellow dragon thrashed against Braatle's hold, and Lisette got two quick breaths before the weight was back. The scale she needed to reach under was pressed flat against her abdomen, with the bulk of a full-grown dragon behind it.

Her vision dimmed.

Remy was going to be so mad if she died this way.

Desperation confirmed her choice. Taking her knife from her belt sheathe, she pulled as hard as she could with her left hand while she reached in to cut the scale free.

The yellow dragon screamed as coppery blood gushed over Lisette's hand. One side of the scale came free. Lisette used that edge as a guide to slice the dragon's hide. By the time she was halfway done, her knife had dulled and she had to resort to sawing back and forth to make any progress.

Just a finger's width to go. But her strength was waning as her panicked need to breathe became the only thing of importance. As her fingers weakened on the knife, she felt another spell detonate. The yellow dragon shifted away, scales scraping on the ground. It was just far enough for her to fill her lungs. After one full breath, she had enough energy to slice down and yank the scale free. Her left hand fell away from the dragon, the bloody yellow scale hanging from the spike, chunks of flesh still attached. Lisette's surgery had been brutal and swift, and she hoped it had been effective.

Everyone froze.

"Braatle?" The yellow dragon spoke for the first time. Lisette closed her eyes in relief. Then the dragon moved away, and she sank down to the floor, eyes still closed, gulping air to regain her breath.

When she could breathe enough to open her eyes, the first thing she saw was the yellow dragon's face an arm's length away, smoke rising from his nostrils.

She dropped the chain and the scale fell onto the floor. "I'm so sorry. It was the only way I could think to get the spell off you."

The dragon loomed closer, the smoke coming from his nostrils hot against her face. "You stink of *Aarat*." His threat was clear despite the impossibly musical voice.

Lisette fought the urge to break into hysterical laughter. They had all assumed that her bond with Aarat would *help*. She'd have to remember to tell Remy later. He would find this funny. But right now, she needed to pull her wits together.

"We're trying to break the bonds draining your magic."

There was no way she could dash past this dragon to the safety of the tunnel. She'd have to talk her way out of this, unless Giselle could throw another spell to distract him.

"And leave me chained in the dark for the next mage to bind?" His anger brought another puff of smoke, hot against her cheek. To emphasize his point, he moved his leg, rattling the links of the chain that bound him to the cave.

Then Braatle appeared in her vision, a streak of soot running along the side of her neck. Lisette realized she'd missed a battle between the two when she'd been pinned against the wall.

"Drelaack." The blue and green dragon used her head to push the yellow dragon away. "The dragon-born will die if we don't allow the mages to help now."

The two dragons rested their heads together. Though the room was silent, Lisette could feel *something* on the edge of her understanding. If Aarat were here, she thought, he'd understand this conversation. Her bond with the largest dragon gave her awareness, but nothing more.

While the two dragons were busy, she would take this opportunity to get to safety. But by the time she'd climbed to her feet, they had finished talking. The yellow dragon — Drelaack, she reminded herself — blew out a puff of steam, then said, "I give you safe passage to do whatever you must to free me."

"Thank you." She wobbled on her first step, but didn't fall. "And I promise we'll do everything we can to free you completely."

On her journey toward the tunnel entrance, Lisette staggered like a drunkard, leaving the two dragons communing at her back. Now it was up to Giselle to break the bond Lord Hanley was using to siphon Drelaack's magic. And she was going to give herself a short break before tackling the next dragon.

But when she rounded the corner, she found Giselle slumped against the wall, her head resting on her knees. The mage waved a hand to let Lisette know she wasn't harmed. "That last spell really took it out of me."

Since the last spell had physically shifted the yellow dragon so Lisette could breathe, she was grateful for the mage's efforts. "Can I get you anything?"

"Eight hours of rest?" Giselle gave a weak smile. "I'll be right as rain after I've had some time to recover." She accepted Lisette's help to stand, and her smile faded. "But I don't think I'll have the strength to free our new friend. I'll try, but..."

"No. I have another idea." Having nearly been crushed by a dragon, Lisette wasn't feeling up to much, but she was still steadier on her feet than Giselle. She held the mage's arm to support her. "Let's go back to Aarat's chamber. Uncle Rye can keep watch while you rest."

She needed to discuss her plan with Aarat. Without a mage able to remove the spell directly, they had only one option.

And she really didn't like it.

CHAPTER 31
NOT A DRAGON TO BE TRUSTED

"Absolutely not!" Uncle Rye was so horrified that he interrupted Lisette before she could finish detailing her plan. Not that there was all that much to explain.

They were in Aarat's cavern, with Sunny and the baby dragon slumbering on scattered coins in the corner, Aarat and Braatle guarding the entrances, and Lisette and Rye arranging a comfortable resting spot for the exhausted Giselle.

"I don't have a better idea," Lisette said. "More than that — it's my *only* idea. If you can think of a better way to break the bonds, please, tell me."

So far, they had found three ways to break Lord Hanley's hold over the dragons: Lisette's accidental smearing of her blood on Aarat's dagger, Remy's use of magic to free Braatle, and dropping a ceiling on the mage holding the bond. "Remy's busy, Giselle needs to rest, and we don't have any extra mages to sacrifice."

Not that they would have done that last one, but it was probably just as well Aarat didn't know about the mages they had captured in the freeholder quarter. The dragon valued practical solutions and wasn't terribly bothered by mages dying.

"It's not safe," Rye protested.

"But would it *work*?" Lisette persisted, looking at Aarat. Knowing that Lord Hanley's forces would be attacking again in the next few hours, safety didn't matter as much as expediency.

Aarat shifted, his amber scales winking like copper in the lantern's light. "I was able to protect you from the magic released because you were bonded to me."

"I'm *still* bonded to you." All the dragons agreed on that, though Lisette managed to ignore it most days. She could only hope that Turtle's bond with Braatle lay so easily upon the girl.

"Dragons are not gears in a watch, "Aarat said, "one replaceable with the other. I can no more absorb Drelaack's power than turn my scales yellow." Something in the way he said the other dragon's name suggested scorn. Giselle tilted her head, as if filing that away to think over later.

Lisette turned over the dragon's words in her mind. "You're saying I would have to be bonded to Drelaack for this to work."

"Stop." Rye held up a hand. "If someone has to take on a bond with that dragon, it doesn't need to be you. The quarter is filled with people who will volunteer. *I'll* do it."

Letting someone else take over that part seemed like a great idea. Maybe not Uncle Rye, who would chafe at being ordered to do anything by dragon, but surely there were scores of freeholders willing to make this sacrifice.

Giselle spoke from her nest on the floor, her voice reedy with exhaustion. "Aarat, how many of them will survive?"

Scales scratched on the rock floor as the giant dragon

turned his head. "No one can know until the deed is upon them. One in ten? Perhaps more, perhaps less. Humans are delicate creatures, and many fail to channel magic."

One in ten would *survive*? Abruptly, the burden was back on Lisette. "Those are terrible odds. We already know I'm capable." She set her shoulders. They didn't have time to dither about this. "Which weapon binds Drelaack?"

From the jumble of sharp objects in the corner, Aarat plucked a short sword and placed it at Lisette's feet. "Drelaack is not a dragon to be trusted," he rumbled. "Take care."

Trust. Were any dragons trustworthy? Yes, Lisette decided, for all that Aarat had different beliefs about right and wrong, she did trust him. So what did it mean that Drelaack could not be trusted? And did it matter? Time was running out.

She bowed her head toward the dragon, picked up the short sword with care, and then held up a hand before Uncle Rye could remonstrate. "Necessity. I'll be back as soon as I can."

When she reached the yellow dragon's cavern, she held the sword before her, tip pointing to the ground. "Drelaack, this is the weapon binding you to the mages. I have no magic to free you —"

"Then what *use* are you to me?" He charged.

As the yellow dragon grew closer, Lisette forced herself to hold her ground. If she was going to be bound to this dragon, he had to believe she wasn't afraid.

Even if she was.

At the last second, the small dragon skidded to a halt, smoke from his nostrils heating Lisette's skin. Before he could speak, she continued, "But I freed Aarat by letting him take the magic back into himself."

Drelaack sat back on his haunches. "You took on the bond and he shielded you."

"Yes." Thank the creatures of the deep that the dragon understood, because Lisette didn't fully comprehend it herself. Her explanation would have been a muddled mess. "And I'm willing to do the same for you, if you desire."

"You would give me your name." Incredulity laced Drelaack's words.

"I would." Lisette steeled herself against the dragon's reaction to what she was about to demand. "But I require your word that you won't use that bond against me."

"Done."

It was too quick, that agreement. Lisette *knew* it was. And yet, what else could she do? She had no means of enforcing *anything,* and Lord Hanley had to be stopped. She cleared her throat, her mouth suddenly dry. "My name is Lisette."

Throwing back his head, the yellow dragon trumpeted savagely. "Lisette," he snarled, his voice a crescendo of beautiful chimes.

The tones expanded within her, drowning out her thoughts and vibrating her bones. *Lisette*, he crooned harshly, this time for her ears alone. Around her, the world dropped away, until all that existed was this golden dragon, pain, and doing his bidding. A tiny ember deep within knew this was wrong, knew there was some reason this shouldn't be allowed, but it was snuffed out and she was swept away by the tide.

Power wrapped around her, buffeting her senses, and Drelaack became the ocean that closed over her head as she drowned.

CHAPTER 32

STOP THIS

Caught in the storm of Drelaack's power, Lisette curled in on herself, just trying to survive. Fire crackled, the sound nearly drowned out by a never-ending roar. With every breath, she choked on dragon smoke. Logically, she knew this was all in her mind — if her body actually burned, she wouldn't be alive to feel this. Lisette clutched at awareness, feeling her sense of self bubbling and flaking away.

By killing her, Drelaack was condemning himself. But expecting rational behavior from a dragon chained and left without language for decades had been a mistake. If he'd been more in control of himself, he would have at least waited until she'd broken the spell stealing his magic. Now Lord Hanley would keep his stolen power and everyone she loved would be in danger.

Trying to get through despite the currents buffeting her, she yelled, "Drelaack! I can't free your magic if you kill me!"

Her words were whipped away by a fiery blast of air. Dragon screams pierced her.

Abruptly, everything went still, cold, and dark.

Lisette waited, afraid to move. Had she finally died? But no, she could feel Drelaack's storm raging on, just outside a bubble surrounding her.

A familiar voice boomed, vibrating her skin. *I told you he was not to be trusted.*

"Aarat?" Lisette tried to look around, but all she could sense was darkness and the surrounding cocoon. Somehow, Aarat had given her shelter. "Can you force him to stop?"

I cannot.

Outside, the hurricane that was Drelaack howled her name and she shivered. "I don't think I can survive much more." The image of Remy finding her like this stabbed through her heart, far more painful than anything Drelaack had done.

Perhaps this will help. Do not make me regret this, friend of the dragons.

Aarat's presence disappeared. At the same time, the cocoon holding her safe turned to flame and sank toward her.

Panic raced through Lisette. "Wait! Aarat, come back!" She flinched, but the flames came inexorably closer.

This was it. This was the moment she would die.

Except... The flames merged with her skin. Power thrummed through her, and her hair whipped around her head like sparks. Drelaack's rage spun her around, but she was strangely insulated.

Irritation bubbled up. "Stop this," she growled at the dragon. A part of her looked on in shock. Not that she didn't get irritated with the various trials of everyday life, but this felt like it was part of the power still seeping into her.

The storm abated.

"No!" Drelaack's cry echoed around her, but once again, it felt oddly distant. "He *would* not!"

With a snarl, Lisette wished the maelstrom away — and found herself back in Drelaack's cavern, facing the yellow dragon. Her skin felt different, somehow tighter, or maybe warmer, but from what she could see, she remained unchanged.

Drelaack inhaled, a prelude to spitting flames in her direction, so Lisette stepped back into the safety of the tunnel. "We don't have time for this," she said, her voice cold as ice. That startled her again. Had she really spoken with such disdain? To a dragon?

What had Aarat *done*?

But it didn't matter, because they really *didn't* have time for her to spar with Drelaack. She hefted the short sword, laid it against her open palm... and then rethought that approach. Damaging her hand was both stupid and unnecessary. She moved the blade higher. Cutting the top of her forearm was awkward, but she finally nicked the skin, and blood welled up to coat the blade.

Magic streamed into Lisette. She remembered this from when she'd bled onto the Dagger of Aarat. But this felt... easier? It was more of a gentle brook than the raging river that had been the magic of Aarat.

And none of that made any difference if she couldn't direct it away from herself. Whatever Aarat had done, he hadn't turned her into a mage. Her discomfort grew with every second.

In desperation, she yelled, "Drelaack!"

What had begun as a cry for help unlocked something between them. The magic flowed away, allowing her to take a shaky breath for the first time since she'd slid the sword across her arm.

Inside the cavern, the yellow dragon bellowed as his stolen magic returned. Power still streamed into Lisette, but it was ebbing now, the bond to Lord Hanley's mages withering. A few seconds later, it stopped.

As the last wisps of power drained away, Lisette staggered, using the wall for support. She peeked around the corner to see the yellow dragon. Magic rippled along his spines as he stretched. For a moment, he glanced toward her. Then he curled up on the stone floor, his head facing away.

"You're welcome," she said with a curl of her lip. And again, she wondered when she had become so antagonistic to dragons. She *liked* the dragons, or, at least, she found them beautiful and she was angry they had been trapped underground by the mages of Harbor Crag. Something inside her had changed.

Using the sword as a cane, she walked back to Aarat's cavern. "One down, a whole lot more to go," she muttered under her breath. As an inspirational speech, it left something to be desired. But at least she was still alive, and Lord Hanley had the power of one less dragon at his fingertips.

When Lisette entered the cavern, Aarat didn't react, but Braatle lifted her head up and back, as if surprised by the sight.

Uncle Rye gave a relieved smile from across the chamber, where he was draping a blanket over Sunny. "You did it!"

From the look of things, one of the freeholders had brought supplies. Steam rose from mugs on the floor next to Giselle. Though Lisette had expected to find the mage sleeping, Giselle sat with her back against the stone wall. She turned her head to stare at Lisette, then frowned.

Lisette patted her hair and shoulders and looked around. "What?"

The mage ignored her question and looked toward Aarat, raising her voice with visible effort. "Why does Lisette give off magic like a dragon?"

CHAPTER 33

MORE TRUSTWORTHY

Giselle's accusation hung in the air as wisps of steam rose from Aarat's nostrils.

Lisette ignored both mage and dragon. "I'm fine," she told Uncle Rye before he could worry about her. "It was necessary. We'll deal with it later." Whatever Aarat had done to her — and she was definitely going to get Remy to explain when they had a free moment — didn't matter as much as *why* it had been done. She'd been trapped and dying; Aarat's gift had saved her life. For now, that was all that mattered.

Turning her attention to the blue-green dragon, Lisette said, "Braatle, will you please help me remove the confusion spell from the next? Perhaps," she said with something like a growl in her voice, "we could find one more *trustworthy*."

Uncle Rye's eyes widened.

In the silence that followed, Braatle skirted around Aarat to pick up a short lance from the pile of spelled weapons, and then strode into the tunnel. "This way."

The cavern remained quiet until Lisette had followed

the dragon into the tunnel. Behind her, Uncle Rye said angrily, "What have you done to her?"

"Nothing that wasn't necessary," the dragon snarled, echoing Lisette's words. Then his voice softened. "It may wear off. Eventually."

Giselle's response was too quiet to hear.

Quickening her steps to catch up with Braatle, Lisette pitched her voice so only the blue-green dragon would hear. "I'm sorry. I didn't mean to be rude."

Not slowing, Braatle said, "You have the magic of a dragon and so you speak as one."

Trying to work out if that was an acceptance of her apology or a claim it wasn't needed — or neither — Lisette nearly ran into Braatle when the dragon stopped at the opening to another cavern. Inside, a large violet dragon watched them with wary eyes.

Braatle nodded at the dragon within. "This is Grelaad, a scholar of the sea floor. Of all of my people, he would be one I would most trust to keep his word."

Lisette's mouth went dry as the lilac dragon shifted and she saw the rest of his body. "He's very... large." This dragon was nearly as big as Aarat. If he smashed her into the wall like Drelaack had, she wouldn't get up again.

"Yes," Braatle agreed. "But trustworthy."

"Of course." Perhaps Grelaad would be slower since he was so large, Lisette told herself, gathering her courage. Except Aarat was even bigger, and *he* could move more quickly than she could follow. "I don't have a better plan than the one we used on Drelaack. Do you?"

"No. I shall attempt to keep his head away from you, though it would be good to hurry. Grelaad is strong enough to dislodge me." Braatle tilted her head to look at Lisette.

"Perhaps he will not fight. Even without language, Grelaad might understand we are here to help."

Lisette wondered if she would have known Braatle didn't believe her own words *before* she'd been given the gift of dragon magic. "Let's hope so." She wiped her sweaty palms on her trousers. "Would it help if you went in more slowly? So he doesn't feel attacked."

"I will try." Magic rippled over blue scales as Braatle walked into the cavern. Grelaad shifted his weight back, but didn't otherwise move until Braatle had nearly reached him. The two dragons touched noses, inhaling in unison. Then Braatle slowly wound her neck around Grelaad's.

That was Lisette's cue.

Squaring her shoulders, she walked firmly into the cavern. *This would be a nice place to live if it had more gold*, she thought. Her steps faltered. Where had *that* thought come from? Was Aarat in her head, or had *she* wondered that?

Across the room, Grelaad's nostrils flared and he whipped his head around to face her, dragging Braatle's smaller body along. Dragon scales scraped along the stone floor as the lilac dragon lumbered toward Lisette.

Lisette dodged, trying to stay away from his mouth, though Grelaad hadn't tried to burn her yet. "Nice dragon," she murmured, when he came to a halt. "I'm just trying to help you."

"Sooner would be better," Braatle said, her neck still entwined with Grelaad's. A blue scale glittered on the floor of the cavern.

Five quick steps brought Lisette to Grelaad's left shoulder, and she passed a gloved hand under the scales to find the spike and chain she knew would be there. At least, she hoped so — the other two had been, but two did not a series make.

Grelaad flinched away. She should have left Braatle to guard the dragon-born and brought Aarat, Lisette realized. If the lilac dragon decided she was a danger, nothing Braatle could do would stop him. Then again, Aarat's appearance might lead to battle. The blue-green dragon's presence was helpful in calming Grelaad, but if Lisette didn't finish soon, she'd be lucky to escape with her life.

Just as her glove encountered the chain, Grelaad side-stepped away from her again, a tremor passing along his scales. "Almost there," she murmured, hoping the tone of her voice would soothe, even if he couldn't understand the words.

"He's becoming more agitated," Braatle said, as if Lisette wouldn't notice the quickened breathing and the plumes of steam rising from Grelaad's nostrils.

Now that she knew which scale had the spike, Lisette moved directly to it. But the cotter pin had bent, as if Grelaad had been trying to dislodge it by rubbing against a rock, and the metal cut into her fingers as she straightened it. Before she could yank out the pin, the dragon sidled away, and the scale pulled away from her gloved hand, slicing into the unprotected wrist beneath.

Anger flooded through her, and blood welled up to drip on the stones by her feet. Two steps took her to the dragon's side. "Hold *still*," she roared, slapping her gloved hand down on the side of the massive dragon as if she could hold him in place.

As her voice echoed around the cavern, Lisette froze. Aarat's gift was going to get her killed. Not that she had hurt Grelaad — even if she'd been using a sword instead of a leather glove, she didn't have the strength to harm him — but dragons were irritable at the best of times.

And now, so am I, she thought.

As soon as Remy was back, Lisette would get some answers. But in the meantime... Grelaad hadn't moved. She wiped her bloody hand on her trousers and levered out the cotter pin with the tip of her dagger. Two hard yanks on the spike going through the scale loosened it enough that she could draw it out.

Grelaad lifted his head and curved his neck to face her. "You *dare*."

Lisette cast the bloody pin and chain to the ground and picked up the lance Braatle had brought. Even through the glove, she could feel the tie to Grelaad and knew that if she went back into Aarat's cavern, she could pair every weapon with the correct dragon.

Gritting her teeth, she forced the alien anger away. Could she even create the bond with this dragon she needed in order to free him? There was no way to know without trying. "I'm here to break the spell stealing your magic. My name is Lisette."

Before she could lose her nerve, Lisette sliced her forearm open with the tip of the lance.

CHAPTER 34
TRAP

The instant Lisette's blood touched the lance, power slammed into her, filling her veins to bursting. She was amazed her skin didn't split open. Where Drelaack's power had been a gentle brook, this was a raging torrent, buffeting her to the point of madness. Lisette opened her mouth to scream, but could only whisper, "Grelaad!"

As if his name opened a channel, the power rushed toward the dragon. Grelaad roared, the sound echoed by a dozen other dragon voices. How many dragons had the mages bound in Harbor Crag? Power still rushed through her, lessening only the slightest. Whether by accident or design, Braatle had chosen a very strong dragon for Lisette to unbind.

All this power wasted on Grelaad, the new part of her that coveted gold and magic whispered. *Surely he wouldn't notice if you kept some for yourself.*

Panic raced through Lisette, because she could *see* how it could be done. Diverting just a trickle would be easy. But feeding that piece of dragon within her would let it take over, and she already struggled to keep it in check.

You need never fear Lord Hanley again, it promised. *No mage would stand against you. You could rule Harbor Crag.*

But with that it had overplayed its hand — Lisette had never wanted to rule over anything more than her watchmaker's shop in the freeholder quarter. *No.*

A grumpy harrumph sounded in her thoughts, and then the temptation vanished. Lisette took a relieved breath. Power still raced through her, but she could sense they were nearing the end. Breaking this bond on Grelaad had struck a significant blow against the attacking mages.

The dragons and residents of Harbor Crag would win this battle.

Suddenly, Lisette had the sensation of being seized and yanked underwater. Her body remained in Grelaad's cavern, but her self had been torn away.

As if from a distance, a stranger's voice said, "There! I have Giselle! Finish the binding!" It was a woman, and she sounded both exhausted and giddy. The slap of water against wood told Lisette the stranger was on a ship in the harbor.

They had mistaken her for the professor, Lisette realized. The attackers had been waiting for another mage to break the bonds on a dragon, and they'd laid some sort of trap. When Lisette concentrated, she could feel a burning net of magic, snagging on the seed of a dragon that Aarat had planted. She thrashed in panic, but the net closed tighter as she struggled.

A second voice cried, "Done!"

The clang of metal snapping into place vibrated her bones.

Forcing herself to stop fighting, Lisette examined the

trap, even as a part of her marveled she could do such a thing. This was what it would be like to be a mage, she thought. It really was too bad she didn't have any training in magic.

On the other hand, taking this net apart felt like it should be similar to taking apart any other mechanical device, even if the tools were different.

That bit *there* flexed as she moved it, but this was a solid design and she could see no way to break it apart unless she could free that piece *there*. Which she couldn't do. Her heart raced. She was trapped and she would *never* get free. The enemy mages would keep the power of the dragons, and they would invade Harbor Crag again and again until any rebellion had been extinguished.

Gritting her teeth, Lisette rejected that thought. Nothing was permanent until she gave up. She would examine a different part of the spell.

As she lost herself in the design that entangled her, her breathing slowed. Why had Remy never mentioned that spells were like mechanical objects? Or perhaps he saw them differently.

Aha! *This* bit was a weak point — not a flaw in itself, but it gave her the slack to twist *that*, which opened a tiny gap. Not yet enough to free herself, but the opening loosened other connections, allowing her access to another weak point. The gap widened.

Vaguely, she was aware that the power flowing through her to Grelaad had slowed to a trickle. No matter what happened here, the lilac dragon was free. Now Lisette just had to extricate herself.

Faster and faster, she worked to enlarge the gap enough to sneak through. Almost there. If she'd allowed herself to take some of Grelaad's power, nothing short of destroying the entire net would have sufficed. But Lisette held the anchor for only a glimmer of dragon magic, and she just needed the tiniest break in the spell to slip free.

There. That had to be big enough. She scraped through, feeling the net slide along her soul. The distant voices were shouting, but she ignored them and twisted away.

The net snapped closed behind her and disappeared.

Lisette opened her eyes to see two dragons staring down at her where she lay on the stone floor. They were close enough that she could have reached up to caress Grelaad's lilac nose or pat the scales between Braatle's nostrils. Resting on the ground between two dragons seemed like a bad idea, but she was still trying to get used to inhabiting her body again. "Give me a bit and I'll leave you in peace."

Braatle dropped her head nearly to Lisette's chest and inhaled deeply, as if she were searching for some odor. Then she drew her head back. "How do you remain unbound?"

As she considered how to answer that, Lisette staggered to her feet. Somehow, the presence of two dragons near enough to touch comforted her, or at least the part of her that had wanted to hold the magic of dragons. "They set a trap for power. And I don't have any."

Grelaad bowed his head. "I am in your debt, Lisette." Her name crackled in the air between them, but it felt more like a blessing than a command.

Remy would have known the proper way to respond to such a statement, and he'd be able to cite the book he'd learned it from, but Remy was down the hill trying to save his mother. "If you promise not to hurt anyone, I'll send a blacksmith to break the chain as soon as I can." Without thinking, she rested one hand on the lilac dragon's forehead and then dropped her arm and walked toward the tunnel, still unsteady on her feet.

The enemy mages would be prepared for her if she freed another dragon now. She and Giselle would need to come up with a different method, because Lisette couldn't face being trapped by Lord Hanley again. It might also give the enemy mages a way to trap Aarat, which they *definitely* couldn't afford.

And if Lisette was being honest, she wasn't sure she could turn away the rush of power again, not now that she'd worked with a spell. The allure of tinkering with other spells, adjusting them in the same way she fixed damaged watches, called to her.

Her boots scuffed along the dusty rock beneath her. Refusing to continue freeing the ensorcelled dragons felt like failure, and the only way to let the others know was to blurt it out as quickly as possible, so the words couldn't stick in her throat. As she rounded the corner into Aarat's cavern, she said, "I can't do this..."

Her voice trailed off as she took in the scene before her.

The dragon-born was awake.

CHAPTER 35
TRIM NOT SCRAWNY

L etting herself relax into Uncle Rye's relieved hug, Lisette stared over his shoulder at the child on the other side of the cavern. Sunny leaned against Aarat's back leg with the boneless grace of the young, rolling a gold coin over her fingers and humming a wordless tune.

Lisette's chest tightened. *Protect the dragon-born.* The need to grab the child and hide her away nearly overwhelmed reason, but Lisette forced herself to stand still. First off, Aarat would never allow that; as much as the magic wanted her to believe she was a dragon, Lisette was only human. The giant dragon would spit her with one claw before she could blink.

But more importantly, where would she take Sunny that would be safer than this cavern? Aarat and Braatle guarded both the dragon-born and the newly hatched dragon. Giselle slept now, but she would add her strength when she had recovered. And Uncle Rye and a horde of freeholders were eager to bash any mage that appeared.

As Lisette stood, paralyzed by her confusion, Sunny

levered herself upright and walked across the worn stone floor toward her. The muscles on Aarat's front leg twitched, as if he wanted to grab the child and pull her back to the safety of his body. For the first time, Lisette truly *understood* the amber dragon.

Sunny peered up at Lisette through a tangle of hair. Then she smiled in delight and stretched out a hand to graze Lisette's arm. "Pretty!"

Warmth flowed through Lisette, and the dragon seed basked in the glow. Sunny had never commented on her looks before — the girl had noticed the magic Aarat had planted. But having a dragon live or lurk or whatever it planned on doing inside her had never been a goal of Lisette's. "I'm glad you're awake," she said to Sunny, briefly clasping her hand over the child's.

Then she moved back a step to break contact and turned to Uncle Rye. "It should be safe to send a blacksmith in to break the chain on Grelaad." Drelaack, the little yellow dragon who had almost trapped her, would have to wait. "I'm going to check on Remy and Anna."

It was only after she'd left the dragon warrens that Lisette noticed the cuts on her hands had been healed.

STANDING at the edge of the green, Lisette picked out Remy, lying face down on the edge of a handcart near the glowing cage that held his mother. Most of the green farther up the hill had an unseasonable layer of frost, but Remy had removed his shirt and boots, and Tiffany worked at the head of a bucket chain flooding the stage with water from the public well two blocks away. The water evaporated nearly as fast as they brought it, but at least Anna didn't look too uncomfortable.

Close to the cliffs at the top end, four people worked to build a bonfire, but the flames guttered out as soon as they were lit. That had to be the spell working against them, because if there was one thing freeholders were good at, it was building bonfires. Every celebration had at least one, even those carried out mid-day during the hottest months.

Though most of the green was unlit, brief flashes revealed white-throated badgers moving toward the heat of the stage. But the citizens of Harbor Crag had prepared for that as well, with a line of gleeful children trapping the animals in sturdy baskets and hampers as the badgers came close. A mound of closed baskets spoke to how long this had been going on. It would be a race to see if they ran out of baskets or badgers first.

If Anna hadn't been in peril, this ridiculous drama would have been the most fun performance Lisette had ever seen on the green. But Remy's mother *was* in danger, and Lisette could do nothing to help.

That wasn't true, though. Maybe Lisette couldn't set foot on the green, but the bucket brigade snaked along the cobblestones leading to the pump. She could fill a gap in the line, or let someone else rest. With a last look at Remy, Lisette went to find a spot in the brigade.

Passing buckets of water from hand to hand was a pleasant change from dealing with dragons and mages. Lisette lost herself in the physicality of it all, hefting a full bucket and passing to the next person, taking an empty bucket and sending it down the line to be refilled. Then she nearly dropped a full bucket when she turned and found there was nobody free to take it, progress having stopped.

Everyone had left the green, other than Remy — still

perched on the cart — and Anna. Lisette put the bucket down and found Tiffany. "What's going on?"

Her friend started, then threw her arms around Lisette. "You're back!" When she stood back, she frowned. "Something seems different. Did you burn off more of your hair or something?"

"Or something," Lisette agreed. "Sunny's awake and they're working on getting another dragon unchained. Why'd we stop the bucket brigade?"

Tiffany pointed at Remy. "Your man, there, is worried that what he's about to do might bring all the badgers out at once, so he wanted everyone off the green."

It was a sensible precaution, though Lisette noted that left Remy in the middle of a potential swarm of grumpy badgers. Her own irritation swelled, making her want to roar at the tiny beasts to leave Remy alone.

Tiffany clicked her tongue. "You're looking quite fierce there, sweets. Want me to find some badgers for you to wrestle with? We have a bunch available."

The earnest offer brought Lisette back to herself, and she and Tiffany dissolved into giggles. "It's been a long, weird day." Lisette held Tiffany's hand as they waited anxiously for a sign of Remy's magic on the green.

Nothing happened.

Tiffany sighed. "He really cuts a nice figure, if you like them on the scrawny side."

Since Lisette had seen her friend weak in the knees after watching her baker — a muscled mountain of a man — walk by, she knew Tiffany's preferences. "Trim. Not scrawny. We don't all —"

A wave of magic radiated from the rock under the cage, light flashing as it traversed the green. It crackled along the wooden cart holding Remy, finally dissipating into the night air. Two seconds later, the cage holding Anna wavered and then disappeared, leaving her free to jump down to the grass. She leaned over the cart's edge to embrace her son.

"He did it," Lisette breathed, her voice inaudible under the cheers of the bucket brigade waiting on the cobblestones. Now maybe they could get some rest and make a plan to repel Lord Hanley's next attack.

And she could get some answers about what Aarat had done to her.

Since the magic hadn't brought out more badgers, the magic-free crowd moved back onto the grass to clean up and release the captured badgers. Everything had the air of an impromptu street festival.

Near the stage, Remy sat up and settled into the center of the cart. He may have dealt with the spell holding his mother captive, but Luella the Difficult's magic still waited to trap mages. As Anna moved to the cart handles, Remy suddenly wobbled and caught himself, a reflexive smile brightening his face as he recovered. But the instability hadn't been Remy, Lisette realized with dread; it had been the left wheel canting sideways. Something was wrong with the cart.

With a hiss that carried to the cobblestones, the cart disintegrated into sawdust, tumbling Remy onto the grass.

CHAPTER 36
BADGER-BLESSED

A collective gasp rose from the onlookers as Remy fell onto the green, then another gasp, louder and higher pitched, when the nearby baskets crumbled into splinters, unleashing a mound of angry badgers.

The child badger-catchers spilled onto the field, yelling and clapping to drive the animals up the slope.

Lisette only had eyes for Remy. "Why isn't he getting up?" His drop to the earth had been graceful enough; he'd landed on his side with both hands breaking his fall, and she couldn't imagine he'd been harmed by such a gentle tumble. Indeed, he was conversing with his mother, a smile on his face.

Of course, Remy smiling didn't necessarily mean things were well. Lisette had noticed his mood lightened considerably when he faced a difficult task. From the way he beamed now, things were dire.

Taking the empty bucket from Lisette, Tiffany said, "I'll go find out." Then she strode onto the grass, using the bucket to nudge a wandering badger out of her way.

More people ran onto the green, encouraging the

badgers to move away from the spot where Remy lay. If the spell had still been moving all the heat down to the stage, their efforts wouldn't have worked, but the temperatures were normalizing, and the badgers were already disappearing down holes into their setts.

Two minutes later, Tiffany was back. "He says Luella's spell has trapped him, but he'll figure out a way around it any minute now. Also," Tiffany added with a frown of puzzlement, "he wants to know when you became a dragon." She threw her hands up. "Does that make any sense to you? Because I can't tell if I'm too tired to understand or if he's trying to get a nickname again. Remy the Bizarre, or something like that."

"He's hoping for something unique. Maybe Remy the Badger-Blessed. Tell him not to worry about the dragon thing. Aarat thinks it may fade."

Her friend looked at her with raised eyebrows, then blew out a breath. "Right." She turned and stalked across the grass.

Around Lisette, the crowds were thinning. It was late, there was no longer a magical cage trapping a woman on the stage, and everyone would need to get out of bed in a few hours. Lord Hanley would know Anna was free — if he couldn't feel it through his magic, Harbor Crag gossip would inform him soon enough. Whether he knew Remy was trapped was another matter. If he *did*, the enemy mages might attack the dragons now, knowing that Remy couldn't go to the warrens until he threw off the spell's effects.

... unless causing Remy to be permanently ensnared by Luella the Difficult's spell had been Lord Hanley's goal all along. Lisette wondered if Remy's words had been overly optimistic to soothe her worries, or if he actually expected to free himself soon.

Tiffany was back. "He says, and I quote, it's very fetching on you." She shook her head. "Do you want anything from the quarter? I need to find out what trouble the girls have gotten into in the past few hours."

"No, thanks. Give Ziggy a kiss for me."

After Tiffany had left, Lisette eyed the grass in front of her. She'd never had a problem standing on the green before, not even after she'd first become bound to Aarat. In order to free his mother, Remy had unraveled the changes Lord Hanley had made to Luella's original spell, so it *should* be safe enough for her to walk on the grass now.

No mage was going to keep *her* from going where she wanted.

By the time Lisette recognized that thought had been influenced by the seed of a dragon, one foot had already touched the grass. She froze, waiting.

Nothing happened.

There. She'd worried for nothing. Luella's spell had been set to trap mages, not dragons or people who worried they might be harboring dragons. Now she'd be able to talk to Remy directly. She kept walking.

Three steps later, magic sizzled up Lisette's leg. That was when she realized the grass had grown beyond the edges of Luella's boundary. When Lisette tried to pull her foot free, it didn't move.

"Huh. That's not good." Lisette looked at her foot and at the ground and considered her options. Nothing came to mind. Letting her own irritation come through, she spoke to the dragon within. "I don't suppose you have any great ideas. *You* got us into this mess." With a sigh, she looked up at the night sky. "Great. Now I'm talking to myself."

Maybe Luella's spell would release her when the dragon seed faded, as Aarat said it might. Having a timeline would have been nice. Fifteen minutes or even an hour would be annoying, though bearable. But if she was stuck here for the next two weeks...

In her chest, the dragon seed snarled. *No.* Magic rippled over her body, flowing over imaginary scales, in the same way it did over Aarat. The two magics clashed near her feet, setting off a shower of sparks that quickly extinguished on the dewy green. Lisette felt a tingle when Luella's spell pulled back.

"Look at me, I'm a dragon," she murmured, trying not to let the edge of hysteria bubble out.

Part of her wanted to retreat to the safety of the cobblestones, but the dragon-fueled remainder walked forward. Long-dead Luella the Difficult would *not* steal Remy from her. Beneath her feet, the earth crackled as Luella's spell reacted to every step, but the magic didn't halt her again.

Remy was surrounded by a small crowd of people, including his mother. When Anna saw Lisette coming, she gave a tired smile of welcome. "I keep saying you two didn't need to go to all this trouble to make my visit memorable."

Lisette hugged her tightly. "I'm so glad you're not hurt. And I know Giselle has been worried, too."

At those words, Anna lifted her head and scanned the people at the edge of the green.

Lisette shook her head. "She's sleeping near the dragons. Overdid it a little with the magic."

Anna pursed her lips. "That woman. She's *supposed* to be resting."

"I'd agree, but she kept me from getting squished by a dragon, so I'm glad she was there." Lisette drew back and looked down at Remy, who reclined on his side with both hands pressed against the earth. "What are we going to do with you?"

Despite his predicament, Remy's smile was warm. "Me? I'm sure I'll figure out something soon. Have you heard? I'm Remy the Badger-Blessed!"

"Remy the Badger-Chewed is more likely if you stay here much longer." Despite all her worries, Lisette couldn't help grinning back. "Let's get you free. I have questions, and you're the only one who might be able to answer them."

CHAPTER 37
EVEN IF YOU DO GROW SCALES

With all the badger catchers and bucket passers gone, the green acquired a quiet peace — aside from the sparks thrown up by Lisette's every movement as the dragon magic warred with the spell of long-dead Luella the Difficult. Lisette had found a freeholder to escort Anna back to their rooms, though she suspected Remy's mother would forgo sleep in favor of checking in on Giselle in the dragon warrens. In the end, it was just Lisette waiting with Remy on the grass, with Simi curled up between them.

Remy remained welded to the earth despite every attempt to free himself. While taking a break from his efforts, he listened to Lisette's account of what had happened in the dragon warrens. "Ah, I'm sorry I missed that."

"Because you might have had a better way to help the dragons?" Lisette kept her face straight with an effort — Remy only had that dreamy expression when he talked of great magical events of the past. He often wished aloud that he'd been present to witness many of them.

His eyes focused on her, and he cleared his throat. "Well, yes. That. Of course."

"Of course."

Remy's lips twitched. "You might find me easier to love if you didn't understand me quite so well."

"I'm sure I would." Careful to keep from touching him, Lisette reached out one hand toward his cheek in an imitation of a caress. The electric crackle that happened whenever Lisette moved on the green also occurred when she made contact with Remy, and he'd yelped the one and only time she'd touched him. "Now tell me what you were really thinking."

"Well..." Remy tried to move into a more comfortable position, then groaned as his attempts failed. "I once found a book in the college library that claimed dragons were originally created from mages." He stopped and gave her a wry look. "You have to understand, the college library had a *lot* of books and scrolls and the vast majority had *no* basis in fact. There was an entire shelf of virility spells that would have killed the recipient if they had worked in the slightest."

"Which you knew because...?"

"Angry notes in the margins from other scholars," Remy laughed. "The library was full of such things. There was a journal by Sipola the Damp who promised his patrons he could create boats entirely of magic. Which he did, a bit, but the boats never lasted long enough to do anything useful. The real problem was that he determined their seaworthiness by sending his apprentices on voyages to test them. His fourth apprentice shoved Sipola out a tower window, and the authorities put it down as an accident."

As much as she enjoyed the anecdotes, Lisette thought it best to get the conversation back on track. "Did this book about the origin of dragons have any thoughts on how to reverse the process?"

"If it did, I missed it. But I doubt it. It was one of those four-volume monstrosities that you had to be careful not to drop so you didn't crush your toes. Picanol tried his best to be accurate, but most of his sources were people who had once talked to someone who claimed to have heard from a dragon that... Still, he also said that some of the sea creatures had been created from horses and goats, which would explain a *lot* about the way they act. So maybe he was right about the dragons as well."

Lisette blinked and tried to take that in. To the east, the sky had turned the milky blue of dawn. Soon, Harbor Crag would wake to face the new day. "Are you saying I'm going to turn into a dragon?"

"No."

Lisette sighed in relief.

Remy frowned. "At least, I don't think so. Physical transformation spells take an *enormous* amount of power. Maybe if you were a mage, but you're not."

Thinking of the power that had flowed through her as she released Drelaack and then Grelaad, Lisette felt her heart skip a beat. Forget evading the trap set by Lord Hanley's mages — if she'd hadn't expelled all that magic, she might be a dragon by now. A tiny part of her wondered what that would be like, and the dragon seed within her trumpeted its joy. "We definitely need to find a different way to free the dragons."

Remy gave her a knowing look. "It's tempting, isn't it? Just to find out."

"Not tempting enough to end up as a dragon for the rest of my life."

"Ah well. I'll still love you even if you do grow scales."

He closed his eyes in concentration. The magic rippling just under the grass wavered, then strengthened. Remy's eyes opened. "Darn. I thought I had it that time."

"Maybe I could ask Aarat to come out here and make you a dragon, too."

Screwing up his face, Remy shook his head. "Better not. We both know *I'd* never be able to resist."

Except... They might *have* to. It had been hours and Remy was still stuck to the ground. That thought triggered another. If she could get Remy away from the green, Luella's spell should let him go. "Maybe I could dig under you and take the ground with us."

"Ooh, I could live in a pot and all the old women will shake their heads and say, 'That poor man. So good looking until he did such a stupid thing.'"

Since the women who ran the fish market probably *would* say something like that, Lisette only winked at him and pulled at the grass near his left hand. Under the layer of greenery, the earth was mostly pebbles clumped together with clay — difficult to dig in with her bare hands, but not impossible. Sparks crackled as she excavated a shallow trench. "A shovel would be nice."

"You would be shocked by how often I've had that thought during my life." He sucked in a breath as Lisette's hands got too close, causing sparks to fly. Then he cocked his head. "Do that again. Put your hand right at the edge of mine."

Lisette did as he asked. They found she could move her hands between the ground and his skin, freeing his hand. "That speeds things up. Are you okay?"

Remy flexed his newly mobile hand and examined both sides in the pale dawn light. "Good as new. Keep going." He vigorously scratched the tip of his nose. "Ah, I've been wanting to do that for ages."

In a few minutes, they had him standing upright, his feet the last thing stuck to the ground. Lisette eyed him doubtfully. "I *might* be able to carry you to the cobblestones, but I can't free your feet and lift you at the same time." She sighed. "If only we had a horse."

With a shudder, Remy said, "No horses."

"I'll find something to carry you in." With a solemn look, Lisette added, "Don't go anywhere."

His mock scowl made her smile.

It took a while to find a cart with an owner willing to part with it — the story of Remy's destruction of the *last* cart had already made it around the city. In the end, Lisette gave all her coins to a woman at the fish market, who promised to return most of them when Lisette brought the handcart back.

As she'd expected, Remy still stood where she'd left him. He waved as she grew nearer. "You found something!" Then he closed his eyes at the smell. "My dignity may never recover."

Lisette maneuvered the cart next to him. "I'm pretty sure your dignity disappeared with the badgers."

"You're probably right."

Lisette freed Remy's feet and helped him flop into the cart where Simi joined him. A few minutes later, Lisette rolled the cart onto the cobblestones. Remy jumped down and stretched. "Right. Let's get the cart back before the tatters of my reputation go up in smoke. Maybe we'll even have time for a nap before the next disaster."

His words still hung in the air when something in the deep waters of the harbor gave an unearthly shriek.

CHAPTER 38
GOATS AND HORSES

As the tortured scream of some great beast echoed off the buildings, the hair on the back of Lisette's neck rose. She stared at Remy. "That sounded a *lot* like that sea creature from the Salty Bookworm."

"A Frisian waterbeast." He squinted to look at the harbor. "But that's coming from the water. If they'd cast that spell again, someone would have seen the waterbeast going into the ocean. Half the buildings would be rubble."

Lisette increased her pace to a jog, and the empty cart jounced along the cobblestones. Simi crouched at the front of the cart, staring into the rosy streets like a feline figurehead. "Maybe they created it on a boat?"

"Only if they wanted to die horribly." Remy took the cart from her and ran faster. "It would sink the boat immediately. And the rocking of the waves would make it nearly impossible to set up a time-delayed spell." They clattered around the corner, heading for the market. Remy added, "I think this waterbeast is genuine."

"You said they were from the ocean beyond the Island of Light."

He shrugged one shoulder. "It must have somehow been *called* here."

Trying to save her breath for running, Lisette gasped out, "Why?"

The waterbeast shrieked again, and Lisette flinched as she ran.

"I don't know," Remy said. People in the apartments lining the streets were awake now, leaning out of windows in their sleep shifts and calling to each other as they looked for news about what had made the sound. "The harbor's not deep enough for it to stay."

They dropped off the cart with its owner, and Lisette pocketed the coins she'd left as a deposit, while Simi curled up in Remy's satchel. Then, they joined the growing crowds of people hurrying to the waterfront to see what was happening. Remy and Lisette held hands to keep from being separated in the crush. As they grew closer to the shore where the crowds were at a standstill, people drew back to let them through.

Remy leaned to whisper in Lisette's ear. "Are they making space because they recognize us, or because I smell like a fish cart?" When Lisette only winked at him, his shoulders drooped. "If I end up being called Remy the Odorous, I'm giving up magic completely and finding a new occupation. Even 'badger-chewed' would have been better."

"Cheer up. Maybe after today you'll be known as water-beast-bane."

He cocked his head, considering that. "A bit unwieldy, but I'll accept it."

They reached the front of the crowd, giving them a clear look at the harbor. Remy held out a hand to a man holding a spyglass. "May I? Thank you." He lifted the spyglass and stared through it for a moment. "Huh. *Sylvain's Slippery Squid*... Do we know that ship?"

"I think it was in the harbor yesterday, but nobody came ashore." When Lisette took the spyglass from him and raised it to her eye, she saw oddly choppy seas though the ocean beyond the harbor was calm as glass. One ship listed, rapidly sinking; its crew piled into rowboats. The other ships — with one exception — clustered at the mouth of the harbor, far too close to each other to be intentional. Something had blocked their exit.

The final ship remained at anchor, undamaged, with no crew on deck other than one man holding a harpoon tied to a rope. Instead of sailors, a dozen well-dressed people stood on the deck in a rough circle. Most had their eyes closed, but she saw one man cast a worried gaze over his shoulder at the water. It took only a second longer to find Lisette's target standing near the mast. "Lord Hanley's out there." She handed the spyglass back to Remy.

The harbormaster strode toward them, shoving anyone who didn't move quickly enough out of her path. "What is a *Frisian waterbeast* doing in my harbor?"

Since Remy was avoiding the harbormaster's one-eyed glare by studying the water, Lisette faced the woman's angry gaze. "I think Lord Hanley and his mages called it and trapped it there."

The sinking ship jolted, as if something had grabbed it, and then the craft plunged under the water, creating a trough that nearly took the rowboats with it. Sailors rowed frantically as the waterbeast breached the surface almost close enough to touch. What Lisette had taken for whiskers running along the pale white body of the miniature water-beast in the bookshop, she identified now as tentacles. One wrapped around an oar mount, dragging the boat lower until a bare-chested sailor with a carved dagger sliced through the flesh.

"Why would they —" Breaking off mid-sentence, the harbormaster growled at Remy, "Can you at least buy the sailors enough time to reach shore?"

Remy brushed at his ear, absently knocking off a dirt clod. "If I could turn waterbeasts aside, I needn't have paid for my passage to Harbor Crag. But maybe..." His head tilted, as if he'd thought of something. "Goats and horses," he muttered, still staring at the water.

After waiting for two seconds to see if Remy would explain, the harbormaster turned to Lisette. "What does that mean? Do I need to drive goats and horses into the water?"

Alarmed murmurs came from the watchers as the waterbeast rose again, and the sailors slashed at more tentacles attempting to grab onto the boat. On shore, a portly man in a silk tunic yelled, "Hit it on the nose!" to the collective eye-roll of half of Harbor Crag.

The benefit of knowing Remy well meant Lisette had some idea of the direction his thoughts were heading. "No. I think he's going to try some sort of spell meant for goats or horses."

With a grunt and a shake of her head, the harbormaster muttered something about mages under her breath. Then her voice strengthened. "Anything that works." She strode off, yelling for the stevedores to distribute oil barrels along the beach and be ready to fire them if the waterbeast came ashore.

"Hold this for a moment," Remy said, handing her the spyglass. Between his hands, a tangle of magic took form. The dragon seed urged Lisette closer, but she pushed its desires down. When the ball of magic reached Simi's size,

Remy tossed it toward Lord Hanley's ship, where it clung to the prow. Three breaths later, a slightly different spell latched onto the stern just above the waterline. He rubbed his hands together in glee. "Now we see if it's true! Remember, front of the ship is goat; back is horse."

Even as Lisette drew breath to ask him what that meant, the waterbeast abandoned the rowboat and swam straight for Lord Hanley's ship. Accompanied by scattered applause, the crowd called encouragement to the rowers. "What did you do?"

Taking back the spyglass, he said, "I paid for a surprising number of drinks at college by putting spells on goats — keeping them out of someone's garden, making them less smelly, that sort of thing. This is just a simple spell to gather them at one spot, which I hope will be strong enough to keep the waterbeast away from the rowboats."

"And the other spell draws horses to it?"

"In a way." He flashed a grin at her, then turned back to the water. "I only know a few horse spells and they're almost all for lameness or toothaches. But I once read a book on animal husbandry that had a spell for reluctant stallions."

Lisette blinked. "You put a spell on the ship..."

"... to make the waterbeast mate with it," he finished. "Yes."

"That can't be good for the waterproofing." Though she'd only caught glimpses of the waterbeast, it had to be the size of at least five ships.

"No, though it looks like they've done something to the wood to protect it from that sort of assault." He sighed, then shrugged. "But it ought to distract them long enough

DRAGON FORTUNE

for me to figure out how to free that poor creature from the harbor."

Lord Hanley's ship jolted, forcing the harpooner to grab the railing to avoid pitching into the water. Then the man recovered his balance and leaned over the side of the ship.

"Horses, it is," Remy said. "I'll have to write a note about that."

Lisette frowned as the man's odd behavior continued. "What is he doing?" There was no way a harpoon would harm a beast that large.

Which meant Lord Hanley had planned something else.

The harpoon flew toward the water, a coil of rope trailing behind it. Then the Frisian waterbeast shrieked, louder than it had before.

As the haunting cry faded, a wave of magic erupted from the beast, arrowing toward the shipboard mages.

CHAPTER 39
GREAT PLANS

L isette watched with horror as magic streamed from the Frisian waterbeast to the mages on the ship. Meanwhile, the harpooner yanked his weapon free and pulled it onto the deck, with the air of one who has accomplished his given task.

"This is what they did to the dragons," she breathed. Presumably, the harpoon had been spelled with the blood stolen from the dragon-born. And now Lord Hanley had access to the magic of the waterbeast.

Remy winced in dismay. "If I hadn't turned it toward Lord Hanley's ship..."

This, she could answer. "If you hadn't, the waterbeast would have killed all the sailors and *then* gone after the *Slippery Squid*, with the same result. Except this way, fewer people died." It was true — even now, the lead rowboat had reached the shore, and the others had reached shallower waters.

"Good point. Thank you." He blew out a forceful breath. "There. I have stopped feeling sorry for myself. Now we should work out how to fix this."

Neither spoke for a long moment.

Finally, Lisette said slowly, "I don't *think* I could give the waterbeast my name and then take over the bond." That had just barely worked for the dragons. Aside from no longer trusting herself to release all that power, the magic streaming across the water didn't *feel* the same to her. Plus, there were practical considerations. "We'd have to steal the harpoon first anyhow."

Remy sighed. "As much as I would love the challenge of invading a mage's ship in waterbeast-infested waters, I think you're right to move that option to the bottom of the list."

Lisette raised one eyebrow. "We have a list?"

"All great plans begin with a blank page," he intoned, clearly quoting something. Then his voice went back to its normal pitch. "Terrible plans, too, but somehow Fortis the Elder never got around to mentioning that. It might explain why he disappeared before finishing his manuscript."

If this conversation had been taking place as they both lay in bed at the edge of sleep, Lisette would have enjoyed hearing of Fortis the Elder's theories and proclamations. But this wasn't the time. "Tell me why the waterbeast's magic tastes different from dragon magic."

"You can feel that, can you?" They watched the second rowboat reach the shore, the sailors piling out to drag the boat to dry land. "It's the source. The waterbeast pulls its magic from the water, while a dragon pulls its magic from air and land." He paused to help Simi climb up to his shoulder. "Lord Hanley — or any mage willing to cast such a spell, really — can use the stolen magic of either. But you're not a mage in the regular sort of way."

"I'm not a mage at all," she clarified. "Back to the list. How can we stop Lord Hanley from gaining more power?"

"Destroy the spell, destroy the waterbeast, or destroy the waterbeast's magic." In the harbor, the waterbeast began wandering farther from the ship and Remy recast his equine spell. "May as well keep them busy while we think."

Sylvain's Slippery Squid wallowed as the beast attempted another seduction.

Destroying the waterbeast Lisette dismissed out of hand. If Remy could do that, he would have done it when the sailors were endangered. Their best bet would undoubtedly be to destroy the spell draining the creature's magic, but... Two mages, multiple weeks, and Aarat's full cooperation had resulted in only five dragons being freed — and one of those had been an accident.

A leather worker who kept her tools on a holster over velvet-covered hips pointed to the harbor mouth, where the clustered ships now departed at full sail. "The harbor is open!"

This had to be part of Lord Hanley's plan. Since the mages had accomplished their task, they no longer needed to contain their prey; as soon as the amorous spell wore off, the waterbeast would flee back to the deep ocean. Lisette frowned at the mage ship, which still sat at anchor.

The harbormaster stomped up. "Why are those thrice misbegotten mages still here?"

"That," Remy said, lifting the spyglass again, "is an *excellen*t question." Whatever he saw made him growl. "They're calling another waterbeast in."

"What?" The harbormaster turned, looking as if she were ready to swim out and take on the mages herself.

Lisette turned her head to Remy. "Block the mouth of the harbor. Now."

Mischief lit up Remy's face, and he began building

another spell, even as the harbormaster eyed Lisette. "With the waterbeast still inside?"

"We can't let Lord Hanley get any stronger," Lisette countered. "And if we have to kill the waterbeast to keep Harbor Crag safe, it's going to be a lot easier if we can find it."

Gritting her teeth, the harbormaster stalked away, muttering about unspeakable acts that should be visited upon mages who put the docking schedule into disarray.

"There," Remy said. "Nothing bigger than myself can get through the mouth of the harbor." Then he shrugged. "At least, not until someone untangles my spell. Which will take them less than ten minutes, so it would be well if our plan took shape sooner."

Worrying at the problem like a cat with a toy, Lisette thought of the options Remy had listed. "If the waterbeast gains its magic from the water, what would happen if it came on dry land?"

"That might cut off the source of magic," Remy allowed. "But surely the question would be, what would happen to the dry land if a waterbeast were here? To which the answer would be: nothing good."

"As a waterbeast, yes," she agreed. Then she waited to see if his thoughts might follow the same journey.

Two seconds later, he snorted. "I see. You think I might undo a transformation by skilled mages hundreds of years ago." His gaze grew distant. "With the beast's magic drained, it might be easier to accomplish. Though it will be temporary if we don't get the horse on dry land." His tone became dubious. "Assuming there still *is* a horse under all that. These things have been breeding in the ocean for centuries. Things may have changed."

Lisette held out her empty hands to indicate she had no

other ideas. "I've added two things to the list. It's your turn."

"No, no. I think Fortis the Elder would be more than impressed with this plan."

"The same Fortis the Elder who disappeared before finishing his manuscript?"

"Minor detail." Remy waved that away. "I'll call the beast this direction. The shallow waters ought to slow it down long enough for me to change it, but we'll have to keep it from retreating back into the harbor." He considered the crowd on the waterfront. "It might be better to move these people to a safer distance."

Convincing bystanders that their front-row seat to the drama might turn into a brief supporting cast role took a few minutes, but eventually the waterfront was clear and the onlookers scattered far enough apart that nobody would be trampled in a panic. During that time, Lisette recruited three horse handlers and borrowed rope for them all. They were nervous about the waterbeast, but confident they could control a horse.

Despite Lisette's misgivings, Remy moved to a spot on the water's edge. "I may have to go into the surf to do the transformation if it can't get on land." He rubbed his hands together with glee. "This ought to be exciting."

Then he cast the equine love spell Lisette had seen twice before, except this time, he attached it to the rocks by his feet. On the hill above them, a horse whinnied and snorted, making Remy cast a worried look over his shoulder and sidle to the left.

They watched the harbor.

For a moment, nothing happened. Then a swell in the water sped toward them, the waterbeast traveling under the surface of the waves. Its head rose into the air as it grew closer, a slimy white nightmare with jagged teeth and tentacles.

"Um, Remy? It's not slowing down," Lisette noted from her spot in the shallows partway down the beach. A second later she realized why — enough of the creature's body was still in deep water, giving it a means to propel itself forward.

The horse handlers scattered, dropping their borrowed ropes in the water as they fled.

With an angry scream, the Frisian waterbeast flew through the shallows, speeding straight toward Remy.

CHAPTER 40
A BIT OF FIRE

L isette watched in horror as Remy tripped and fell backward on the sand. The waterbeast reared up, its head towering over the mage, tentacles along the side of its body writhing.

But instead of fleeing, Remy rolled to the side and waited, one hand out. Quick as a snake, the waterbeast struck the ground.

"Remy!" Lisette sprinted across the sand straight toward the beast, even as she questioned what she could possibly do to help. Because it didn't matter — both Lisette and the dragon seed within needed to do *something*.

Before she had covered the distance, the waterbeast threw back its head and screamed, a haunting sound that crumbled into a whinny. At the same time, the waterbeast shimmered and then shrank in a haze of magic. Suddenly, the beach was empty, with Remy lying on his back in the sand, tentatively moving his limbs as if shocked nothing was broken. Of the waterbeast, there was no sign. Remy waved Lisette weakly toward the water. "Don't let it get away."

Lisette stumbled to a stop and looked around. "Don't let *what* get away?" Then she noticed movement in the surf. She'd assumed it was driftwood snagged on shore since she'd been looking for a *horse*. But the animal struggling to its feet in the shallow water barely came to her hip.

Though the only equine experience Lisette had was feeding apple slices to cart horses, she'd prepared herself for a rampaging full-size steed. This tiny stallion was... *cute*, with a tousled forelock hiding one eye and a handful of white speckles on his wet black coat. They wouldn't need ropes to control him — he was so small Lisette could almost pick him up.

By the time the pony had gained unsteady feet, Lisette had pushed through the surf to stand by his side. "Hello there. I don't suppose I could convince you to move out of the water?" Taking a handful of white mane, she tugged the pony toward land.

He ignored her, all four legs braced, nostrils flaring. Saltwater lapped around his fetlocks.

This would be the first time he'd ever stood on four legs, Lisette realized. He might not know *how* to walk, and would certainly be terrified in this new environment. In fact, someone might *need* to pick him up to get him out of the water. Unfortunately, the horse handlers were long gone; she really could have used their experience. Lifting her gaze to Remy, who had climbed to his feet, she called, "How do you make a horse move?"

"Hire someone?" He shook his head and stayed on dry sand. "Have you tried slapping its hind end?"

"I'm not about to *hit* the poor thing."

"Your *poor thing* nearly squashed me." With a sigh, he waded into the surf. "I suppose we'll have to lift it."

From the corner of her eye, Lisette saw a ball of fire arc

toward them from the mages' ship. It landed in front of them on the beach, and a fishing boat exploded into flames.

Suddenly, the pony knew *exactly* how to move his legs. With a snort of alarm, he wheeled around and bolted toward the harbor. Only Lisette's grip forcing him off-balance kept him from dragging her into deeper water. When his attempt to run failed, the tiny stallion bounced onto his front end and kicked Remy squarely in the knees with dainty little hooves.

"You little..." Remy bit off the last word, whipped off his cloak, and wrapped it around the terrified pony's eyes. "We're trying to save your life, you ungrateful creature." He glanced back at the ship. "You pull and I'll push. Once we get on dry land, Lord Hanley won't be able to keep pulling power from it."

Another fireball landed on the sand, but this time, Lisette ignored it. "It's just a bit of fire," she crooned to the pony as she urged him forward. "The bad mage is trying to scare you."

Remy had both hands on the pony's rump, arms straight, which kept him out of range of the hooves. "Just a bit of fire?"

Lisette shrugged and pulled harder, because there was no easy way to explain how nonchalantly the dragon seed treated fire. It wanted her to reach out a hand to steal the flame.

Two more blasts landed directly in front of them before they dragged the pony onto dry sand. Lord Hanley was attempting to herd them — or at least the transformed waterbeast — back into the harbor.

But the citizens of Harbor Crag weren't without defenses of their own. A tremendous splash in the harbor distracted Lisette. At first, she thought Lord Hanley had lured a second waterbeast, but then she saw a rock plummet into the water near *Sylvain's Slippery Squid*.

Someone on the cliffs had manned a trebuchet. As far as she knew, nobody alive now had deployed them against an enemy; the mages of Harbor Crag had possessed so much stolen dragon magic, there had been no need for mundane defenses. But the trebuchets were kept in working order and used to fling blazing oil-soaked bundles into the ocean during festivals, mostly because everyone wanted an excuse to set something on fire and hurl it across the water. Normally, the missiles were aimed wide of the harbor, with no specific destination other than unoccupied water. But whoever was in charge on the cliffs was refining their aim quickly, and while they weren't using incendiaries, the rocks flying into the harbor could put a sizable hole in the hull.

The mages on the ship must have agreed, because they turned their attention to the trebuchet. During the distraction, the harbormaster ran forward with the largest man Lisette had ever seen. "Careful," she ordered the stevedore.

He knelt down, leaned forward, and then stood with the pony draped over his shoulders. The muscles in his forearms bulged as he caught the stallion's front ankles in one hand and his back feet in another. Even as they walked forward, the harbormaster looped ropes around the pony's feet until he was trussed up like any other package being taken ashore.

Lisette and Remy followed along behind, their wet clothing dragging at them as they walked beyond the nearest cluster of warehouses. Once they were shielded from Lord Hanley's view, they stopped. Simi raced over and jumped onto Remy's shoulder.

The harbormaster helped get the pony down on the

ground and transformed the rope from hobbles into a halter with a loop around the stallion's rear. "How long will it stay like this?"

"Until it gets back in saltwater," Remy said. "I think." He looked uncomfortable. "It might be smartest to dispatch it now, but..."

To Lisette's surprise, the harbormaster shook her head decisively. "No. It's done nothing wrong and I'll not bring that sort of luck down on my harbor. We'll wait until *they*," she waved her hand to encompass the hidden harbor and Lord Hanley's ship, "are gone, and then I'll take *this* out to deeper water and put it overboard where it will be safe."

Remy nodded, looking relieved. "Good. They have no reason to stay now. We have the waterbeast, we can keep them from binding another one, and they can't sneak back on land without someone noticing. I'm sure they'll be gone with the tide."

Ridding Harbor Crag of Lord Hanley and the mages he'd gathered would be the best thing, but something in Lisette's chest tightened at the thought. She knew exactly where the ship was, even though she couldn't see it, and that helped her figure out the source of her unease. "Not yet."

Remy, the harbormaster, and even the musclebound stevedore, stared at her.

Tilting her head at the unseen ship, Lisette explained. "They have the dragon-born's blood on that ship. We need to get it back."

CHAPTER 41
NAVIGATION HAZARD

Taking advantage of their distraction, the tiny stallion wheeled and kicked Remy's kneecaps. The harbormaster stared at Lisette. "You want to go on that ship full of mages?"

"It's not that I *want* to, but..." Lisette looked at Remy.

He nodded, though he kept a wary eye on the former waterbeast, who clearly bore a grudge. "If those mages escape with blood from the dragon-born, they'll have so much magic, we'll never be free of them. We need to get on that ship and steal Sunny's blood back." His eyes unfocused as he thought. "Or sink the ship and its contents."

Since Lord Hanley was on board, sending the ship to the bottom of the harbor seemed like an excellent plan to Lisette. "I like that option better."

With a scowl, the harbormaster shook her head. "Let's not add a navigation hazard to my harbor."

Remy spoke again before Lisette could argue her point. "I'm not sure we even *could* sink that ship. The hull has so many protective spells on it, they almost don't need the wood. Sipola the Damp would be proud."

The quiet from the water on the other side of the building suggested the trebuchet had been damaged beyond use and the mages were conserving their remaining power. The harbormaster raised her spyglass and leaned around the corner. "Well, they won't be going anywhere soon. Not until they fix the mast and the anchor windlass." She lowered the spyglass. "I owe Pierre a drink. He said he could hit that ship from the cliffs and I bet him he couldn't."

"All thanks to Pierre," Remy murmured. "He's bought us some time to figure out how to board the ship and search it from stem to stern." He gave Lisette a wry grin. "I know I said it would be exciting to sneak on board, but I didn't expect you to call my bluff."

Lisette stepped between Remy and the pony as the latter made another assault on the mage. "If I can get on the ship, I can find the dragon-born's blood."

The harbormaster cocked her head. "Before or after you feed your breakfast to the fish?"

Right. The harbormaster had been there when she'd had to go out to the *Dancing Eel*. "Trust me, I'd be happy to let someone else do it if they can feel the blood, too." She turned a hopeful glance toward Remy. Maybe the mages could feel the dragon-born's blood, too.

His reply was full of regret. "Sorry, my love. I don't feel a thing."

Lisette resigned herself to another stint on the water. "Maybe Giselle will know how to sink the ship without creating a navigation hazard," she said, without much hope. "I should probably let the dragons know what's going on and check on Anna."

Remy put a hand on her shoulder. "I'll stay here and make sure no other waterbeasts come into the harbor." He leapt to the side to avoid the pony's teeth. "And add another layer of spells on this little man."

Lisette leaned in to touch her forehead against his, while Simi rubbed her cheek against Lisette's hair. "Stay safe."

"Of course. I promise I won't sneak onto the boat without you."

Lisette grinned and headed up the hill toward the dragon warrens.

THOUGH THE MORNING had started with a waterbeast screaming and a ship of mages hurling fireballs through the air, life in Harbor Crag trundled on. The bustle of carts and people created a pleasant background hum as Lisette inhaled deeply. Scents of tea and spices wafted through the air, competing with the salty tang of the harbor and a hint of goat manure. She paused to buy a fruit-filled breakfast roll before continuing her climb.

With any luck, the mages would be busy fixing their ship all day. Perhaps she could take a few minutes for a nap, or even fix one of the clocks waiting in her workshop. She craved the quiet feeling of certainty that descended when she worked on mechanical devices. And she now had the remains of the automaton Bralinost to explore.

Maybe after she'd spent an hour or two at her workbench, she'd know how to live with the dragon seed Aarat had set within her.

The rapid click of metal against stone from a quiet side street brought her back to her surroundings. She slowed her steps, trying to see what had made the noise. If she hadn't dug the remains of Bralinost from the ashes of Lord

Hanley's mansion... But no, it was a tiny object, no bigger than her palm, scuttling around on eight legs, its metallic body shining. A glance along the street showed her no obvious owner, yet this work of art would not be let loose on its own.

Despite the sleepless night, Lisette felt a smile tugging at her mouth. The challenge of making and then coordinating all those limb movements! Truly, it had been built by a genius. She walked closer, marveling at the precise gait of the gleaming metal as it wended its way along the street. The person who commissioned the piece had to be nearby — surely they would be willing to tell her who had created it.

So intent was she on the automaton that she didn't notice the man turning the corner until she ran into him. "Oh! I *am* sorry. Is this yours?"

The man grunted in reply, and then picked up the automaton in one hand and held it out to her.

Lisette held out her hands and laughed in delight as the automaton crawled onto her palms, the tiny feet so light that she could just feel the pressure on her skin. "But this is wonderful! Who created it?" The mechanical creature stumbled and caught itself, one foot pinching her skin as it recovered its balance.

"A cousin of a friend." Then the man gazed at her, as if waiting for her to remember the next lines of dialogue in a play. He wore a heavy purple cloak with a hood that cast his eyes in shadow, but she could still feel his stare.

Suddenly uncomfortable by the combination of deserted street and odd behavior, Lisette held out the automaton to its owner. "It's a lovely piece. Someday I'd love to meet the person who designed it."

The buildings around her wavered, and she put out a

hand to the nearest wall to keep her balance. "Something's..."

Before she could finish the sentence, her knees collapsed, and she felt herself falling.

Everything went black.

CHAPTER 42
DELIGHTED

L ight filtered through Lisette's closed eyelids along with a vague sense of unease. Opening her eyes seemed impossible. When she blearily wiped at her face, her hand encountered strange bedding, linens that smelled faintly musty, as if they needed airing after being stowed and forgotten. With rising panic, she searched her memory to determine where she was or even what time of day it might be. But it was her stomach, insisting everything was moving despite lying absolutely still, that gave her a clue, and she sighed in relief as she figured out what was going on.

Sickness. *That* explained why she was sleeping during the daytime and why she had such a hard time opening her eyes. Remy would be so worried about her.

She finally cracked her eyelids, only to find she was in a tiny room with just a narrow bed, a bare desk, and a scarred wooden trunk. Wood creaked as sunlight streamed through a round window placed high on the wall...

Her heart sank as reality set in. She hadn't taken ill.

She'd been drugged and kidnapped. And the rocking deck beneath her belonged to a ship.

That realization had her stumbling out of bed to look through the salt-encrusted glass of the porthole. In the distance, the city of Harbor Crag rose above the water. Knowing she was still in the harbor was a minor comfort, though it was swamped by dread. Even if she hadn't been able to feel the dragon-born's blood nearby, Lisette would have known who was behind this. After all this time, Lord Hanley's obsession had never dimmed.

She was on Lord Hanley's ship, *Sylvain's Slippery Squid*, and somehow she had to get off this ship before it left the harbor.

The porthole was too small to squeeze through, but Lisette opened the pane anyhow, inhaling deeply as the cold air hit her face. Perhaps she could signal people on shore so they could...

What? Rescue her? From a ship full of powerful mages?

No. She'd have to get herself out of this. Setting her shoulders, Lisette lifted her chin. She and Remy had been looking for a way to steal the dragon-born's blood, and now she had the perfect chance.

Behind her, the cabin door creaked open. Lisette whirled to find herself face to face with the man she'd wanted to avoid forever. Lord Hanley's gaze darted from the bed to where she stood at the porthole, eyes glittering as he smiled. "Awake so soon? I'd hoped you'd sleep a while longer, my sweet."

Magic crashed over Lisette, clawing at her will, but her tie to Aarat protected her just as it had in the past. With a bravado she didn't feel, she said, "You know that won't work against me. Let me off the ship and maybe you'll get out of the harbor alive." She brushed one hand against her waist, feeling for her dagger, but it wasn't there. No matter. Lord Hanley had one — she'd take his instead. *And sprout wings so I can fly to shore while I'm at it*, she thought, aware of the absurdity of her plan. She had no experience wielding weapons, while Lord Hanley had been raised with a nobleman's training in the arts of war.

He waved her words away with a languid hand. "With you on the ship, that useless mage from Galfigon won't dare attack us for fear of hurting you." He sniffed twice, as if scenting the air. "What have you done to yourself? You feel like a *dragon*."

Having Lord Hanley learn to exploit the dragon seed within her was the last thing Lisette wanted. "All those years of being warped to look like a Hanley have taken their toll," she said. "You're imagining things. But since we're on the subject... Do you really think Aarat will just let you leave Harbor Crag with me aboard? You just barely escaped with your life the last time you met."

For an instant, the madness in his eyes spread to his entire face. Then it was snuffed out, harnessed behind the aristocrat's bored gaze. "Would he tear the ship apart looking for you? I'd be delighted if he tried."

The malice in his voice took her aback. This wasn't an act. Lord Hanley really *did* want Aarat to attack the ship. While he might not be completely sane where Lisette was concerned, this mage had been the true ruler of Harbor Crag for years, even while the Duke sat at the head of the council. He wasn't stupid.

Then it dawned on her. Lord Hanley had a weapon prepared with the blood of the dragon-born. If Aarat came close enough to be pierced, the mages would bind the dragon to them again, stealing his magic and gaining the power to retake Harbor Crag.

Lisette was suddenly glad she hadn't been able to send a signal. Better for her friends and family if they didn't know she was here... at least until she recovered the dragon-born's blood, stole a rowboat, and made her way to shore, she added silently.

A tremendous splash sounded just outside the porthole, and the ship jolted. Lisette grab at the edge of the table to keep her feet. Outside, a man shouted, "Trebuchet. There!"

Lord Hanley's face reddened, a vein throbbing at his temple. "Excuse me. It seems I have things to do before we leave."

"Don't let me stop you." Lisette crossed her arms and leaned against the wall, acting as if she had nothing to do other than sit and wait.

The mage shook his head sadly. "Forgive me, my sweet. For your safety, it would be better if you slept until we were underway." He reached into a pouch at his belt and pulled out the mechanical spider she'd seen in the alley.

The skin of her hand twinged in remembrance. The spider had *drugged* her. Lisette drew back as the little automaton scuttled across the uneven floor.

If she could push past Lord Hanley and lock him in the cabin, maybe the spider would drug him instead. But before Lisette could act on the thought, Lord Hanley stepped into the hallway and slammed the door. She heard a bolt ram home.

Lisette regarded the mechanical spider as she tried to predict its movements. "I don't suppose you would let me..."

Tiny legs clicking against the planks of the deck, the spider skittered forward.

CHAPTER 43
NO PROBLEM

As the mechanical spider lunged across the ship's cabin, Lisette jumped onto the bunk, pulling her feet away from the decking. Part of her wanted to study the tiny creation, to learn how the legs achieved their rapid movements — some sort of piston instead of gears? — but the rest of her screamed that if the spider drugged her again, she might not wake until the ship was in the open ocean, and then she would be stuck here *with Lord Hanley* until they raised the Island of Light. That was not a future she was willing to contemplate.

Barely slowing, the automaton clung to the bed linens and climbed. Really, this tiny mechanical amazed her, and the fact that she couldn't spend hours examining the details was just one more fault to cast at Lord Hanley's feet. But she had to be practical. Grabbing the blanket, she brushed the mechanical to the ground and trapped it by holding the rough wool against the planks of the floor.

As the tiny machine searched for a way out of its fabric prison, Lisette considered her options. When they had disabled Bralinost, she and Remy had removed the magic powering it. But she'd had Bralinost's schematics ahead of time and knew what she needed to do. And even then, she and Remy had nearly been killed. On the other hand, Bralinost had wielded sharp blades. As long as she kept this spider under the blanket, it couldn't —

At that point, a metallic limb poked through the wool, nearly skewering Lisette's finger, and the rest of the spider followed. She yanked her hand back. Apparently, the mechanical spider had its own blades. Time for her backup plan. "Sorry about this," she told it as she dodged another lunge.

Throwing the edge of the blanket over the spider, Lisette rolled it in layers of fabric, scooped up the bundle, and shoved the entire mess through the porthole before the automaton could fight its way out. Then she slammed the porthole shut.

There. First problem solved. Now she just needed to get out of the locked cabin, grab the dragon-born's blood, fight her way through a group of mages, and get back to land. All with no tools or weapons.

"No problem," she said aloud. "I can do this." *Burn the ship down*, suggested the dragon seed. Perfect sentiment, even if it wasn't practical.

The room didn't offer any obvious resources, so she turned to the contents of the desk. The top drawer held a leaking bottle of iron gall ink, a smattering of quills, and a tiny knife for cutting the quill nibs. Though the blade seemed too small to make a useful weapon, Lisette kept it.

The second drawer held a logbook with entries full of dates, coordinates, weather reports, and sea monster sightings. Whoever had been keeping the log had doodled pictures of mermaids in the margins with more enthusiasm than talent. Lisette paged through the book, looking for something that might help her.

Unfortunately, there wasn't a diagram of the ship with handy arrows pointing to secret passageways, though she did find a fascinating description of a ghost galleon that the writer had seen multiple times during storms. Lisette closed the cover regretfully. If she ended up trapped in this cabin, it would be entertaining reading, but for now, she had other goals.

The bottom drawer was locked, and Lisette could feel magic radiating from something inside. With visions of a powerful weapon or a lifesaving floatation device running through her head, she used the penknife to force the latch. Wood splintered and the drawer slid open.

Inside, three bottles of rum sat on a pile of coins. She ignored them in favor of a tarnished silver disk underneath that seemed to be the source of the magic. Hoping it wasn't a trap that would instantly kill her, Lisette took hold of the disk.

Light flared, then resolved itself into a moving image of a woman looking over her shoulder at Lisette as she coquettishly pulled her dress off one shoulder.

"Really?" Lisette let go and the image disappeared. Of all the useless things to find...

She picked the disk up again, hoping to find another object under it that was the real source of the magic leaking from the drawer. This time, a young man appeared and began the same seductive routine, drawing his shirt away from well-muscled shoulders.

There was nothing under the disk. This was the source of the magic she'd felt. She temporarily let go of the disk to tap the back of the drawer, looking for secret compartments. Nothing. When she picked up the disk again, this time a mermaid appeared, slowly removing a completely impractical corset. Obviously, the person who'd created the spell hadn't considered what would happen if a mermaid tried to swim in such a thing.

Irritation flooded Lisette's veins. *Burn the ship down*, the dragon seed repeated, and this time, she was in complete agreement.

Without conscious thought, Lisette inhaled the magic powering the alluring tableau. The mermaid flickered twice and then winked out. Lisette's lungs were suddenly filled with flame. *Burn the ship down.*

Panic flooded her. She wasn't a mage — the dragon seed had taken the magic. If Lisette didn't release this fire, she'd be ash long before the ship sank beneath the harbor. But if she let the dragon take over, it would burn the ship down around her. Worse, she was fairly certain that if the dragon took control, she would never wrest it back.

The air took on a rosy haze. She needed to find a path forward that suited them both.

"Burn the *door* down," she said, altering the dragon's words. She pushed it to focus on just the bolted door blocking her escape.

Crossing the room, she put her hand on the wood and pushed, feeling the planks give everywhere but the spot where the bolt held it in place.

Burn the door down, the dragon agreed.

Power surged from her body and the planks beneath her palm burst into flames.

CHAPTER 44
SINGLE-MINDED

When the door ignited under her palm, Lisette yanked her hand back, expecting blisters. But aside from the warmth leftover from the magic that had filled her, she was unharmed.

The door, however... The fire she had started had burned in a curious pattern. Most of the door remained untouched, the sanded planks smooth under her fingertips. But the wood that had anchored the metal bolt fastening the door had disintegrated. Ashes drifted like snow. Lisette pulled on the door and it swung open.

A quick glance revealed the hall to be mercifully empty of people, and she crept out. Not having the layout of the ship or knowing where the crew was quartered meant she didn't know the best path to remain hidden. But it didn't matter yet. Both the bond with Aarat and the dragon-seed within told her the dragon-born blood was somewhere to her left.

She couldn't leave without it.

Another jolt rocked the ship, making her stomach lurch. "This is why people dedicate their children to the god of the depths," she muttered, after swallowing down the bile that threatened to come up. Though, technically, children dedicated to that god were merely protected from harm, not seasickness. But surely it would help.

Ignoring the stairs leading to the deck, she followed the tug of the dragon-born's blood past two more cabin doors. At the third door, she stopped. This was it.

Though the door had a lock, it opened when she turned the handle, revealing a smoky room taken up by a table covered with dried herbs, loose sheets of paper, and a brazier in the center. The brazier and table were bolted down — a sensible precaution on a ship, she supposed — and someone had tried to mitigate the fumes by adding a metal pipe funneling smoke out the porthole. In a crate next to the table waited a jumble of metal rods.

No, not metal rods. *Weapons*, waiting to be coated with the dragon-born's blood and used to bind dragons or waterbeasts to steal their magic.

Lisette's hand went unerringly to the chest next to the brazier. Once again, there was a lock, but whoever had been here last had left it unlatched. Probably interrupted when boulders began falling near the ship, she realized. Which meant they would be back soon to finish their work.

Inside the chest was a stoppered bottle of crimson liquid. Sunny's blood, either mixed with something or spelled to keep it from clotting. Lisette picked it up and considered what to do with it. If the porthole had been open, she'd have dumped it out into the water, but the exhaust pipe blocked access to the outside. *Burn the ship down*, the dragon-seed snarled.

"You are remarkably single-minded," Lisette noted. Burning the liquid wasn't a terrible suggestion, but she didn't know what was mixed with the blood and what fumes it would produce if she dumped it onto the glowing coals in the brazier. She shoved the bottle down the side of her boot to keep her hands free and then turned to leave.

Lisette allowed herself a small moment of triumph. Lord Hanley thought he could kidnap her and make her his prisoner, did he? She'd teach him the error of his ways — against all odds, she'd escaped the cabin and found the dragon-born's blood. Now all she needed to do was get off the ship and she'd be free.

Halfway to the door, she realized she still felt the tug of the dragon-born's blood behind her. "How much did they...?" She wheeled around, ready to search for a second bottle. But it was the crate of weapons next to the bench that caught her attention. She'd assumed they were waiting to be used, but now that the bottle wasn't distracting her, she could feel faint traces from the weapons as well.

Unlike the weapons stored in Aarat's cavern, these had no spells binding them to another creature, but the blood was there just the same. If Lord Hanley found another place to call waterbeasts to him, he would have all the power he needed before the ship reached the Island of Light.

"Well, that's a problem." Lisette crouched to look. There had to be at least thirty daggers, arrows, and spear tips in the pile. She couldn't carry all those with her. Pulling an arrow out at random, she examined the metal tip. Yes, there was the dull red gleam that pulled at the dragon-seed.

As an experiment, she thrust it into the coals of the brazier. Acrid smoke billowed up, most of it going into the pipe to the outside, but a thin stream added to the fog near the ceiling. Lisette coughed. If that was what just a drop or two did when burned, she was grateful she hadn't tried to pour the bottle over the coals. But when she pulled the arrow from the heat, she could no longer feel a link to the dragon-born. It was just a metal arrow tip. She tucked it under her arm in case she needed to defend herself.

So fire would indeed purify these weapons. The dragon seed had been right.

Taking a deep breath and holding it, Lisette pulled weapons from the crate by the handful and shoved the tips into the coals. Smoke billowed, making her eyes water, but she persisted until all the sharp objects were among the glowing embers. Her eyes streamed as she hurried to the door, desperate for the relatively fresh air of the corridor so she could take another breath.

Lisette threw open the door, moved into the hallway, then slammed the door behind her, leaning against the frame as she bent nearly double and coughed, sucking in untainted air to fill her lungs.

It was only when she stood, eager to find a way off the ship, that she realized she wasn't alone in the corridor. A dozen people in fine clothing silently lined the hallway in front of her — the mages, with Lord Hanley at the rear.

"Grab her, you fools," Lord Hanley growled.

Jabbing with her single arrow proved no match for people who knew how to fight, and in less than a minute, Lisette's arms were held behind her. She lifted her chin. "They won't let you leave the harbor."

Lord Hanley strode forward and smiled. "It's too late," he said. "We're already on our way."

CHAPTER 45
MAGIC EATER

Restrained by the enemy mages, Lisette's thoughts were a jumble of regrets and rapidly discarded plans. If only she had dumped the dragon-born's blood onto the burning coals of the brazier! The smoke might have destroyed her lungs, but at least the dragons would be safe. Now it was only a matter of time before a mage noticed the bottle she'd stashed in her boot. Could she somehow get close enough to throw it overboard? If not, the mages would be able to steal the power of water-beasts and dragons. And underneath the blur of thoughts was the heart-stopping fear of being trapped on a ship by the man who had stalked her for years.

But Lord Hanley's attention was fixed on the cabin door she'd burned. "I would have sworn she wasn't a mage," he said to the gray-haired man standing next to him, "and yet now..." Tapping the charred edge with one finger, he turned his head to gaze speculatively at Lisette.

Her skin crawled. *Burn the man*, the dragon seed snarled within her. If only she could. The ship lurched, and Lisette wondered how many of the mages she could splatter if she lost the contents of her stomach. Maybe that would lessen Lord Hanley's fascination with her. She looked at the mage standing next to her, a woman with a snub nose and auburn hair in perfect ringlets. "Why do you follow him? You must see how unstable he is."

Lord Hanley ignored her words and turned back to examine the charred door. "Let's continue this conversation in fresh air. I'd like Marlon to have a look at her."

Lisette let herself be manhandled along the corridor, tipping her head back to inhale the fresh breeze coming from above. Then they reached the deck, and she turned her back on the setting sun so she could look toward Harbor Crag. The *Slippery Squid* was just passing the mouth of the harbor, and the buildings were already so small that she could just barely pick out landmarks.

Intense longing swept over her as she spied the main road leading to the freehold quarter. Remy, her friends... By now, they would be searching for her in the city, but they would never think to look for her on the departing ship.

Hoping she could surprise the men holding her, Lisette twisted her body and yanked her arms back. If she could get to the rail, she could fling herself overboard and swim back to shore. One man lost his grip, and she turned, kicking at the other captor. Their brawl became a noisy scuffle, with everyone calling commands or grabbing at her. "Hold still!" "Grab her hair!" "Watch out for her — ow!"

Through sheer determination, she dragged the group halfway to the rail. Another arm's length and she'd be close enough to throw herself over. Lisette bit the hand of a man who'd been bold enough to grab her shoulder, and he let go with a howl.

Then magic squeezed her arms to her body, a distraction that let someone grab her elbow. She could feel the spell sliding off her, as all magic had since she'd first given her name to Aarat, but before the magic slipped away, the dragon seed inhaled, the same way it had done with the artifact in the cabin. Lisette's lungs burned as the power settled in her body. *Burn the ship down*, the dragon seed snarled.

Now that she had a little experience, Lisette knew she didn't have enough power to burn more than a hand-span of wood. That wouldn't help. But more important than escaping was keeping the dragon-born's blood from these mages, so she modified the thought. *Burn the blood in the bottle*, she ordered. Another spell buffeted her, and more power heated her chest.

Lord Hanley's voice broke through the commotion. "Stop throwing spells at her, you fool! She's absorbing everything!"

Burn the blood in the bottle, the dragon seed agreed. Abruptly, the pain in her chest eased, replaced by a burning of the skin at her ankle. With a pop, the cork flew off the bottle and acrid smoke poured out. Lissette took advantage of the coughing and confusion to leap to the railing. Her fingers clutched at the rope.

But she was hauled back by a firm grip on her tunic. "You aren't going anywhere," Lord Hanley breathed into her ear. Then he raised his voice. "Marlon. I want whatever it is that makes her feel like a dragon taken *out*." His fingers dug into her arms as someone else tied her wrists behind her with hemp rope, and he spoke into her ear again. "Marlon trained as a magic eater. It makes him useful to me."

Lisette had never even *heard* of a magic eater. If Remy were there, he could have explained in a way she would understand, probably with historical footnotes and a funny anecdote or two. She blinked back tears. It seemed unfair to be stuck on this ship without him.

Lord Hanley spun her around, and Lisette found herself face-to-face with a young man whose exposed skin was covered in a dense patchwork of linear scars, as if someone had taken a blade to his flesh over and over. His green eyes shone with a malicious light as he raised a boning knife between them. "It will be my pleasure," he crooned, taking hold of her chin in his free hand.

"*Not* her face," Lord Hanley interrupted.

Marlon's nostrils briefly flared, but he turned his attention to her shoulder, slitting her sleeve open to expose the flesh of her upper arm to the cool ocean breeze. He pulled his own sleeve up to expose his arm. Before Lisette could jerk away, he sliced once into her skin and then again into his own. He followed by placing his palm over her arm as blood dripped from her elbow onto the deck.

Burn them all, the irritated dragon seed insisted inside Lisette. To her surprise, Marlon laughed excitedly. "Yes," he exclaimed. "Yes, burn them all." His gaze bore into her eyes.

Lisette's chest burned like someone was carving into her ribs. She couldn't help the grunt of pain that escaped. "Stop!"

"No, you don't need this." The pain increased as Marlon's smile widened. "Almost... There." He dropped his bloody hand from her arm and stepped back, still smiling.

Lisette ignored the blood dripping down her arm. "What did you do?" But she could feel the change, a hollowness in her chest that she wouldn't have noticed a few days ago.

The dragon seed was gone. And from the satisfied look on his face, Marlon had stolen it for himself.

CHAPTER 46
NEW PATHS

Ever since Aarat had given her the dragon seed to save her from Drelaack's attack, Lisette had been wondering how she could make it go away. Now that it was gone, she missed the smoldering anger and power that had been her only company on this ship. The empty spot in her chest ached more than the cut on her arm.

She'd never thought she would miss any kind of magic.

In front of her, Marlon threw back his head and laughed. Even his chin and neck were lined with scars, a visible record of the magic he had stolen. And now Lisette could see power swirling around him.

"He'll have the power of the dragons," Lord Hanley said next to her ear, jealousy coloring his voice.

Forget the power *of the dragons*, Lisette thought, remembering how the dragon seed had acted, *he'll be lucky if he doesn't...*

But Marlon's outline had already blurred and grown as the magic coalesced. The ship wallowed in suddenly rough seas, and the sails went slack. Fighting against Lord

Hanley's grip, Lisette struggled to keep her feet under her as all the mages took a step back. Even the sailors on deck pressed against the rails to get farther away from the thing Marlon was becoming.

With a flash of light and the crack of thunder, Marlon disappeared — to be replaced by a slate gray dragon with lines of silver scales, giving him the markings of a tabby cat. He was small, only the length of two men from nose to tail, but Lisette could see the muscles play under his hide as he crouched. He growled, "Yes!" Throwing back his head, the new dragon released a torrent of flame.

The envy of the other mages made Lisette's skin itch, and their muttering was audible beneath the dragon's roar. Meanwhile, the sailors were screaming for a different reason — the main sail was ablaze. "Fire!" As one man unhitched the lines to lower it, four others were raising buckets of sea water to douse the flames.

Lisette waited for the voice within her to exult in the ship's burning, but it was... gone. The breeze gusting in from the open ocean sent a shiver down her spine, and she struggled against the ropes binding her wrists behind her. She was stuck on this ship with no allies.

A mage in red velvet robes waved a hand and the fire snuffed out, though the sail remained charred and tattered.

With one hand locked around Lisette's arm, Lord Hanley took a step toward the dragon, pulling Lisette along. "Fascinating." He crouched and ran his fingers over the mottled scales. "And can you replicate this in other mages, Marlon?"

The dragon growled. *That*, Lisette recognized. If Lord Hanley expected a dragon to behave as meekly as his tame magic eater had, he was likely to be burned to a crisp.

And Lisette alongside him since she couldn't get away.

"Perhaps," Marlon finally replied, his voice beautiful even though it carried only a hint of the power Aarat wielded when he spoke. "Though I find it hard to work with magic in this form."

That, too, made sense. For all the magic that Aarat held, casting spells was solely the purview of human mages. Remy might know why. Lisette wished he were here, telling her about some manuscript he'd read that explained the theory behind why dragons couldn't cast spells and also a ridiculous method for keeping goats lactating or some such nonsense.

Lord Hanley straightened. "Change back. This opens new paths for retaking Harbor Crag." He wheeled and walked toward the wheelhouse, where the captain stood, dragging Lisette along with him. "Drop anchor here," he called.

"It would be better to return to the harbor, sir," the captain replied. "The baromancer says there's a storm brewing. We risk washing up on the rocks if we stay here."

With a wave of his free hand, Lord Hanley said, "Fine, yes, whatever. Take us back into the harbor. But keep us out of range of those blasted trebuchets."

"Of course, Lord Hanley."

The mage turned around. "With an army of dragons, we'll be able to retake the city by nightfall," he gloated. But though he spoke it loudly enough for the other mages to hear, they remained focused on Marlon.

Marlon was still a dragon. And becoming increasingly agitated.

"I can't!" Marlon roared and spat fire again, this time burning a rope. A smaller sail flapped and dropped to the deck.

If they continued to have a dragon on board much

longer, perhaps Lisette needn't worry about the ship leaving for the Island of Light. At this rate, they'd have no sails by morning.

"You can't what?" Lord Hanley's voice held no patience.

"I can't change back."

The mages looked at each other without speaking. In the silence, Lisette tried to remember everything Remy had told her about the origins of dragons. The first dragons had been human mages, she knew, but had the transformation been voluntary?

More to sow discord than to be helpful, Lisette smiled. "It's a prison," she said, pretending a confidence she didn't feel. "That's how they dealt with mages who had become a problem."

"Be quiet!" But Lord Hanley didn't immediately refute her words, and the other mages noticed.

"If I were you," Lisette said to the dragon, ignoring the man digging his fingers into her arm, "I'd leave before they decide to chain you and steal your magic like the others."

The tableau changed as the dragon shifted to keep all the mages within sight. He took a step back and flinched as he ran into the mast.

"Don't listen to her," Lord Hanley said. "Relax, Marlon, we'll get you changed back."

For a moment, it looked like the dragon would settle. But then a sailor passed by with a coil of rope. It was undoubtedly meant to replace or repair the line that had burned, but the dragon was already wary. When the man walked behind him, Marlon jumped, his wings unfurling.

Lisette had seen Aarat leap into the air and fly, but even *he* had taken a running start. In a panic, Marlon flapped, hitting rigging and falling awkwardly. His claws scrabbled against the deck.

The other mages jumped backward, adding to the chaos. Only Lord Hanley — and Lisette, because he had a bruising grip on her arm — stayed in place. "Marlon, halt!"

But the frightened and confused dragon wasn't listening anymore. He flapped harder, gaining enough height that he could almost clear the railing. One wing hit the mast and he careened sideways, twisting his body to keep his balance.

Lisette saw the dragon's tail sweeping toward her, but there was no way to evade it. And then it crashed into her and she went flying.

CHAPTER 47
I'VE GOT HER!

T ime slowed as Lisette flew through the air. She had a perfect view of the dragon spewing fire, the panicked mages jumping back, and the ship's crew scrambling for safety. There was a certain peace found in watching from a distance while not being involved.

Then the moment passed, and she crashed into a wooden crate on the deck. "Oof." She fell to the rough wooden planks amid a shower of cloves, the spicy and sweet scent overpowering the background odor of fish and rotting kelp. Across the deck, the dragon that was Marlon spit flame at his former colleagues and a mage screamed as his robes caught fire. But the other mages had enchanted a spool of thick rope, and even as Lisette watched, a loop whipped around the dragon's hind end and slammed him to the deck. The planks shuddered.

This was Lisette's chance. While everyone was busy with the out-of-control dragon, she could steal a rowboat and escape. Or just jump overboard and swim toward shore. Even if she didn't make it, drowning would be far better than whatever Lord Hanley had planned for her.

From her spot on the deck, she couldn't see him, but he was around somewhere. This might be the last chance she ever had to elude him.

Except... If she left now, Lord Hanley would have a dragon to play with. Lisette had destroyed all the weapons coated with the dragon-born's blood in one room, but she couldn't be sure they didn't have a few more stashed elsewhere on the ship. There was magic *everywhere* and she could no longer feel the dragon-born's blood.

And while Marlon couldn't reverse the spell himself, the other mages might do it for him. The thought of this group learning how to create dragons at will sent a shiver down Lisette's spine. "Monsters of the depths take it," she cursed under her breath.

Lisette needed to get the dragon off this ship.

But first, she needed some place to hide. After it got dark, she'd figure out some way to free the dragon. And *then* she'd get off this ship and make her way back to Harbor Crag.

Taking advantage of the smoke and chaos, Lisette pried open the damaged crate to reveal burlap sacks full of spices. She hefted two bags of nutmeg seeds and tossed them over the railing, wincing at the loud splash below. Luckily, another sail erupted into flames and sailors screaming commands covered the sound. Having made space, Lisette crawled between the loose slats and burrowed beneath a sack of cinnamon bark. A casual search of the crate wouldn't find her, and a gap in the boards let her see the rest of the ship.

The chaos continued for another few minutes, but the mages finally gained the upper hand. After the dragon had been restrained, it didn't take long for Lord Hanley to notice she was missing.

"Where's the girl?" he yelled. He glowered at everyone around him, as if they might be concealing Lisette in their cloaks.

Nobody wanted to meet his eyes, but eventually the gray-haired man he'd been talking to below deck spoke up. "When I saw her last, you were holding her."

"That was before I was almost knocked into the water," Lord Hanley snarled. "Did nobody think to see where she went?"

The silence stretched. Pinned by Lord Hanley's gaze, a young woman winced. "We were containing the dragon?"

"And the fires," the equally young man next to her added.

Lord Hanley glared at the trussed-up dragon, then wheeled on his boot heel. "Find her!"

Hiding until everyone was asleep had been a good idea, because searching an entire ship for one person was nearly impossible — Lisette's ancestor had used that to her advantage as a stowaway on the voyage to Harbor Crag. But Lisette hadn't counted on the crew being certain she hadn't gone below. All access had been blocked or in use during the dragon's rampage, so they only needed to look on the deck. Sailors began opening crates and baskets, muttering curses under their breath, and Lisette's heart sank.

Still complaining, the crew finished with the first pile, tied down the netting holding it in place, and moved to the next group — Lisette's hiding place. She forced herself to breathe quietly. They had just pried open the crate next to Lisette and were removing bolts of brown cloth when the cabin boy whispered to the captain. "Something splashed on starboard side, sir, when the beast was scuffling."

Everyone stopped and stared at the child.

Snatching the captain's spyglass, Lord Hanley moved to

the railing and scanned the water. "If she's drowned, I'll have the lot of you keelhauled." He thrust the spyglass back at the captain and raised both arms. Magic swirled around him and then streamed from his fingertips over the side of the ship into the water.

As the magic continued to flow, the crew put down the cloth they held and edged away. Lisette wondered how many would choose to abandon the ship to avoid the punishment of an angry mage. Given the option, *she* would have found another berth the moment the mages set foot on the gangplank back at the Island of Light.

Lord Hanley's arms trembled as the magic faltered. *Perfect*, Lisette thought from her hiding space. *He'll use up all his magic and retire for the night. I'll cut the dragon free and slip over the side before anyone notices.*

Then the streams of magic converged. "Aha!" Lord Hanley shouted in triumph. "I've got her!"

Within her snug hidey-hole, Lisette's eyebrows raised. It certainly didn't feel to *her* as if anything had happened. But Lord Hanley was making wide motions as if he were reeling in some heavy catch. A giggle threatened to erupt as she imagined him thinking he had recaptured her and instead, dragging some large fish on board.

But when the mage made a final yanking motion, it wasn't a fish that landed on deck, but a man, his clothes dripping as he bounded to his feet. Though his back was to Lisette, she would have known that figure anywhere. Her breath caught in her throat.

Remy spun in a circle to take in the entire ship. "Nice of you to welcome me aboard!"

CHAPTER 48
ANGLES

L isette watched helplessly as the other mages bound Remy with both magical and mundane means. If she emerged from her hiding spot to help, that would just leave both of them prisoners. It hurt to see him restrained. And yet... For the first time since she'd woken up on the ship, she didn't feel alone. She wished she could let him know she was there.

As usual, Remy seemed unbothered by the activity around him, merely shifting his shoulders so the bindings were more comfortable. His attention was on the dragon, trussed up and tied to the mast. A faint frown line formed between his brows. "*You're* not what I was expecting."

"Silence!" Lord Hanley turned away from the railing where he'd been staring toward Harbor Crag. "If we didn't need a mage for experiments... Bah!" He strode closer to Remy. "How did you get her so far away without a boat?"

Lisette held her breath. One wrong word from Remy and the interrupted search for her would resume. She'd be caught before sunset.

But this was Remy. Only someone who knew him well

would notice the curious twitch of one eyebrow or the momentary hesitation as he changed what he'd planned to say. "Underwater breathing spell combined with a compulsion on a shark to pull her toward shore. If I'd been able to find a second shark for myself, you'd never have caught me."

Lisette held her breath.

Remy had nearly been expelled from mage college because he refused to perform compulsion spells. But these people didn't know him. If they questioned anything, it would be the breathing spell, and *that* sounded exactly like something Remy would have run across in some forgotten book.

As if he'd been reading Lisette's mind, Remy continued earnestly, "Found that one in Dibred's *Wonders of the Deep*, which probably would have been more popular if he'd hired an artist instead of doing his own illustrations. Someone had used it to prop up a wobbly table in the college kitchens, and I only found it by accident when I was being punished for sending a flock of chickens into the masters' dining hall. I'll admit, it's hard to trust your life to someone who draws something as easily verified as a starfish with eyes and a mouth on top, but I found that Dibred is actually quite sound when you—"

"Be *quiet!*" Magic drifted around the hand that Lord Hanley thrust in Remy's direction, but nothing happened.

Remy nodded sympathetically. "I expect that's because that net spell tired you out. It was quite well done. A bit wasteful, but then I'm sure you will have had a good reason for it."

Having experienced Remy in a chatty mood before, Lisette felt just the slightest bit sorry for Lord Hanley, who must have thought he could intimidate the other mage into silence. That was an impossible task. Lord Hanley obviously reached the same conclusion, because he exhaled sharply and then went belowdecks, yelling, "Tomorrow morning, we'll examine Marlon more closely and decipher this dragon spell."

By the time the sun dropped below the horizon and the crew had set their lanterns on the stern deck while they patched sails, the other mages had also gone below. The odor of fried fish wafted through the air, and Lisette's stomach rumbled, though she wasn't sure if it was because she hadn't eaten all day or because the ship bobbed on the increasingly rough waters.

After an hour of quiet only broken by the murmur of sailors talking as they worked, Lisette wiggled out from between the sacks of spices and exited the crate. She took a few moments on the deck to straighten her limbs, and then she crept to the mast, where both Remy and Marlon were tied. The dragon had struggled so much that the twisted ropes had to be cutting off circulation. In contrast, Remy appeared only mildly inconvenienced.

When Lisette slid next to him, Remy briefly closed his eyes in relief. Then he returned to his usual insouciant self. "Ah, excellent," he murmured. "I thought I might have to search the entire ship for you."

"After you freed yourself, you mean," she replied, scooting behind him to examine the knots by feel. The darkness made it easier to sneak around unnoticed, but she could have used a little more light to see what she was doing.

"I disposed of the spells. I was just taking a little break while I worked out how to untie the ropes."

"You didn't happen to bring a knife, did you?"

"Two, in fact, but they took both of them away. It's almost as if they don't trust me."

"Shocking, I know." Lisette abandoned her attempt to untie the knots — they'd been tightened beyond her ability to loosen the rope — and considered where she might find something to cut it with. She missed the little knife she'd stolen from the desk belowdeck, but it had been taken from her when she'd been recaptured.

Though the sailors would be carrying knives, she doubted her ability to steal one without someone raising the alarm. And there weren't all that many sailors left. Given the furtive movements and quiet splashes near the prow, the captain would be lucky to have any crew remaining in the morning. Assuming he didn't abandon the ship as well.

The dragon stirred, and Lisette leaned away so she wasn't in danger from the sharp scales... which gave her an idea. "I'll be right back."

"I promise I won't go anywhere without you," Remy said.

Lisette snuck back to her former hiding place and pulled a bolt of cloth from a nearby crate. Using the fine green silk to protect her hands felt wasteful, but she didn't have a choice. When she had made her way back, she lifted a scale on the dragon's shoulder and whispered to Remy. "Lean this way."

As she'd expected, the dragon scale cut through the hemp rope faster than the sharpest boning knife. A few minutes later, Remy was on his feet, crouching beside her. "Much better than my plan to magically age the hemp until I could rip it apart," he said, pulling the coils of rope from his frame.

Lisette paused for a moment, considering that. "You

were planning to limit your spell so the entire ship didn't rot away to nothing, right?"

His laughter was a whisper on the wind. "Truth be told, it was my worry that the mast would fall while I was still tied to it that held me back. The angles were a problem."

Across the ship, the captain raised his lantern. "Olivier! Get over here!"

Remy and Lisette froze. But after a moment of staring into the darkness, the captain set down the lantern and turned back to the patched sail. Lisette squeezed Remy's shoulder and whispered, "We can't leave the dragon here."

"No, of course not." The comforting combination of pepper and vanilla tickled Lisette's nostrils as Remy grasped the ropes securing the dragon's tail. A moment later, the rope dropped to the deck, a section in the middle frayed and worn. "See? If the angles are right, this isn't a problem." He moved to the next set of knots. "From the looks of this, tying him up was a last-minute decision."

"Marlon couldn't shift back and everyone suddenly realized he'd be a great source of power." Glaring at the dragon, whose head was tied so he couldn't do more than blink, she added, "And he should remember that when we finish untying him."

A wisp of smoke from the dragon's nostrils was Marlon's only response.

"I left a camouflaged raft tied to the anchor chain," Remy whispered. "If we're quiet enough when we leave, we should be able to get to shore before anyone notices we're gone."

More ropes fell away as Remy continued working his way along the dragon. "Almost there."

Suddenly, light from an abruptly unshielded lantern reflected from the dragon's scales, and the captain's voice boomed from behind them. "Olivier! What are you doing over there?"

As she wheeled around, Lisette saw the exact moment when the captain recognized her and noticed the ropes lying on the deck. He opened his mouth, but before he could make a sound, the last rope snapped. Marlon roared as he shook himself free.

Lisette turned back to the larger threat. And found herself face-to-face with an angry dragon.

CHAPTER 49
I DID SAY

L isette stared at the slate gray dragon a mere arm's length away. Angry silver eyes stared back at her. The dragon leaned forward, forcing Lisette to take a step back. Remy grabbed a handful of her tunic. No way could she run far enough to escape the claws or flames, so she'd have to trust that Remy had a plan. She cleared her throat. "Remember who released you. You may need us again."

The dragon's voice was musical, even in its rage. "It's your fault I'm like this." He inhaled deeply, and Lisette responded to Remy's tug and dove for the deck behind a stack of crates. Flames licked over her back, and the crates caught fire, scorching Lisette's sleeve before she yanked it back.

"That way," Remy whispered, pointing starboard at another stack of crates a short sprint away. He made a gesture in the opposite direction and the port railing exploded into splinters. The dragon whirled and spat fire at this unexpected attack, leaving Remy and Lisette to run to their next spot of safety. A man's scream told them the dragon had discovered someone creeping up on him.

Crouched next to Lisette, Remy whispered, "Climb down the anchor chain to the raft. I'll be there in a few minutes."

Lisette grabbed his sleeve. "Where are *you* going?"

"I just need to grab something from the hold." He winced at her expression. "I meant to say, *we* just need to grab something from the hold."

"That's what I thought." More yelling near the port side of the ship gave them enough warning to see Marlon launch himself through the gap Remy had made. His wings unfurled, and after a shaky start, he began climbing. In two seconds, the slate gray dragon was lost to the darkness, leaving the group of sleep-tousled mages screaming threats into the sky.

Shoulder to shoulder, Lisette and Remy hurried down the aft stairs, past the cabins and into the hold. Remy closed the door, shifted a crate to block it, and floated a mage light above their heads.

The space was vast, far larger than Lisette had expected. Then she realized why — most of the hold was below the waterline, which explained the sound of water slapping against the hull coming from above her head. Wooden crates and canvas sacks were lashed in place between hanging nets, the planks of the hold creaking as the ship rocked in the waves. Lisette swallowed and tried to think of anything but the movement of the ocean.

A harpoon with its point swaddled in burlap dangled from a hook on a beam. It both felt a little like dragon magic, but also not. Then she recognized it as the weapon used to bind the waterbeast-pony. "One problem solved."

She grabbed it as the ship rocked and had to take a careful breath, willing her stomach not to betray her.

Remy eyed her doubtfully. "It's not too late to head for shore."

"I'll be fine," she said, swallowing again as she rested the harpoon on her shoulder. "What are we looking for?"

"Ah, yes, that's the question, isn't it?" Remy pushed between two nets that formed a makeshift aisle. "Aarat insisted there was something calling to him from the ship."

"The dragon-born's blood? I destroyed that." Lisette trailed after him, the rough rope of the nets scraping against her skin. "And I think I got rid of most of the primed weapons, too."

"Yes, Aarat noticed. That was our first clue that we should be looking for you here instead of in the city." A heavy canvas bag had shifted against the nets, and Remy climbed over it, turning at the top to offer Lisette a hand. "How *did* you end up on this ship?"

"There was a mechanical spider," she started. "In an alley."

"Ah," he said, his tone understanding. "So you followed it."

"It was a mechanical spider." Lisette jumped down and resumed pushing her way between the nets behind him.

"Completely understandable. And then you were attacked?"

"No. It injected me with something and I passed out." She quickly recounted everything that had happened from the time she woke until Remy had been brought aboard.

"Marlon's a magic eater?" Remy zeroed in on what he thought was the most interesting part of her adventure, though it clearly should have been the mechanical spider.

There was no accounting for taste. "I've never met one before."

"Well, now he's a dragon and he can't eat spells anymore." Lisette shuddered as she imagined being stuck as a dragon for the rest of her life. "Did you know someone who changes into a dragon can't reverse the spell?"

He paused to smile at her over his shoulder. "I did say that I'd love you even if you grew scales."

Despite the situation they were in, Lisette answered with a grin of her own. "So if we're not here for the dragon-born's blood, what *are* we looking for?"

"Something else. Aarat told me something or someone called to him, and I couldn't allow this ship to leave Harbor Crag."

Lisette stopped and looked around the hold in despair. "Without knowing what it is, how do we know when we've found it?"

"Well, I was *hoping* I'd have someone with dragon magic to help me search. But you seem to have given that to Marlon. So now," he said, straining to shift a crate with straw poking between the slats, "I'm starting on the assumption that it's the thing exuding magic over in that corner."

What Lisette had taken as a stroll through the hold to look around actually had a destination. She scrambled to catch up, reaching his side just as he patted a smaller pile of crates. These had been stacked with more care than the other cargo, and had their own section of netting, which Remy climbed up to unhook. Lisette put out a hand to steady the pile as the hemp rope thumped to the planks.

Remy jumped down, light on his feet. "There we go," he said, rubbing his hands together in front of the first crate. "Do you want to take bets on what's inside?"

"I *want* to be on dry land," Lisette replied. She swung the harpoon down from her shoulder and let it thud on the wood. "Let's open it and find out."

"No sense of adventure," he said, shaking his head, but he took the harpoon, wedged the tip under a slat, and leaned on it until the nails popped free. When he'd loosened all four sides, he set down the harpoon. "Let's see what we have."

The wood chips shifted to expose a silk-wrapped bundle the size of his head. With a deft flick of his wrist, he exposed the contents, a cedar box with inlaid ivory showing a dragon in flight.

Giving in to impulse, Lisette put a hand on the box. Whatever was inside recognized her bond with Aarat and pulsed magic in response. "I think this is probably it."

Remy angled the box to look for a seam. "I hope so. We may have to take it on faith. As much as I want to find out what's inside, it will be a bit tricky to open in these conditions. And Lord Hanley might notice our raft if we overstay our welcome."

As if conjured by his words, the hold reverberated with the sound of fists beating on the door.

CHAPTER 50
WORKS OF ART

The sounds from outside the hold grew more frenzied. Remy bundled the silk coverings around the cedar box and pushed it into Lisette's arms. "That's our cue to leave! Give me one second..."

This could be their only chance to retrieve what Aarat had noticed, so Lisette merely nodded and tied the ends of the silk together so she could loop it over one arm and keep her hands free. The sooner they could get away from the *Slippery Squid*, the better.

Meanwhile, Remy broke open the remaining crates in the pile, not bothering to minimize the damage. Jewels and coins scattered on the planks. A glowing pendant went into Remy's pocket, along with a heavy silver ring with an oily sheen. He made a distressed sigh when he read the label on a bottle, but placed it back among the straw reverently and stood. "Let's go."

Grabbing the harpoon again, Lisette followed him through a narrow aisle running along the length of the hold. "You sure you don't want to bring that bottle?"

"If I broke it, I would never forgive myself." He shifted a

244

pile of staves to create an opening and held them out of the way until she'd passed through. "This way, I can hope the ship goes aground before they reach the Island of Light and someone who appreciates fine brandy will salvage it."

A herd of goats appeared when they waded past the next netted pile. Despite the urgency, Lisette's steps slowed. They'd been in the hold for at least ten minutes, and she had heard no noises other than the creaking of timber and pounding on the door. More, she hadn't *smelled* goats — Lisette and Tiffany had spent hours cleaning the windows and pavement in front of her shop when an escaped herd had spent the night in the street. And nobody would leave a herd of goats near anything valuable, which presumably included everything in the hold.

Then she noticed the unnatural stillness of the herd.

"It's a stay spell," Remy said, seeing her interest. "Easiest way to move livestock on a ship, though there has to be a mage aboard to renew the spell every few days." He gave the nearest doe a gentle pat. "Only works on goats and cattle, though. Simi walked in front of me when I was learning to cast it, and all she did was blink. Then she took a nap in a sunbeam, but I'm fairly certain that's why she was walking there in the first place."

As Lisette walked by the herd, the box tied to her arm warmed. "Uh, Remy?"

"Hm?" His response was a distracted murmur, as he was busy tipping a heavy barrel back so it didn't crash down on them.

Tiny magic darts erupted from the box, shooting around the goats and then returning. The pattern reminded Lisette of the probing she did with a pick when faced with an unfamiliar lock. The magical exploration changed, the probes becoming stronger and more focused, purple threads moving in a complicated weave before fading. For two seconds, nothing happened. Then magic streamed from the goats into the box, and whatever was inside hummed in satisfaction.

Remy finally succeeded in balancing the barrel and turned toward her just as twenty goats shook off their torpor, bleated, and scrambled away. With a quick step to the side to avoid being butted, Remy laughed. "Someone hasn't been renewing their spells."

"Not exactly," Lisette replied, pushing a curious goat away with the side of the harpoon. It occurred to her that the hull had likely been reinforced with magic, and the sudden removal of those spells could very well lead to a catastrophic structural failure — while they were still below the waterline. Her skin prickled. "More like *this*," she said, raising the silk-wrapped box, "decided to undo it."

Remy cocked his head. "Ah. *That's* interesting." His eyes unfocused as he considered.

"Dry land," Lisette reminded him. "You can look at it later." Preferably when they weren't at risk of drowning.

He came back to himself with a start. "Yes, of course." The goats had scattered, so Remy and Lisette resumed moving in the direction of the forward door. They were now close enough that a hunter could have thrown the harpoon and lodged it in the doorframe. "In a perfect world, I would have had a chance to wander around a bit before I was tied up, but sometimes these things don't go according to plan."

"Have you ever had one that *did*?" In her experience, Remy's strength lay in improvising after his original plan fell apart. "I'm not saying that you come up with terrible plans, you know, but..."

The creak of ungreased hinges cut through the banging on the aft door. Remy and Lisette backpedaled and crouched behind a stack of crates. Remy whispered, "My plans are works of art. It's not my fault reality intrudes."

Hoping her motion would be lost in the chaos of the goats roaming the hold, Lisette leaned to look around the corner. Three of the younger mages stood uncertainly in the forward doorway. She eased back into their hiding place. "Is there another way out?"

Remy looked doubtfully at the hull. "Creating an exit isn't the problem. It's the drowning part that worries me."

Any hole in the hull would cause a blast of seawater that would only stop when the space had filled. "So the breathing underwater spell...?"

"Had a wine stain obscuring important sections of the text," he replied. "I'm sure I could recreate it, given enough time, but I'd rather not test it in field conditions."

"Sensible."

"Also, I'd feel bad if the goats drowned." He sat down and shimmied further into the pile. "I think our best bet is to stay here and hide."

Suddenly, the toe of his boot was the only part of him Lisette could see. Her heart skipped a beat before she remembered the invisibility spell he'd cast once before. She scooted closer. When she'd passed the spell's perimeter, he reappeared. It took a bit of wiggling to get both of them and their belongings inside the border, but they managed.

"The things we have to do to get a bit of privacy these days," he murmured into her ear.

Lisette grinned and kissed the angle of his jaw. "I know places we could go. You only had to ask."

He opened his mouth to reply, and then closed it as two pairs of embroidered slippers came around the corner accompanied by a furiously whispered, "It wasn't me who was in charge of the goats!"

A woman's voice whispered back. "You were next on the rota. Never mind. Unblock the other door and let the rest inside. Maybe I can round up the goats before his lordship notices."

Remy and Lisette exchanged dubious glances. From the looks of her footwear, this woman wasn't a goat herder, and rounding up a bunch of goats in a space with so many hiding places and areas to climb would be difficult for someone with experience. This woman was about to learn some important lessons about goats.

Then the box cradled in Lisette's arms warmed up again. "Stop that," she whispered, panic making her skin tingle.

But her admonishment went unheeded. Purple darts of magic swarmed through the air around them.

CHAPTER 51
VERY ROMANTIC

Remy blinked at the purple magic swirling around them even as Lisette slapped the box tied to her arm. "Stop that," she hissed again. She had no idea if it understood her, though she was certain it was alive. After watching it undo the spell holding the goats, she suspected it could learn to untangle other spells — including the one keeping them hidden.

"That's amazing," Remy murmured. He waved a hand through the flurries, and the tiny sparks inspected his fingers.

"That's what released the goats," she warned.

"Ah," he said in sudden understanding. "Perhaps we might interest it in something else." He pursed his lips and blew a quick puff of air toward the harpoon at their feet. The magic sparks tumbled to the metal in disarray, then swarmed around the shaft.

On the other side of the cargo they crouched behind, someone tripped and stumbled, the muffled sound accompanied by the startled bleat of a goat. "Get over there, you stupid thing," a young man said.

A white goat with tiny horns hopped down from a crate, nearly landing on Lisette. It nibbled her hair and ignored her attempts to push it away. Given its position, the animal was halfway in the sphere covered by the invisibility spell; having the back half of a goat with no front half would expose their hideout to even the most casual search.

She pushed at its chest and hissed, "Shoo!" All that did was make the goat butt her arm.

Remy was more practical. He leaned forward and wrapped his arms around the goat's neck and shoulders. Then he dragged it closer, so it was lying on its side, half in Lisette's lap. "Everything's fine now," he murmured, and even though Lisette knew he was talking to the goat, his words eased the tension in her shoulders.

A plump youth rounded the corner, his embroidered orange slippers covered in fresh streaks of dirt and pitch. "Where did it go?" He clutched at his blond hair, and its resemblance to a haystack suggested this was not the first time. "I could have gone off to Galfigon," he muttered as he stumbled by, "but no, I let Monique talk me into *this*."

Concealed by the invisibility spell, the goat bleated in sympathy. Remy's head dropped forward as his shoulders shook in silent laughter.

The young man swiveled his head and hissed, "Where *are* you, you stupid thing?" He stared right at the spot where the group was hiding, and Lisette held her breath.

A woman's voice called from farther away. "Antoine, hurry up!"

"I can't find it," he replied.

"Goats don't just disappear."

That was a little too close to the truth. Only when Antoine walked away did Lisette turn to look at Remy. "We can't stay here."

"Agreed." Then he was distracted by the probes going from the box to the harpoon. "Now *that's* interesting."

With a pop, a stream of magic flowed from the harpoon into the box, and Lisette felt a pleasurable fullness and then nothing. The air was clear of purple magic. "I think it's sleeping now."

Remy took one hand from the goat to run a finger along the metal of the harpoon. Flakes of dried blood crumbled and dropped to the floor. "The spell stealing the water-beast's magic is *gone*."

Across the hold, Lord Hanley bellowed in rage. "Find them! Bar the doors. They're in here somewhere!"

Despite the invisibility spell, a concerted search would find them. Remy pushed the harpoon to the side. "At least now we can leave that behind." He cast a wary glance at the quiescent box. "*That*..."

Lisette nodded and tightened the knots holding it to her arm. "It's coming with us." No matter what was hiding inside, Lord Hanley couldn't be allowed to keep it.

Remy pointed at the nearby cargo net attached to a huge vertical beam. "Climb slowly and don't get too far away from me. I'll maintain the invisibility spell."

One eyebrow raised, Lisette whispered, "The goat's not coming with us, right?"

"Not unless she really wants to."

"Just checking."

After a quick check to make sure nobody was looking in their direction, Remy urged the goat to its feet. It trotted toward the door, climbing and jumping off barrels along the way, which meant it was quickly spotted. During the resulting outcry, Remy and Lisette crept in the other direction, alert for anyone who might blunder into them. The only people searching seemed to be exhausted mages —

Lisette wondered again how many of the ship's crew were left.

Remy had sweat on his brow from the effort of constantly recasting an invisibility spell designed to work in one spot. Then they reached the net and immediately found another problem. The net moved from their weight as they climbed — anyone looking in their direction might deduce their presence by the strained ropes. The only way to avoid making their movement obvious was to slowly shift their weight from one knot to the next, a nerve-wracking and exhausting exercise. Thankfully, the box remained quiet.

"This reminds me of the night we met," Remy whispered into her ear. His body covered hers as they inched their way up the net together.

"Very romantic," she whispered back, "though I'd prefer to be climbing down a tower than stuck in a ship's hold."

"Not stuck," he said. "I just thought it would be better to make a new hole in the top of the hold than the bottom."

Lisette couldn't argue with that logic.

They had climbed high enough that they no longer needed to worry about a searcher running into them by accident, though she felt more exposed the higher they went. Down below, Lord Hanley used a sharp rod to poke into any space where they might be hiding. Given the force of his thrusts, he'd skewer anyone he found, though all he'd managed so far was to damage sacks holding grain and other goods. The rats would feast well during this voyage.

As long as Lord Hanley kept everyone searching at floor level, nobody would notice a hole in the ceiling before Remy and Lisette had escaped. Unfortunately, Lisette wasn't the only one to have that thought.

"Dissolve the nets!" Lord Hanley yelled. "They must have climbed higher."

"Time to pick up the pace," Remy murmured. At the end of the hold, a stack of crates and baskets crashed down as the net securing them crumbled to dust.

Lisette abandoned any hope of stealth and pulled herself up, the rough nets abrading her palms. A second net to their left crumbled, and a mage yelped as boxes fell. The aft end of the hold was now a jumble of broken crates and split canvas. A chorus of bleats and swearing heralded the escape of the rounded-up goats, and the herd took advantage of the poor footing, climbing over the wreckage of what had previously been orderly cargo.

A man with two goats chewing on the hem of his robes reached the base of the net Lisette and Remy were climbing. A spell wrapped around the fibers of the rope under the enemy mage's hand... and then he fell over in a dead faint. One goat chewed on his sleeve.

Remy blew out his breath in relief. "That's what happens when you try to use magic you don't have. He's going to have the world's worst headache when he wakes up."

"Any chance of Lord Hanley falling over soon?"

"Sadly, no. He's still pulling magic from the dragons. We're just lucky most of the mages still on board are low level."

Lisette smiled even as she found her next handhold. "I love the way you look at things."

They reached the heavy iron hooks that secured the netting to the central post. Remy paused a moment with his hand on the rough planks of the ceiling and viewed the chaos. It looked as if the ship had weathered a deadly storm, with fabric unrolled, a cask of wine spilled, jagged splinters sticking up from the wreckage, and atop it all, a herd of goats scampering around.

"I think our work here is done," he said with satisfaction. He looked up at the planks and narrowed his brows as he concentrated. An area just big enough for both of them to climb through slowly crumbled.

At that moment, the box on Lisette's arm warmed. "Uh oh."

Purple magic streamed out and mixed with Remy's spell, and Lisette got the sense that whatever was in the box was trying to be *helpful*, like a small child sweeping up in the shop.

The hold's entire ceiling disintegrated, leaving Lisette and Remy with nowhere to go.

CHAPTER 52
DO YOU SMELL SMOKE?

As they clung to the pole, Lisette met Remy's gaze. "Did you know," she said wryly, "I was worried about your mother coming to visit because I thought she might not like me. Other disasters hadn't crossed my mind."

"Which just goes to show you that worrying isn't worth the effort," he replied. "Can you climb up to that beam, or do you need me to pull you up? I think we can get to the stairs leading to the deck. Assuming our friend there doesn't dissolve that as well." He gave the box tied to her arm a disappointed glance.

Below them, goats scampered over the debris that had fallen from cabins that no longer had floorboards. Further back, Lord Hanley scanned the hold, searching for any sign of them, while the other mages continued dissolving the remaining cargo nets, including the one Lisette and Remy had climbed. But the mages were too late.

Lisette swung her legs up, locked them around the crossbeam, and dragged herself to the top, all the while hoping she was still within the sphere covered by Remy's invisibility spell. When she finally made it to the top of the beam, she straddled the wood, her arm muscles burning from the unaccustomed usage. The skin of her hands and inner arms was covered in splinters, but at least she was in no danger of falling, though the swaying of the ship had her empty stomach complaining.

As soon as Lisette was stable, Remy levered himself up next to her on the crossbeam. He sniffed. "Do you smell smoke?"

With her arms still wrapped around the beam, her nose was right next to the oak, and the only thing Lisette could smell was the tang of wood preservative. Like everything else on the ship, it was probably flammable. She sat up, straddling the beam, and caught a whiff of burning wool. "There was a brazier in one of those cabins." The coals would have been cooling for hours, but it didn't take much to start a fire.

"Ah, yes, that would do it."

Remy urged her starboard, so Lisette crawled on the beam, her progress slowed by the narrow width and the need to be sure Remy wasn't far away. As she inched forward, the air grew more acrid. Her eyes watered from the fumes.

The smoke didn't go unnoticed for long. A man whose red robes were now covered in bits of straw and goat droppings pointed toward the source. "Fire!" Magic collected around his fingers, but before he could release the spell, his eyes rolled up and he collapsed amid the debris in the hold. Remy was right — the other mages didn't have access to the power of the dragons, and they'd exhausted their reserves.

Before another mage could try to magically douse the

embers, Lord Hanley stood atop a sealed barrel. "Stop! Let it burn for now. And be *quiet*!"

Letting a fire burn unchecked on a ship filled with flammable materials seemed like a terrible idea. From the surreptitious looks the other mages were giving each other, they agreed. But it only took a moment for Lisette to understand Lord Hanley's logic. Even with the hatches to the deck open, the smoke was thicker near the top of the hold. Lisette muffled a cough in her sleeve. She and Remy would be tracked by the noise long before the embers turned to open flame.

Remy put a hand on her ankle to halt their progress. "Get ready to move quickly," he whispered. "I'll have to drop the invisibility to smother the fire."

Lisette nodded and flattened herself against the beam to minimize her silhouette. With a flick of his hand, Remy toppled a pyramid of wine casks onto the smoldering wool. Wood splintered and liquid sloshed to saturate everything.

But instead of fizzling out under a deluge of wine, the flames roared to life. Smoke billowed up, along with the sinus-clearing smell of brandy. Goats bleated and scrambled away, followed by panicked mages.

"The labels on those barrels *lied*!" Remy sounded more offended than anything else, even as he urged Lisette forward.

"Dodging taxes," she choked out as she scrambled toward the stairs, all pretense of stealth gone. Distilled spirits were often taxed at a higher rate than wine and mead, and the cooper in the freeholder quarter occasionally made double-walled barrels for special clients — wine on the outside and a hidden cask for stronger spirits within.

Lord Hanley bellowed in rage, but not even *he* could

ignore a conflagration on the ship where he stood. A spell flew through the air, sending up clouds of black smoke from the wool, but the flames had leaped to another pile of goods soaked in brandy. Another spell arrowed to the new flames, and then a third. If the cargo had still been in orderly piles netted together, it would have been the work of seconds to douse the fire, but the chaotic mess left pockets where the brandy had soaked through to other flammable items, causing a potent distraction for Lord Hanley.

By the time her head hit the side of the ship, Lisette had forgotten everything except her need for balance and oxygen. She'd lost track of Lord Hanley, though the billowing smoke had lessened, so she assumed he'd smothered the fire. She looked down through burning eyes. The stairs were directly below her, just a short drop away. A river of smoke flowed through the deck hatch. Lisette swung down to land on the stairs, narrowly avoiding a mage who fled toward clean air without looking back.

Remy landed lightly beside her, coughing. "Shall we?" He took her hand and they hurried up the steps.

Lisette's first gulp of the fresh night air was as sweet as anything she'd ever breathed. Around her, she could hear other people coughing, but the deck was cloaked in darkness, with just one lantern gleaming at the stern. The ship rocked as powerful waves slapped against the side. Sailing a raft to shore wouldn't be pleasant in these conditions, but Lisette didn't care. If that was what it took to get away from Lord Hanley and this ship, so be it. She let Remy pick their path toward the anchor chain and tried not to trip over the ropes on the deck.

A dazzling light flared in front of them. Lord Hanley stood in their path, a mage light burning above his palm. He smiled. "Not so fast."

Lisette gripped Remy's hand more tightly. Remy's magic had saved them from tricky situations in the past, but if he had to fight Lord Hanley directly, he didn't stand a chance. For the first time, she wished she'd allowed herself to transform into a dragon. She could have kept Remy safe.

Lisette opened her mouth to say whatever was necessary to convince Lord Hanley to let Remy go. But before any sound came out, leathery wings scraped against the mast. Clawed feet encircled Lisette and Remy, dragging them up into the night sky. The box tied to Lisette's arm bounced against her thigh.

Behind them, Lord Hanley bellowed in rage, but the dragon was out of range before the mage could stop them. With her eyes struggling to adjust to the darkness, it took Lisette a moment to realize who had saved them. Then she recognized the gray scales and smaller stature of the dragon flying them through the night.

Marlon, the magic eating co-conspirator of Lord Hanley, the only living dragon born as a human, had snatched them from the ship and was now flying over open water.

CHAPTER 53
RESCUED

Rushing through the chilly night air left tears streaming from Lisette's eyes, but even so, she could see the lights of Harbor Crag — and Marlon wasn't flying in that direction. She yelled to the dragon above her. "Where are we going?"

Marlon didn't reply. Lisette felt churlish complaining. *Anyplace* was better than staying on that ship with Lord Hanley.

Remy reached over and clasped her hand, his skin the only warmth she could feel.

They flew just above the water so that the spray dampened her clothing. The lights of the city were no longer visible when Marlon dropped them on a rocky beach. Luckily, those rocks had been smoothed by the never-ending tumbling of the waves, so it didn't hurt much when she pitched forward and skidded on her elbows. The magic box tied to her arm clattered against the stones, but its inhabitant didn't complain.

Remy groaned softly. "That was faster than a boat," he

said, wiping at his face, "but the landing lacked a little something."

After they had stood and assured each other they were unhurt, they peered at the starry sky. Lisette frowned. "I doubt Marlon flew us here without wanting something in return."

Remy hummed in agreement. "At a guess, he wants me to change him back to his previous state. Which could be a problem." He paused. "Or maybe not, if that thing you're carrying is what I think it is."

Now that they weren't running and climbing, Lisette untied the fabric, releasing the scent of cedar. She clamped the box under her elbow as she pulled the silk around her shoulders for warmth. "What do you think it is?"

"A god."

The box clattered to the stones before Lisette could catch it.

There were plenty of small gods in the world, of course — every temple in the city had originally been built around one, and there were thousands, or maybe millions, in nature, unbothered by humans. Most had limited influence, granting small favors to their acolytes until the god's presence faded away a few generations later. Lisette had felt the presence of various gods in Harbor Crag and on her travels, but to her they had always felt like an impersonal hum of magic — something to be avoided, like sensible people avoided all other magic, but not something she particularly worried about.

The thing in the box had felt *alive*.

She crouched to scoop up the possible god. "Outside of a temple? Moving around like this? I thought they inhabited one place." Standing, she thrust the box into Remy's hands, eager to be rid of it.

"There's some debate about whether it's possible. Espasa the Short wrote a book of poems about traveling the coast with a god living in a wine bottle." He tilted his head. "Some scholars claim that was a metaphor and it just meant she enjoyed drinking. It's a little unclear. And Hoot the Odd tells a story of a younger god traveling with a trader until it found a spot to settle down, which turned into the Temple of Dog Island. The temple and the rest of the island are abandoned now, of course, but I can't think of any other reason for people to settle there."

Lisette cleared her throat. "So... You're saying we just stole a *god* from the cargo hold."

"Well..." Remy shrugged, the movement just barely visible in the dim light. "I wouldn't be surprised if it was stolen from someone else. And Aarat did say it was calling to him. So really, you *could* say that we *rescued* the god from the cargo hold."

"Somehow I don't think Lord Hanley's going to take it that way." Lisette shivered, partly from the cold and partly from the remembered madness in Lord Hanley's eyes.

"Well, no, likely not." Remy wrapped his free arm around her. "We probably shouldn't mention it to Marlon anyhow."

"Good idea."

They huddled together on the beach, waiting for Marlon to return. Five minutes later, the dragon landed next to them, smelling of charred flesh and damp wool. "Change me back," he commanded. "Now."

"I'll try," Remy said. "Though if I'm successful, we're going to have a long walk back to Harbor Crag. Maybe we should move a little closer while you still have wings?"

"If we move any closer, the dragons will attack me again," Marlon snarled.

Since Marlon had likely been siphoning dragon magic for years, he was probably right about that. The dragons were unlikely to forgive him in the next few centuries. Lisette decided not to tell him that Aarat had felt called by the contents of the box Remy was holding, or Marlon might decide to take them even farther away.

Remy leaned toward Lisette. "I'm not sure how long this will take," he said apologetically. "You might want to get comfortable." Then he walked to the dragon's side, the box cradled against his chest. "What have you tried so far?"

While Remy and Marlon spoke, Lisette found a dry spot to sit, not so far away that she couldn't hear them over the sound of the water, but not so close that an errant swing of the dragon's tail could catch her.

Remy and Marlon stood unmoving as waves rolled onto the beach. Occasionally, a crackle of magic flared between the two, but the dragon remained a dragon. The box in Remy's hand stayed quiet. If Lisette had been a little warmer and the pebbles a little softer, she thought she might have been able to sleep.

Hours later, the sky had just gone the gray of pre-dawn when Remy took a step back. The dragon had become increasingly irritated as every attempt had failed. "Give me a moment to clear my head," Remy said. Marlon snorted in reply, smoke carried away by the breeze.

The tide had ebbed, leaving strands of kelp on the pebbles.

Dropping to the ground next to Lisette, Remy murmured, "Can we try having you hold our friend? I think it may be more excited about you." When Lisette nodded, he spoke more loudly. "Perhaps with your bond to Aarat to guide us, we'll be able to reverse the transformation."

As they walked over to the dragon, Remy casually

handed the box to Lisette, as if it had no value and he needed to have both hands free. She tried not to think about why a small god would be excited about her. Maybe because she had a bond with multiple dragons? While she didn't know of any connection between gods and dragons, there was a dragon inlay on the box holding it.

It suddenly occurred to her that without the dragon seed for protection, any of the dragons who knew her name could command her obedience.

They stopped by Marlon's mottled silver shoulder. Remy glanced at Lisette. "Ready?"

She nodded.

Holding one palm above the gray scales, Remy closed his eyes. His breathing deepened, and Lisette saw the magic pooling under his hand. She'd seen variations of this throughout the night, and it hadn't transformed Marlon. Lisette wondered if the next step would be fleeing from an angry dragon.

The box in her arms warmed.

Purple strands of magic darted out and through the dragon. Marlon threw back his head and roared, sending flames into the sky. The strands became more and more numerous until it looked as if an entire net of purple magic rushed into the dragon and back to the box again.

Gray scales under Remy's palm glowed purple.

Suddenly, the dragon collapsed to the sand, and then his form kept shrinking and changing until the man emerged, dressed in the same clothes he'd been wearing on the ship, with scars covering every inch of his skin.

Lisette blew out a relieved breath. "It worked!" She took a step back and relaxed, waiting for the purple glow to fade.

But the magic coming from the box hadn't stopped. As Lisette watched, each strand embedded itself within a scar before cavorting back to the box, leaving unblemished skin behind and erasing the physical signs of Marlon's magic eating gift.

Somehow, it was taking the magic that Marlon had eaten.

"No!" Marlon writhed on the pebbles, clutching at the disappearing scars. "Stop!"

Lisette stared at the cedar box in her hands, wondering if the process would end with the mage dead on the beach. "What do I do?" She shoved the box at Remy.

He took it from her, but the magic didn't slow until Marlon's skin was as smooth as a child's, every sign of his special talent erased.

The box's occupant gave a satisfied hum and went back to sleep. On the rocky sand, Marlon covered his face. "My magic!" he screamed. "You took my magic!"

Remy looked down at the box he held, then over at Lisette. "Oops."

CHAPTER 54

PERSISTENCE OF BELIEF

The wet sand sucked at Lisette's boots as she trudged along the beach. A night of little sleep after the events of the previous days had left her exhausted and sore. She looked left to throw a dark look toward Marlon. "Surely we could have gone a *little* closer without the other dragons attacking."

Marlon didn't answer. After his magic had been stolen by the small god, the mage had raged at the cedar box for an hour while Remy and Lisette watched. Nothing had happened until Marlon had grabbed a rock, intent on smashing the box open. Before Remy could intervene, the inlaid ivory dragon glowed. Marlon dropped the rock and sank to the sand, sobbing. When Lisette and Remy had picked up the box and begun walking toward Harbor Crag, Marlon followed, all his attention fixed on the small god Lisette carried.

Remy waved an arm at the cliffs on their left and the clear blue sky beyond. "It's a beautiful day for a walk along the beach with my love."

Lisette raised an eyebrow. "And another mage and

266

something that might be a god." But his words had lifted her spirits, and her strides lengthened. "Do you think your mother would want to tour the waterfront? When this is all over, obviously."

"Obviously," he agreed solemnly. "And I think my mother would like to spend time with us both, no matter what we're doing."

"Oh, then maybe we should take her with us to search among the ashes of Lord Hanley's estate." When Remy didn't immediately laugh with her, she added, "I wasn't being serious."

"And yet," he said, detouring around a clump of seaweed swarming with tiny flies, "my mother happily played in the mud with me when I was a child. Given a choice between a guided tour and digging through ashes, she might indeed choose excavation."

"Your Professor Giselle would probably jump at the chance, too," Lisette said, working to keep her face straight. The small god dangling from Lisette's wrist suggested that it, too, would enjoy finding magical items in the wreckage of the estate.

"My mother and Giselle know *entirely* too much about my early years." Remy shuddered theatrically. "Surely the two of them finding each other on that ship is some sort of cosmic punishment for my wrongs."

Lisette smiled at him. "I think they make a good pair. Though, to be fair, I may think that because they don't know every wrong-footed or embarrassing incident from *my* first twenty years."

Remy groaned.

Lisette continued before he could comment. "But they don't need to, because we have Rye and Barlow twenty

267

paces away. They know everything I've ever done *and* Barlow loves to gossip."

Taking one skip closer so he could grasp her hand, Remy said, "Shall we stow away aboard a merchant's ship and travel south to find an island where we can both be safely anonymous? There's a long tradition of mages doing so, you know. Though," he added after a moment's reflection, "their stories are collected in various histories, which suggests they were not *entirely* successful in their anonymity."

"Surely some of them must have managed it."

"Yes." Remy paused. "Maybe." After another three steps, he laughed. "Most of the stories consist of the mage making a good start and then failing wildly in the execution. Bertold the Talkative vowed to leave the college after a particularly acrimonious spell exchange. He disguised himself as a fisherman and lived in a village on the coast for a few months, rowing out in a boat every day and using magic to fill his nets while he napped on the water. Then he would stay up all night in the pub talking. Finally, one of the villagers travelled to the college and asked them to please come get their mage as he was drawing the wrong kind of attention and they were tired of listening to his stories."

"Did it work?"

"Oh, yes, the head of the college, Donato the Thoughtful, a man who was by all accounts the most pleasant mage of his generation, went on a walking tour of the coast, where he — purely by chance — ran into his old friend, Bertold. After a few drinks, Bertold gave his boat to the barmaid and went back to the college. There's still a shrine to Donato in the village. I've seen it."

Lisette lifted the arm with the box tied to it. "Maybe

that shrine would like to have a god? Or better yet, we could send it along with the traders going overland. That would keep it away from Lord Hanley and make Harbor Crag less of a target."

A wave, braver than the ones before it, foamed over her boots. Lisette automatically angled her steps higher up the beach to drier sand, only then realizing she'd done that without noticing multiple times as they walked. The cliff face, a comfortable wall at her left shoulder earlier in the morning, now loomed menacingly. Damp seaweed and barnacles at eye level gave evidence that the water regularly reached the cliff. There was a reason no army had ever invaded Harbor Crag from the beaches on either side. At high tide, they'd be dashed against the rocks or pulled out to sea.

The tide was coming in.

Lisette lengthened her stride. "If we can get to the edge of the bay, we might be able to signal a fishing boat." How long would the beach still be walkable? She wasn't sure they had enough time.

Next to her, Remy kept pace, but he looked beyond the waves when he clicked his tongue. "We may have another problem."

On the horizon, the outline of a familiar ship was visible through the haze. The *Slippery Squid* looked worse for wear, with patched sails and a canted mast, but it was still seaworthy. As they watched, a rowboat splashed into the water.

Lord Hanley hadn't set sail for the Island of Light; he was coming after them.

Lisette turned toward the cliff face, assessing the handholds. There was a reason nobody bothered to patrol the cliff top. "We *might* be able to climb it," she said doubtfully.

She would certainly take her chances scaling the nearly vertical surface if her choices were down to that or returning to Lord Hanley, but that was likely just choosing between two forms of death. They were closer to Harbor Crag, but not yet close enough to attract help.

Another wave washed over her boots.

Behind her, Marlon splashed through the receding water. "Return my magic, and I'll hold off the boat *and* the tide."

He sounded serious, which suggested it might be possible. Lisette tilted her head toward Remy without slowing her steps. "Can you do something with your...." She waggled her fingers.

Remy captured one hand in his. "My love, you are adorable in the persistence of your belief that magic might go away if you ignore it."

"I live in hope. And you didn't answer the question."

Remy heaved a sigh. "I might be able to hold back the water for a time, but not long enough for the tide to go out again." He looked thoughtful. "The boat, though. I might be able to do something about that when it gets closer."

"If we haven't been dashed against the cliffs by then," Lisette suggested.

"Yes." He squeezed her hand. "How would you feel about a romantic *run* along the beach?"

They sprinted for Harbor Crag, Marlon at their heels.

CHAPTER 55
ĤIGHLIGHTS

L isette had lived a stone's-throw from the water her entire life, but she had never really understood why sailors personified the ocean as a capricious lover. Until this moment.

Now, it seemed the waves couldn't decide whether to crush her against the rocks, drag her back to the deeps, or merely hold her in place so she could be once again captured and given to an insane mage. The ocean's insistence on hurting her felt *personal*.

Or perhaps the ocean wanted to punish Marlon, and she and Remy were merely victims of circumstance. That was the problem with feeling victimized by inanimate objects — perhaps the object's aim was skewed. Lisette pondered that as she splashed through the water. Marlon was a far more likely target. If one believed in that sort of thing.

The next surge went over her knees. Soon, they would have to stop walking and grab the stones of the cliff or risk being knocked from their feet.

She surveyed the cliff face. "Maybe we could make it to

that ledge?" She pointed to a spot a quarter of the way up the cliff. It was near the high-tide line, but there was no obvious path from there to the top of the cliff. And it would leave them stuck in one place as they waited for the tide to ebb.

The next wave nearly lifted her from her feet.

"I think we'll have to," Remy said, though he glanced at the boat getting ever nearer. "I'll see what I can do to make life more difficult for them while you find the best handholds."

The night Lisette and Remy had met, they'd climbed the outside of the duke's tower. Surely they could climb this cliff, and they would help Marlon up if he couldn't manage by himself.

Lisette's stomach growled as she scrambled onto a waist-high stone to plan her next steps without worrying about the waves.

"I heard that," Remy said.

"Who planned this outing?" Lisette grumbled. "No food, water rising, enemies approaching..." Two possible paths to the ledge offered themselves. She pulled herself up to follow the longer of the two because it seemed easier; as tired and sore as she already was, she wasn't looking for a challenge. The instant she left the large stone, Marlon jumped onto it.

"... and me," Remy added absently.

Lisette glanced down at him. He wove strands of magic between his fingers as water lapped the cliff face. "Are you listing yourself as a drawback?"

His lips curved up, though his focus didn't move from the spell forming around his hands. "Sorry. I thought you were pointing out the highlights."

Lisette rolled her eyes and climbed, but she couldn't hold back her grin.

A few seconds later, a tremendous splash out in the water drew her attention, but she couldn't turn to look without falling.

"That should take care of them," Remy called up to her, his voice laced with satisfaction. Then, a few seconds later, he said, "Or... maybe not."

Hands aching, Lisette wedged her fingers into an opening so she could drag herself up. Just as she began to slip, her free hand reached the ledge she'd been aiming for. From there it was just a matter of pulling herself up and wriggling onto the plateau, which was just large enough for the three of them to sit. A dark crack in the cliff behind suggested there might be a cave; Lisette offered up a prayer that it wasn't a badger den. Still, a small perch above the water was infinitely better than being dashed against the rocks and dragged out to sea, even if they might need to share the space with badgers.

Marlon's hand grasped the ledge, and Lisette moved sideways to give him room to climb up.

Down below, the rowboat bobbed on the waves, close enough that she could pick out Lord Hanley seated in the stern and two young mages inexpertly manning the oars. All three were soaked through and wore the same disgruntled expressions. Magic swirled around Lord Hanley's fingers and a chunk of rock exploded from the cliff face.

Remy yelped and laughed slightly hysterically from his spot on the cliff. "Try again! That gave me an easier climb!"

Lord Hanley couldn't possibly have understood Remy's words over the roar of the waves, but another blast rocked the cliff. After a pause, during which Lisette held her breath, Remy laughed again. "His aim is improving!"

Stuck on the ledge, they'd be sitting ducks. "I'm going to check out the cave," she called to him. "Try not to drown."

"Anything for you, my love," he called back.

Entering the cave required squeezing through the opening, but the space inside was larger, allowing Lisette to move so she wasn't blocking the light. No badgers in sight. She breathed a sigh of relief. The back of the cave was lost in darkness, but there was a reassuring lack of animal debris. If they could keep Lord Hanley away from the ledge, they could rest here in relative comfort while waiting for the tide to go out. The stone under her feet trembled as another blast rocked the cliff. At this rate, Lord Hanley might bring the whole cliff face down.

Lisette crawled back out onto the ledge in time for another shower of pebbles to rain down on her head just as Remy pulled himself up. "There's a cave."

"With badgers?"

"Not that I saw."

"Good. Sooner or later Lord Hanley is going to account for the movement of the waves, and I'd rather not be in sight when that happens." He climbed to his feet. "Shall we?"

Marlon slithered in first, as if he was afraid they might leave him behind. Lisette went next and quickly moved out of the way.

Remy's shoulders were too broad to fit through the opening. After a few tries that only succeeded in wedging him more tightly, he sighed in defeat. "Let me try going in feet first. If nothing else, it will make me a smaller target."

Light flooded through as he moved back, and then his booted feet came through. Lisette sidestepped to give him room. "Would it help if I pulled?"

Before Remy could answer, the cliff shook. Inside the cave, pebbles fell and dust billowed up. An ominous rumble suggested larger movement of the cliff face. Lisette grabbed Remy's legs and *yanked*.

Remy slid into the cave, and there was a brief glimpse of daylight. Then rocks tumbled.

Lisette dragged Remy further from the opening, until he reached over and patted her hand, the first sign that he was conscious.

The rumble of shifting rocks had stopped, but daylight no longer streamed through the cave opening. After listening to the crash of waves for hours, the sudden silence felt ominous.

The cave opening had collapsed. They were trapped.

CHAPTER 56
SECOND TO NONE

A mage light rose from Remy's hand, highlighting the dust hovering near the low ceiling. Blood trickled from a cut on his brow, mixing with the dirt on his face. "If Lord Hanley keeps throwing magic at me like that, I might start thinking he doesn't like me."

Lisette helped him to his feet. "I can't decide if it's better or worse that he wants to destroy *you* more than he wants to capture *me*."

"Worse," Marlon said. It was the first word he'd spoken in hours.

Nodding at the cedar box Lisette carried, Remy said, "He's panicking about losing our friend there."

Lisette sighed as she looked at the rocks blocking the cave opening. "Now we have something to work on while we wait for the tide to go out."

Remy bumped his head when he took a step toward the rear of the cave. "How far back does it go?" Ducking, he went around a bend, the mage light floating above his shoulder. "Aha! Now *this* is interesting."

"If you find wild animals back there, you have to deal

with them," Lisette warned. But she followed behind, winding around the rocks that hid a narrow passageway, Marlon on her heels.

Running her fingers along the rocks, Lisette felt evidence of claws or tools. Her elbows brushed both sides when she lifted her arms, but the consistent width of the passage felt deliberate. "I think this must be a smuggler's cavern." Remy's footprints in the dust suggested it wasn't currently in use. At least they would have plenty of air while they cleared the cave entrance.

"Maybe we'll find another way out."

Lisette smiled at his optimism. "As long as we don't get lost along the way."

"My sense of direction is second to none." He paused. "Also, there really doesn't appear to be more than one way to go. Though this may still dead end — we seem to be heading farther away from the water unless I've gotten turned around."

While reaching Harbor Crag was still a hike of multiple hours if they traveled along the beach, a straight line through the cliffs wouldn't require much time at all. Rumors of such tunnels were part of the city's lore, but Lisette had never met anyone who claimed to have traveled through one. "This *might* go into the city. Assuming the tunnel hasn't collapsed somewhere along the way." After all, there had to be a reason it was no longer in use. The need for smuggled goods hadn't changed in hundreds of years.

"Let's go find out, shall we?"

As they walked farther, Lisette became more convinced this had been a smuggler's route. The tunnel might have occurred naturally, but at every point it narrowed, there were tool marks on the walls where it had been widened enough to let through a single person carrying a moderate burden.

Ten minutes later, they received confirmation of the tunnel's purpose when they reached a tiny cavern stuffed with a dozen wooden crates. Remy rubbed his hands together before unbuckling the leather strap on the closest crate. "What have we here..." He lifted the lid expectantly, and then looked confused.

"What is it?" Lisette leaned forward to look inside.

The crate was filled with three-cornered cocked hats some sized to fit heads and others smaller as if meant to be worn atop wigs, fancy monstrosities of a style not worn since the dances of Lisette's grandmother's day. Dyed leather and velvet formed the bases; each had been individualized with feathers, metal trinkets, and fabric folds that hid the scaffolding so well that they looked like entirely different creations. But each held a glimmer of magic.

"Why would anyone smuggle hats?" Remy lifted one to peer at it more closely. "It's a simple cosmetic spell, the sort of thing that hides blemishes and changes the color of the wearer's eyes."

It was that last detail that gave Lisette the clue she needed. "The green eyes of Amalfi!"

Remy and Marlon stared at her.

"Historical politics," she explained.

Marlon immediately lost interest, but Remy looked intrigued. "Someday you'll have to tell me the story."

"Barlow can tell it best. I'll get half the details wrong."

Generations ago, the Amalfi family, rich merchants who had recently expanded to Harbor Crag, became famous for their green eyes and their fierce opposition to the duke's economic policies. Having lived through the whims of a different duke, Lisette sympathized even if she didn't know the specifics. Sporting green eyes indicated support for the Amalfis, which made the duke threaten to imprison any magic user who created a spell that altered a person's eye color. Despite that, green eyes continued to appear, up to the day when the duke choked on a caramel apple and his heir exiled the Amalfis while also choosing more moderate advisors.

The small god tied to Lisette's wrist roused long enough to explore the magic still present in the hats, though it left the spell in place. Probably still trying to digest all the magic it had taken from Marlon, Lisette thought. But instead of immediately going back to its quiescent state, its purple darts probed the cavern, the same way Tiffany had looked around her new rooms before she'd moved her family there.

Remy cocked his head and watched the probing magic. "If the god settles here, we wouldn't have to worry about Lord Hanley stealing it again."

Aghast, Lisette shook the box. "This is practically under Harbor Crag! Wait until we have a chance to get you on a caravan going across the mountains. I'm sure there will be far better places to stay." The last thing her city needed was a new god attracting more attention.

Whether it understood her words or just didn't like what it had found there, the god went back into the box with what felt like a sigh.

Lisette ran a finger over a decaying feather. "Tiffany would love to see these. I wonder why they were left here." Even after the duke's sudden demise, the hats would still have had value. "I hope that doesn't mean the tunnel caved in..."

"I'm positive it didn't," Remy said, letting the crate's lid down gently. "At least not completely." He walked toward the other opening in the cavern, the tunnel that presumably led to some hidden portal within Harbor Crag.

Lisette followed, one hand out to the side as she tried to feel an imaginary breeze on her fingertips. "How can you tell?"

"Listen."

At first, Lisette heard nothing other than their footsteps and the rubbing of fabric abused by salt and sand. But then she heard the faintest whisper — the annoyed chatter of a cat who had been separated from her person for far too long. "There's a cat in front of us."

"Not just any cat. That's Simi."

Lisette couldn't have picked out Simi's noises from other cats, but she trusted that Remy could. "How could she possibly have found us?"

"I told you," Remy said, lengthening his stride. "She was exposed to a lot of magic as a kitten. She's not entirely normal."

And then a calico projectile crashed into Remy's chest and the next few minutes were given over to trills and chirps and Remy's assurances that he hadn't meant to leave her behind for so long and apologies for having done so. There was a brief pause for Simi to greet Lisette before she jumped back to Remy. Marlon received a stare accompanied by a tail twitch before he was ignored completely.

Ten minutes later, the odors of fish and woodsmoke filled the air. "I recognize that smell," Lisette said slowly. It had taken a week for her cloak to lose that stench after they'd gone searching for the dragon egg. "Coincidence?"

Inhaling deeply, Remy turned so he could watch her. "Perhaps. We never got a good look around the house."

Lisette shuddered, remembering the interior of the dead mage's house. "I'm not sure I would have stayed to look for a tunnel entrance even if we'd had the time." Back then, she'd just wanted to get the dragon egg to safety.

"It *would* explain why the tunnel stopped being used." Remy looked past her to Marlon. "Jasque the Mad had a house in this area."

"Jasque the Mad?" For the first time in hours, interest infused Marlon's voice. "Did you find his book of spells?"

"Sadly, no." Remy whirled around so he was facing forward again. "Though I'm not sure I would trust anything he wrote down. He wasn't called 'the mad' on a whim."

Marlon grunted once and lapsed back into silence.

The tunnel twisted in a serpentine, dirt and ash getting thicker on the floor. After one final turn, dust motes glittered in a ray of sunshine. Remy let his mage light wither and they walked up a stone staircase, through the ruins of a house, and into a small, weed-tangled front garden. This had been the home of Jasque the Mad.

Lisette leaned on the crumbling garden wall, exhausted now they had reached safety. "Almost home."

A few people passing in the street gave them incurious looks, automatically sizing them up as a source of danger rather than wondering why they were coming from the house that had been impenetrable for decades before its sudden collapse. Lisette inhaled deeply. The odor of fish warred with the smells of animals and cooking food, a definite improvement over anything on a ship.

Simi jumped down from Remy's arms and stalked in the direction of the fish market, tail held high as a clear invitation for them to follow. Since the fish market was on the way back to the freeholder quarter, the group followed.

"Rye and Barlow will know someone trustworthy leaving overland," Lisette said, lifting the box still tied to her wrist. "The sooner we can get this thing away from

Harbor Crag, the better. After that, I'm going to sleep for an entire day and *then* we can get back to normal."

"Maybe not entirely normal," Remy suggested. "There are a few stray mages to deal with and a waterbeast disguised as a pony that needs a place to live."

Lisette glanced up at him. "I'm pretty sure that *is* our normal."

He snorted. "You may be right." They'd reached the wide boulevard and turned to begin the climb past a row of carts and stalls holding the evening's catch. Simi jumped on his shoulder and meowed sharply. Remy scratched the calico's neck as she nuzzled his face. "Yes, let's go find you a treat." Glancing at Lisette, he said, "Give me a moment." He walked to a small cart, conversing with the cat as he went.

As Lisette waited, she considered Marlon. The mage who no longer had magic looked around at the market as if it was the first time he'd ever seen such a thing. She raised the box with the ivory inlay. "Do you want us to find you a spot on the caravan that takes this thing?" Perhaps he had a talent a caravan might need, though she'd noticed most mages had few practical skills — Remy being the obvious exception.

Before Marlon could reply, a shadow passed over the street. A cart horse shied and bolted, dragging a full load of grain bags up the hill despite the brake keeping the wheels from turning. Patrons scattered. Even some of the fish sellers, a stoic bunch, drew their wares closer to the edge of the road.

Drelaack, the dragon who had tried to trap Lisette, landed on the street in front of her, his talons dislodging a line of cobblestones as he slid to a stop. The last time she'd seen him, the yellow dragon had been chained under the earth, sick from years of having his power drained by the mages of Harbor Crag. Now his scales glowed gold with health, magic rippling from nose to tail. There was no sign of the chain that had bound him, or the suppurating wound that had lain beneath the shackle. Lisette hoped nobody had been injured while freeing the untrustworthy dragon.

After his attempt to destroy her while she was undoing the spell that freed him, Drelaack was the dragon Lisette liked the least. But Harbor Crag needed to live with *all* dragons in their midst, not just the likable ones. Drelaack wouldn't have sought her out without a good reason.

Worried about what had brought this dragon to the middle of the city, Lisette straightened her shoulders and, with a calm that was entirely feigned, said, "You look healthier today." She wished she could look to Remy for clues on how to handle this interaction, but he was on the other side of the dragon. Marlon sidled behind a cart heaped with mackerel, as if trying to avoid the dragon's notice.

Scales scraped on stone as Drelaack stretched like a cat. "This is how a dragon should always look. Aarat, with his age and strength —" The dragon spat the descriptors. "He has been free for weeks and *still* lingers in sickness." The smell of charred flesh clung to his scales, and the nearest vendors abandoned their wares and fled.

Lisette hadn't noticed Aarat looking particularly weak since he'd broken his chains and left his cavern, but she kept that to herself even as she wondered where the amber dragon was. Keeping her voice light with an effort, she asked, "How did you recover so quickly?"

Sunlight glinted off golden scales as Drelaack lowered his head to look Lisette in the eye. "Power that was stolen can also be returned."

Heat washed over Lisette as the dragon snorted,

making it a struggle to stand her ground. If she ran, as every part of her screamed to do, Drelaack would lose all respect for her. And that respect might be the only thing keeping her alive. "Returned?" She had a bad feeling about the dragon's choice of words.

"A bargain," Drelaack said. "Instant freedom for dragon-kind with no attempt to enslave us again. And all they want in return is you and the god you carry with you."

The god and Lisette — the only two things left for Lord Hanley to salvage from his disastrous attempt to regain Harbor Crag.

Forget respect. Running had been the better option. But before Lisette could move, Drelaack breathed, "Lisette."

CHAPTER 57
FIND YOUR HOME

H er body froze.

Lisette had given Drelaack her name, and she no longer had the seed of a dragon to protect her. His mind smothered all thought. She couldn't even breathe as a golden claw darted out and caged her. Then the hold on her mind relaxed, but she slammed against scaled toes as Drelaack took to the sky. His wings skimmed the buildings beneath them as he worked to gain altitude, and she pulled her dangling legs higher to avoid colliding with a chimney.

"Those mages won't keep a bargain with you," she screamed above the rushing wind and the pounding of her heart. Lisette had never heard that mages could harness the power of a small god, but if they could, Harbor Crag would fall. "If you deal with Lord Hanley, you'll never be free!" And she would never escape from him again.

Black-tipped talons tightened. "Once my people are unbound, we will return to our islands. No mage would survive that journey."

In some ways, that prospect was appealing. With the

dragons gone, there would be nothing to draw Lord Hanley or the mages from the Island of Light back to Harbor Crag. Life would gradually return to a new normal, one without dragons or magic or gods.

It was the Harbor Crag that Lisette had always thought she wanted.

But it was a tempting lie.

Harbor Crag might be a better place with Drelaack gone, but Lisette actually *liked* Aarat, even though he frightened her at times. Despite everything that had happened, Aarat had stayed in Harbor Crag. In the past, before the mages had enslaved the dragons in the warrens, dragons had lived in Harbor Crag of their own free will.

Magic and dragons and yes, even the occasional small god, were the core of Harbor Crag, along with the people who lived there. The newly hatched dragon Dinaat belonged. Remy was a mage, and *he* belonged. Maybe even the small god in the box tied to her wrist belonged.

The ornate mansions of the rich merchants passed beneath Lisette's feet as Drelaack flew toward the harbor. The dragon banked to the right to take advantage of an updraft, and they circled lazily, going higher as they passed over the duke's palace and then the ashen ruins of Lord Hanley's estate.

At her wrist, the small god woke long enough to test the magic buried in the rubble and Lisette stifled her reaction to tell it to stay in the box. Far better for the god to find its permanent home before ending up in Lord Hanley's clutches, even if that home was Harbor Crag.

Perhaps, *especially* if that home was Harbor Crag.

After all, the box had a dragon inlay and the inhabitant had called to Aarat. Perhaps the god desired a home near dragons. It might even be a small god *for* dragons.

Up and up they went. Lisette could see all of Harbor Crag. Down near the fish market, she thought she could see Remy. It was too far to make out his expression, but she knew him so well, she didn't need to see. Remy would be running through his options, searching for a way to bring her back safely, probably nattering on about an obscure manuscript he'd once read to anyone who would listen. Lisette would have given anything to hear his forays into ridiculous and unlikely history, which he thought might have a grain of truth hidden in the details.

But there was nothing Remy could do. Even if he had the magic to bring down a dragon — which he didn't — if she fell from this height, she would be dead when she hit the ground. A cleaner death than the one which awaited her at the end of her current journey, but Lisette was desperate enough to believe she still had a chance of escaping, no matter how terrible the odds.

Somewhere down in the dragon warrens, Giselle rested, gathering her strength and protecting Sunny and the baby dragon. She wouldn't be aware of what was happening to Lisette, and besides, the professor needed to save her strength — Lisette didn't believe the attacking mages would keep the terms of any bargain, and Giselle would be the last line of defense for the dragons... and Remy's mother, Anna.

A dark speck speeding above the water was almost certainly Aarat, returning from his regular patrol. Drelaack abruptly abandoned the updraft in favor of winging away, crushing Lisette's brief flare of hope. Drelaack's betrayal — and she had to believe it *was* a betrayal and not a thing the dragons had agreed upon or Drelaack wouldn't have waited until Aarat was away — meant Aarat couldn't leave Harbor Crag unprotected to hunt them down. The mages who had made a deal with Drelaack might even now be corrupting some other dragon. Though Lisette thought they would have a harder time with Grelaad and Braatle.

No. Lisette couldn't rely on anyone else to save her, and she didn't yet see a way to save herself. The small god *might* help her when they arrived at their destination, though she couldn't count on it. But she could do the one thing that might prevent Lord Hanley from gaining more power, even if that would doom her and enrage him to the point of insanity.

Before her thoughts warned Drelaack, Lisette pried up a scale from the dragon's chest. Blood welled from her fingers. Lisette slid the fabric tied to her wrist against the razor edge, cutting the pouch open and scoring the box. Blood from her fingers stained the ivory dragon inlay. The fabric slipped away from the box, and Lisette let go of the scale.

"Find your home here," she whispered to the god. "Harbor Crag will welcome you."

For a moment, the box hung from Drelaack's scale. Then something — the rushing wind or a movement of the god or maybe just gravity — dislodged the box and it dropped, tumbling as it fell toward the buildings below.

"No!" Drelaack bellowed, tightening his grip on Lisette as he banked sharply and dove after the falling god.

Rushing wind blurred Lisette's vision as the world tilted. Her stomach lurched. With Drelaack's wings tucked, they were hurtling toward the ground.

Drelaack abruptly leveled out and made another sharp turn, tossing Lisette back and forth. Talons dug into her ribs. She struggled to breathe as darkness crowded the edge of her vision. The dragon bellowed in triumph, dove, and snatched something from the ground with the foot not holding Lisette. His wings beat against the air as they climbed toward the sky.

She had failed. Lord Hanley would regain the god, Lisette would never see Harbor Crag again, and all the dragons, even tiny Dinaat, would be bound to power-hungry mages for the rest of their lives.

Suddenly, magic saturated the air.

Lisette's view of Harbor Crag disappeared beneath a haze of sparkling purple that surged through her body and filled her lungs, heavy and warm, until she was drowning in the magic. Drelaack's claws spasmed.

Lisette knew the feel of this power. It wasn't the playful nudge of Remy's spells, or the irritated surge of energy from Aarat. This magic... She'd seen it free a herd of goats and extract knowledge from Marlon's scars.

But now it seemed less questioning and more... insistent. It didn't want to go with Drelaack. It wanted to stay right where it was.

The small god had chosen its home.

CHAPTER 58
PROMISE

P urple magic washed over the dragon, seeping under golden scales and through yellow skin. Drelaack shuddered. His wings slackened and then he flapped in an uncoordinated panic as he tumbled through the air. Lisette pushed at the talons crushing her chest, but her struggles did nothing.

Then the talons holding her dissolved under a wash of purple magic.

Lisette was suddenly completely alone and unsupported, taking huge gulps of air as she fell from the sky.

Thoughts flashed through her mind as the ground grew closer: at last, she could breathe again; the god had chosen Harbor Crag; hopefully Remy had been close enough to see the god change; someday scholars could read his observations and silly asides. She clung to the distractions because underneath it all was the certainty that she couldn't survive this fall.

Lisette hurtled toward the ruins of Lord Hanley's estate.

There was something deeply unfair in dying on that piece of land, even if the building had burned and the owner had fled Harbor Crag. Perhaps she should have given in and become a dragon when she'd had the chance. At least it would have kept her away from any association with Lord Hanley.

On the far edge of Harbor Crag, she could see Aarat barreling toward her, but he would be too late.

Lisette wished she'd had more time with Remy. But then, she would have felt that way if they'd been granted an entire lifetime together.

The ground rushed up. Lisette squeezed her eyes shut and waited to die.

And then... she landed, but not on ashes and jagged rubble. Instead, she felt warmth and the sensation of dragon scales under her palms. Lisette opened her eyes.

Beneath her, an enormous purple dragon spread its wings, spiraling slowly down toward the ruins of Lord Hanley's estate. The dragon's body felt as solid as Aarat ever had, but Lisette could see the ground through the scales beneath her.

Blood oozing from the cuts on her hand swirled over the scales and disappeared. That couldn't be good.

After two lazy circles, the dragon glided to a stop amid the ruins.

"Uh, thank you," Lisette said, wrapping her injured hand in the hem of her shirt. She slid off the magical being, still in shock over surviving the fall. The dragon form of the small god moved to curl around the border of the property, with just a small space between the nose and tail tip.

The air over the entire estate shimmered and Lisette gave up all pretense of dignity as the ground shifted beneath her feet. She sprinted for the street. Just as she reached the cobblestones, a chime resonated in her bones. When she turned, the ethereal dragon had become a solid crystal wall, though it retained its dragon shape. In the center was a gleaming white building. Or perhaps, it was less a building and more a hill. The space between the dragon's nose and tail opened into a solid stone cave that reminded Lisette of Aarat's cavern.

The whole thing was impossible — stone had appeared where none had been before — but the entire area radiated with the power of the small god.

Remy's voice sounded behind her. "I should have known you would find an escape."

Lisette whirled and threw her arms around him, careful not to disturb Simi's grip on his shoulder. "I thought I'd never see you again."

He stroked her windblown hair even as he held her close. "I would have followed you to the ends of the earth." Then he kissed her forehead. "Though I have to admit, your solution is far more convenient. It would never have occurred to me to ask a god to transform Drelaack into a man."

Lisette leaned back so she could look at his face. He didn't appear to be joking. "Wait, what happened to Drelaack? I thought he'd just..." She waved a hand. "Disappeared."

"No, the god took away the dragon magic and changed him back to a man. I could see it from where I was." Remy cocked his head and looked into the distance as he thought. "Though I'm pretty sure he was born a dragon, so I guess he wasn't really changed *back*." He shrugged and looked at her again. "In any case... While you were riding through the air in style, he was hanging from the tail of a dragon god. I suspect he bounced a few times during the landing."

Lisette looked around at the empty street. "Where did he go?"

"I don't know, but I'm sure someone will let us know when he turns up."

Before Lisette could protest that Drelaack had her *name* and she needed to know if that meant anything in his new form, a gust of wind accompanied Aarat's arrival.

The dragon peered suspiciously at the temple that hadn't been present a few minutes before, reminding Lisette of a cat examining a new toy. He sniffed at the dragon form and the cave opening, then scuttled back in shock when the wall came to life long enough to snort at him.

Remy drew Lisette farther away, so they weren't in any danger of being accidentally trampled under dragon feet. "I'm sorry," he murmured. "I know you had hoped to send the god overland before it settled."

Aarat took another cautious step toward the shrine and sniffed again.

Lisette winced as Simi's rough tongue groomed her brow, but she didn't pull away. "Where else would it go? It belongs here." She reached up to scratch the calico's chin, enough of a distraction that Simi settled on Remy's shoulder and began to purr.

Magic crackled over amber and black scales as Aarat stretched his head forward.

The normal sounds of the city slowly increased in volume as they watched the dragon inspect the small god. By morning, most of Harbor Crag would act as if there had always been a shrine where the ruins of Lord Hanley's house had once stood. More interesting gossip would replace talk of recent events. Harbor Crag continued on.

Lisette blew out a breath, muscles already aching at the thought of climbing the hill again. "I know you probably want to stay here and record everything for posterity, but after that, we should go home and let everyone know we're alright."

"Then food and a warm bath," he said, guiding her steps toward the main road which led up to the freeholder quarter.

"And a bed. On dry ground."

They were quiet for a dozen steps. "And then you'll disappear into your workshop until you understand how Bralinost was made."

Lisette took a breath to protest, and then blew it out. "Just for a little while. I promise."

Remy grinned and kissed her cheek. "Never change."

Lisette already had, and Remy must have noticed. But she merely rested her head against his shoulder as they walked, and allowed her feet to carry her home.

I ʜᴏᴘᴇ you've enjoyed Dragon Fortune! Want to read a short story ("Persuasion Magic") about Remy's time at college? How about when Lisette and Remy found the dragon's egg? ("The Curious House of Jasque the Mad")

Join my newsletter at https://tmbaumgartner.com/subscribe/ — *you'll get those short stories and more, plus book news and foster kitten pictures!*

ACKNOWLEDGMENTS

This book took far longer to create than it was supposed to. I had so much fun writing *Dragon Freehold* that it was a forgone conclusion the adventures would continue, and continue they did. *Dragon Fortune* started as a serialized story. But then I got busy with other projects and this story got shoved on the back burner. And then the serial site got shut down. And then there were more projects and... All I can say is that I'm terrible at sticking to deadlines and I apologize to all the readers who have been waiting for this book. It's finally here — thanks for your patience!

A big wave of gratitude also goes to my critique group who read the manuscript and pointed out its flaws. Some of them are fixed, and you're probably right about the rest, but that's what book three is for.

Finally, thank you to my brother Eric who somehow found typos in what I could have *sworn* was a pristine manuscript. Might he have added them himself just so he'd have something to complain about? Maybe. Who can really know?

ABOUT THE AUTHOR

T. M. Baumgartner is a speculative fiction writer who has difficulty following directions. This probably explains why the IRS recalculates her tax refund after she files it every year. At various times she has been a veterinarian, Unix system administrator, software developer, and after-hours book-shelver in a medical library.

Theresa currently lives in Northern California in a house with too many animals. She knits hats for garden gnomes and fails to grow tomatoes despite living in the perfect climate.

She also writes cozy mysteries under the pen name Tess Baytree.

Want updates about new releases? Silly dog anecdotes? Free stories? Join the newsletter mailing list! Go to https://tmbaumgartner.com/subscribe/ or point your phone's camera at the QR code above.

The marketing department here at Speculative Turtle Press is great at tail wagging, but a little challenged by tasks that require thumbs.

If you enjoyed this book and would like to help other

readers find it, please tell your friends and consider leaving a review at your favorite site.

ALSO BY T.M. BAUMGARTNER

As T.M. Baumgartner:

Shift Happens

The Chaos Job (Jackpot Drift #1)

The Chaos Connection (Jackpot Drift #2)

The Chaos Nexus (Jackpot Drift #3)

Dragon Freehold (The Dragons of Harbor Crag #1)

Dragon Fortune (The Dragons of Harbor Crag #2)

All Gremlins Great & Small (The Portal Storms #0)

All Rocs Wise & Wonderful (The Portal Storms #1)

All Basilisks Wild & Sparking (The Portal Storms #2)

Theoretical Magic (The Floodmouth Files #1)

Independent Flight

As Tess Baytree:

Death Walks a Dog (Penelope Standing #1)

Death Tracks the Scent (Penelope Standing #2)

Death Smells a Rose (Penelope Standing #3)

Death Trims the Tree (holiday novella)

Death Crashes a Wedding (Penelope Standing #4)

Death Paints a Picture (Penelope Standing #5)